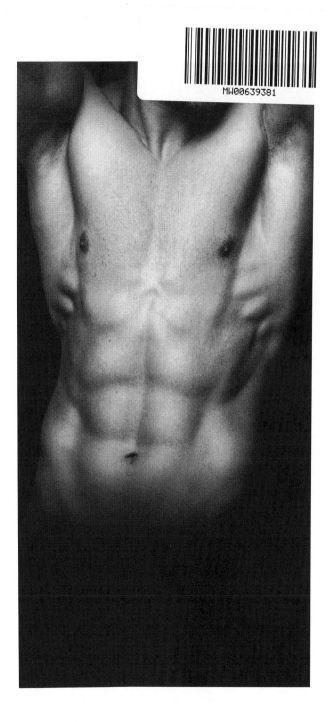

MW00639381

PUBLISHER'S NOTE
This is a work of fiction. Any names, characters, places,
and incidents are the product of the author's imagination
or are used fictitiously, and any resemblance to actual
persons, living or dead, business establishments, events
or locales is entirely coincidental.
The scanning, uploading, and distribution of this book
via the Internet or via any other means without the permission of the publisher is illegal and punishable by law.
Please purchase only authorized electronic editions, and
do not participate in or encourage piracy of copyrighted
materials. Your support of the author's rights is
appreciated.
www.sacredforestpublishing.com
P.O.Box 280
Moyock, NC, 27958
Digital ISBN- 978-1-941315-38-5
Print ISBN- 978-1-941315-39-2
Sacred Forest Publishing

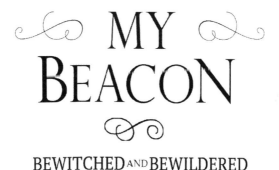

MY BEACON

BEWITCHED AND BEWILDERED

ALANEA ALDER

DEDICATION

~Omnia Vincit Amor- Love Conquers All~

~Thank you for waiting~

The past couple years have been hard on all
of us, but like Meryn and the gang, try to keep
your thoughts positive, things always get better.

PROLOGUE

G AGE WATCHED IN HORROR AS the flames rose in front of his mate. He could hear her scream, but the intensity of the fire prevented him from taking even a single step forward. The flames rose higher and he could no longer see her. He blinked and he was now in a hallway, watching the scene before him from behind a doorway. The flames died down long enough for him to see her turn his way, reaching for him. Suddenly, the door slammed shut.

Gasping he woke and sat up kicking off the blankets. He didn't want anything next to his skin. He could almost still feel the heat from the flames. Feeling frustrated he flung himself back down on the bed.

How could he save his mate, if he couldn't reach her?

CHAPTER ONE

G AGE LEANED AGAINST THE WALL as he listened to those sitting around the large table sound off about the dimming of the city's lights.

Yesterday, after sprinting back to the palace, chaos ensued as the queen sent out runners everywhere. This morning, his unit was summoned back so that Ari could attend meetings.

Covering his mouth, he tried to stifle a yawn. An elbow in his side had him rolling his eyes as Kincaid scowled at him.

"*Pay attention*," the witch mouthed at him

"*Yes, mother*," he mouthed in return.

"So, what you're saying is that y'all don't have seasons? Doesn't that get boring," Meryn asked.

"Meryn, we are called the City of Eternal Sun," Brennus reminded her gently.

Meryn tilted her head to one side. "So, like, no fall? No, bonfires and pumpkin spice?"

Izzy eyed the shorter woman. "Pumpkin spice? Really? I wouldn't have pegged you as one of 'those' people."

"What?" Meryn protested. "That shit is good, I don't care if it makes me a basic bitch."

Izzy rolled her eyes and smiled.

"Bitch?" Aiden growled. "No one better say that about you."

Meryn made kissy noises up at her mate. "Don't worry babes, no one would say shit with you nearby."

"They probably wouldn't say shit with him on another continent either, Meryn," Brie added.

Meryn nodded in agreement. "True."

"Back to the new crisis at hand," Kari said, bringing them back to the reason for the meeting.

"I think it's a crisis to stay in summer forever. Let it cool off a bit," Meryn mumbled under her breath, snuggling into her sweater.

"It's not that simple, Meryn," the queen said, sighing.

"We're already having to make arrangements to cover and warm some of the more delicate plants around the kingdom," Portia added.

Molvan closed his eyes and sat back in his chair. "It's been a logistical nightmare."

Meryn turned to Kendrick. "Isn't this your sort of thing to handle?"

Kendrick stared at her, a flat expression on his face. "Normally, yes. However, I have no idea how the lighting here works," he admitted, looking disgusted with himself.

Kincaid's eyes widened. "That happens?"

Anne stifled a giggle as Kendrick growled.

"Yes, fetus, it does happen, even to the best of us."

Kincaid flushed, but was smiling at the admonishment. Gage knew that the younger witch felt a bit of relief that even Kendrick ran into problems with magic every once in a while.

"*And*, fire is your primary element," Thane added, further rubbing salt in the wound.

"I know *that*," Kendrick shot daggers at the other witch.

"Maybe you just have to change the batteries," Meryn suggested.

Everyone at the table turned to look at her in unison.

She blinked at them. "Turn it off, then turn it back on again?"

Once again, silence met her suggestion.

She shrugged. "I got nothing then."

Izzy tapped her fingers to her lips. "Meryn may not be that off in her ideas. This one time, when I accidentally flooded the walls and had water coming out of the electrical sockets, I had to call an electrician, then the plumber. Couldn't you call the ones that installed the lights?" she suggested.

Oron stared down at his mate in horror. "What? How?"

She held up her hand. "Long story."

Portia turned to the queen. "Though not exactly the same, the suggestion does hold merit. I have been scouring our city archives for anything that may help. According to one of the city journals the Fire Temple of Storm Keep are the ones that designed and installed the lights of the city."

Kendrick nodded. "Mikel, as the Fire Temple Head, would be invaluable in troubleshooting this." He frowned. "I think he left some time ago, but they should be able to recall him."

Aiden smiled. "It would be nice to see him again."

Darian laughed. "Just like old times."

Meryn bopped her head back against Aiden's chest. "Old times?"

Aiden kissed the top of her head. "Mikel became Alpha's witch when I became Unit Commander. When he had to return to Storm Keep, we got Keelan."

Meryn's eyes widened. "A Keelan, before Keelan."

Kendrick shook his head. "Not really, they're nothing alike. Mikel is much older for one and a more serious individual."

"Damn fine witch, though," Darian added.

Kendrick just nodded his agreement.

"Portia, could you contact the Fire Temple and have them send the Fire Temple Head as soon as they can possibly spare them," the queen requested.

"At once, Your Majesty," Portia inclined her head and hurried from the room.

Darian reached over and placed his hand over the queen's. "I'm sure it's nothing."

She smiled wanly. "As much as I would love to believe that, the lights dimming after our enemy's attempts at infiltrating our city has me pessimistic."

"I wonder if it's like how I used to help Law get into buildings. Cut the security and the lights, then bust in," Meryn mused out loud.

Once again, heads swiveled to her, this time varying looks of horror on their faces.

"Meryn, you're a genius," Law admitted. Unlike everyone else at the table, he looked thoughtful. "It's exactly how we would try to infiltrate a location." He turned toward the small menace. "Flip the script. What would you do if you were running security of the building and noticed lights and security cams were fritzing out?"

Gage was officially impressed. Law seemed to know exactly how to engage Meryn, to get her thinking in her own special way.

Meryn frowned. "It's not that simple. Had I truly been in charge of the building, I would have countermeasures already in place. That's not the case here."

The queen leaned forward. "What would you add?"

Meryn was silent a moment, then turned to Kendrick. "Do portals accumulate any type of measurable energy before forming?"

Kendrick's mouth dropped open.

Gage watched in fascination as one of the most powerful witches he had ever met sat there slack-jawed.

A moment later, Kendrick broke into a huge grin before he jumped to his feet, whooping. He moved around the table and picked up Meryn, swinging her around. "Such a clever mind!"

Aiden stood growling before he plucked Meryn from Kendrick's hands. "She's not a damn doll."

Kendrick ignored him. "Boys, Kincaid, Justice, you're with me." He was still muttering to himself about energy signatures as he practically sprinted from the room.

Nigel, Neil, Kincaid, and Justice looked at each other before breaking into a dead run after the master witch.

Gage blinked as his friend disappeared from sight. "What just happened?"

"We're mixing technology and magic," Meryn explained as she settled back down in Aiden's lap.

"I need a bit more than that," Brennus said, looking confused.

Meryn shrugged. "Since I haven't been able to use wands for magic like in Hogwarts, I have been approaching magic from a scientific standpoint. To me, it makes sense that there would be a gathering of energy to form a portal. If we're able to measure and track that energy, we can pinpoint when and where these dark portals will pop up. That would be step one in my defense plan," she explained.

Thane and Law turned to look at the doorway with envious expressions. Gage could tell that they wanted to play with the experimental magic too.

The queen sat back, looking stunned. "What would be your step two?"

"Death and traps," Meryn answered succinctly.

Thane sprang to his feet a second before Law stood. "We can handle that," he volunteered.

Meryn tapped her chin with her pointer finger. "It will have to be easily moveable. We don't know where these portals will show up."

Law said excitedly. "Sounds like a fun project."

"Come on, Law, we can't let the prissy librarian show us up," Thane said, heading toward the door.

"Thanks, Red Queen," Law grinned wickedly and followed his brother.

Brennus sat back next to his mate. "We should just leave Meryn in charge."

Aiden exhaled. "I've been saying that for months."

Kari lifted her stylus. "We still don't know why the lights are dimming," she reminded them.

"And we probably won't until Mikel gets here. Until then, we're working on countermeasures," Declan said, before kissing his mate on her neck.

Izzy turned to Oron. "So, what do we do now?"

Gage couldn't have been more surprised when Kari turned to him an apologetic look on her face. "When you have a moment, I have a message for you from your family."

Declan rolled his eyes. "Leave the boy be." He looked him in the eye, smiling. "And it's not your entire family, just your mother."

Kari scowled up at her mate. "Maybe he would like to discuss this later," she reprimanded diplomatically.

Gage winced and rubbed the back of his neck before turning to Kari and Declan. "I know what you're referring to. Ever since the shadows have been sighted here in Éire Danu, my mother has been calling to see if I could return to Noctem Falls," he paused, then continued.

"She seems to forget that I'm grown and unit warrior," he looked around the room. Those from Éire Danu were well aware of his mother's overprotectiveness toward him. The others, recently from Noctem Falls, had met his uncle and aunt. As embarrassing as it was, he felt like he should just get everything out now, to get the conversation over with.

Meryn looked over to him. "I remember meeting Simon and Leana and Beth's bodyguards, but I don't remember meeting anyone else from that family. Your mom lives there, right?" she asked.

Gage winced. "Yes, she lives with my uncle and my aunt, but she keeps to herself. My mother is Leana's sister, so, technically, I am not related to the Géroux by blood, but Simon has always treated me the same as his nephews, Tarak, Kuruk, and Bastien." He stopped, took a deep breath, and re-centered himself. When he looked back over at Meryn, he smiled wanly. "It is a difficult conversation to have. My mother's mate, my father, is not the most caring of individuals. Growing up, I constantly heard that people were surprised she had not faded due to the lack of love between them. But, for all his faults, he is a fair leader and does well by House Fabre," he sighed.

"Unfortunately, my mother did not want a fair leader. She wanted love. Without a mate at her side, she became that much more protective of me. She transferred all the love she had to give to me."

Next to him, Ari snorted. "And became a bit obsessed," he added playfully.

Gage smiled. "Something like that. It was nothing inappropriate," he clarified, "and it meant she was able to raise me, and I got to know and love my mother, but sometimes it can be daunting."

Meryn nodded. "That makes sense. You're her son. She's lived for you, and now she's worried you might get killed by random ferals popping up in shadows in a city that is supposed to be impenetrable."

To Gage, her lack of pity was almost refreshing, and he found himself liking her just that much more. "Thank you, Meryn. I think we all needed that recap," he teased.

Kari lifted her stylus. "I can be a point of contact for her if that is easier. I do send updates to Magnus, and I am sure he is meeting with Simon often," she offered.

Gage thought about it a moment before nodding. "You know, that might not be a bad idea. If it comes from you, via Magnus and my uncle, it's mostly coming from official channels. She wouldn't be able to argue. It wouldn't be a mat ter of just not wanting to visit her. Thank you Kari. I'll take you up on that."

Out of the blue, Priest wrapped his arm around his neck and pulled him down to rake his knuckles across his scalp.

"He's just a baby vampire, who needs his bot bot," Priest teased.

Laughing, Gage drove his elbow into Priest's solar plexus, and his unit brother grunted. "And you're just our little baby bird, Dora," he countered.

At the table, Meryn spoke up. "That's Pandora," she corrected.

Ari stepped between the two of them, and they both straightened, remembering that they were in the Queen's chamber. Ari placed a hand on his shoulder. "You know it wouldn't be a bad idea if you wanted to invite her here," he suggested.

Gage just stared. "You want me to invite my mother to the city? We've been having these strange portals pop up out of nowhere. Are you out of your mind?" he exclaimed.

Ari simply raised an eyebrow. "And both of my parents live here. She could stay at the Lionhart estate with them."

Gage shook his head. "I love my mother, I do, but I can barely handle her in a whole other pillar city. I'm not sure what I would do if she were down the road," he said, sighing.

"Paranormal helicopter parent," Meryn announced. "I wonder how much more that's amplified than in the human world." Groaning, Gage buried his face in his hands.

Ari removed his hand. "I'm telling you, it will do a lot of good if she can see for herself how safe you actually are. Maybe a lot of her anxiety is from not knowing."

Gage straightened. "I see your point. All I can promise is that I'll think about it."

Behind Ari's back, Priest was making faces at him. Just as he was about to reach over and slap him one, an alarm sounded.

Meryn blinked. "That's new. What is it for?" she asked.

Around the table, everybody looked a bit confused. Not getting an answer, Meryn looked up to Aiden. "Babe, do you know what the new alarm is?" she asked again.

Aiden was already reaching for his walkie-talkie. "Ben, report!" he barked.

"Adonis," Meryn whispered.

Aiden ignored her.

"Commander, another one of those shadow portals appeared in almost exactly the same location as the last one. Citizens saw it and reported it to Dav," Ben replied. "The Old Guard is in place and Gamma is heading there now. We'll be on standby."

"Stay alert," Aiden ordered. "We'll be right there." Switching channels on the walkie-talkie, he stood then started speaking again. "Kendrick, a new portal has been sighted at the perimeter. Grab your witches and head there. We're leaving the palace now. Tell Nigel and Neil to come back and guard Meryn."

"Got it," was the quick reply.

Aiden turned to them. "Tau unit move out," he ordered.

And just like that, Gage was moving. They ran through the palace, Kincaid meeting up with them in the hallway.

Since the appearance of the first portal and with them not knowing when they were going to get deployed to warehouses, the units had taken to wearing a lot of their regular gear as they patrolled. Luckily, they didn't need much as they headed toward the perimeter.

Gage pulled out his sidearm and checked it as they ran. "What do you think we'll find when we get there?" he asked.

Ari glanced back at him, a wicked gleam in his eyes. "Hopefully, our enemies," was the cheerful reply.

The city proper flew by, and as they rounded corners in the Border City, they soon found themselves at the perimeter.

The Old Guard and Gamma was standing in formation, looking up at a large shadow portal. As they ran up, the guard saluted Aiden.

Aiden waved off their formality. "What do we have?" he asked.

Dav stepped forward. "One of my patrons saw something flickering in the field. They came in and told us, so we ran out here and watched the damn thing form. It was like every shadow and piece of darkness in the area just solidified into that thing. So far, nothing has come through."

Aiden reached for his walkie-talkie. "Meryn, update the palace. We're here at the portal. So far, nothing's come through. We're going to establish a perimeter and monitor this thing."

"If they came through invisible, and the Old Guard doesn't have thermal goggles, would they have seen anything passing through?" Her chirpy response had the men wincing.

Dav paled, his normal golden tone draining to a milk white. "We didn't see anything…" he said, stumbling over his words. He then smacked his forehead with his palm and exhaled. "And we wouldn't if they were invisible."

Frowning, Aiden brought the walkie-talkie back up to his face. "Meryn, can you put in another order of thermal goggles?"

Seconds later, Meryn answered, sounding as frustrated as Aiden looked. "It's going to be a few more days for that. It's not like you can order this shit off of *Amazon*, and we're in a pillar city," she reminded him.

Kendrick looked at the Ashleigh brothers. "I guess we can start studying this thing while it's still open," he said, pointing to the portal. "I wasn't expecting to get data this quickly."

"I have my goggles," Brie announced, adjusting them on her face. Lifting her left hand, she pointed to the tree line. "I've got movement." She took off on a dead run, Ari, Kincaid, Priest, and Gage, right on her heels.

There was no way in hell he was going to let anything happen to his unit brother's mate. Behind them, he heard Aiden give orders to Gamma to hold the perimeter as he tossed his set of goggles to Dav.

The thundering footsteps behind him moments later had him turning. Aiden, along with the witches, Darian, Oron, and Declan, were following close behind.

A gunshot up ahead had his head turning back forward where he saw Brie run over to a spot in a clearing, gun pointed down. "I got him," she announced. Moving her foot, she seemed to nudge something. Sighing, she removed the goggles. "Sorry guys, I think I killed him, though I can't tell for sure, he's kind of laying on his face," she added.

Aiden looked around at the men. Gage shook his head to answer Aiden's unasked question. They could all see blood pooling, but without putting on their own goggles, they couldn't see a body.

Gage reached for his and adjusted them on his face. Looking around, he kept an eye on their surroundings while his brothers investigated the body.

Aiden turning to Brie. "Brie, do you see some sort of a necklace on the body?" Aiden asked.

Brie shrugged. "I can try flipping him over, I guess." Putting the goggles back on, she went to step forward, and Ari growled. "Let me," he ordered.

Rolling her eyes, she shot daggers at her mate before stepping back. Once he had his own goggles in place, seeing what Gage assumed was the image of whatever was on the ground, Ari kicked it hard. "There," he said. "It's flipped."

Brie removed her goggles and looked down.

"There is something there." She squinted. "I don't see the body, but there's like a flicker, right….. there," she went to lean down, and once again, Ari stepped in front of her.

Releasing a small growl of her own, which was impressive for a human, she punched Ari in the back. "This shit is getting old."

Ari sighed and stepped aside. "I'm sorry, go ahead."

Taking out her gun, she emptied her ammo into the body. "There, baby, feel better now?" she asked.

Exhaling with relief, Ari just grinned. "Thanks, hon."

Shaking her head, she went to her knees in the dirt and reached forward. They heard a distinctive snap, then the body was suddenly visible. "Is this what you're talking about?" she asked, holding up a leather beaded necklace.

Aidan nodded. "That's it," he replied, sounding resigned. Standing in a circle, they were all looking down.

Gage pointed. "Does anyone recognize him?" he asked.

Unlike Ari, he had grown up in Noctem Falls. To him, the man was just blond hair, golden skin, and tall. He didn't recognize any features that might belong to a certain fae family.

"Mother may," Darian responded. Pulling out his phone, he took a picture. "I'm sending this to Meryn to share." He looked down at the body and shook his head. "What do we do with it?" he asked.

Aiden straightened. "Brie, you're assigned to the portal area. For now, Ari will be your escort."

Brie exhaled loudly. "I don't need a damn escort."

Aiden's expression softened. "It's not because you're female. We'll all be moving around using the buddy system. Who better than your mate to protect you?" Looking a bit mollified, she nodded. He continued. "Right now, you're the one with the most experience with the goggles. Until we all get more comfortable using them, I would feel better with you taking point."

Nodding, both Ari and Brie turned and started to run back toward where the portal was. Aiden looked his way. "Priest, Gage, if you could bring our new friend back, we need to secure him or whatever is left of him," he added, looking at all the bullet holes. "The queen may need the body for further identification." Aiden turned and looked further into the woods. "Where was he going?" he wondered out loud. He glanced over to Darian. "What's out there?" he asked.

Darian grinned wickedly. "That's the Dark Forest. Only goblins and dark creatures live there. Frankly, I feel sorry for any feral dumb enough to take them on."

Aiden shook his head, smiling at Darian's answer. "Darian, you and Kincaid find a way of warning the goblins. If anything happens to them, Meryn will have my balls." Aiden winced, thinking of the repercussions.

Darian nodded. "Easily done. We have a point

of contact there now, thanks to Meryn." He paused, frowning. "What was his name again?"

"Gilheim," Kincaid answered, then smiled impishly. "Evidently, according to Meryn, he also has an amazing ass."

Aiden growled.

Ignoring him, Darian straightened and turned to look into the forest. "That's the one. I heard he is a fierce warrior and defended her amongst his people. It would be beneficial to have him on our side to act as a liaison for the goblins."

Gage sighed. "Why do we have to mess with the body, and Kincaid gets to go meet the goblins?" he muttered.

Priest shrugged. "We're just that lucky, I guess."

"Commander, the portal just collapsed. We'll stick around just in case it reforms," Dav called out over the walkie talkie.

Aiden lifted his comms unit. "Roger that," he replied, then looked around one last time. "We're done here. Let's move out," Aiden ordered.

As the rest of the team began to jog back toward the city, he exchanged looks with Priest. "Drag it back?"

His unit brother nodded, and they each bent down, picked up an ankle, and proceeded to drag it back towards where the palace was, heedless of any damage it might take along the way.

CHAPTER TWO

❦

"MY LADY, DON'T FORGET THAT you have a one o'clock with Rodney Mandrake. He wants to discuss a heating system proposal suggested for Noctem Falls."

Zoe held back a sigh as Andrei looked down at his notes and continued. "Lunch is at two. You will be having roast and vegetables. After lunch, you have your daily maintenance checks of the temple's fires…"

Every day was the same. Each minute planned and accounted for. She barely had any time to breathe. If it weren't a hereditary obligation, she would have walked away from being the Fire Temple Head and traveled instead. But, as she was next in line to serve when she came of age a month ago, all the responsibilities and burdens fell to her.

"My lady, are you listening?" Andrei's sharp tone had her wincing. She hated it when he got angry. Yet another decision that had been made for her. Andrei, her council-appointed assistant.

"I'm sorry, what was it you said?"

He sneered. "I said that you also have your

weekly visit with the council's physician to check on your, *condition*." He seemed to savor the word as if relishing in discussing her huge failing.

"I understand," she replied meekly. It was best to agree and get the meetings over with.

Andrei placed a large stack of papers on her desk. "And those need signatures before the day is out. I'll be at my desk if you need me."

You mean you'll be at your desk watching, as usual, she thought to herself.

"Thank you," she said, pulling the stack closer. It would take her until at least midnight to read and sign each request. She hid her smile. Reading each document was her tiny way of rebelling. Andrei couldn't leave until she did, and she refused to sign anything unless she had read it. Looks like they were both in for a long night.

Just as she was enjoying her small victory, someone knocked as they opened the door slowly. "Zoe, do you have a minute?" a female voice asked as they entered.

Smiling, Zoe stood and hurried over to one of the few friends she had in the council building. "I always have time for you, Caroline. What can I help you with?"

The older witch smiled before her eyes darted to where Andrei listened in. "Queen Aleksandra of Éire Danu has requested the assistance of the Fire Temple Head as soon as you can leave."

"She has appointments through the end of the month," Andrei protested, immediately standing, his arms crossed over his chest belligerently.

Her friend's expression turned frosty. "I wasn't speaking to you."

"You know good and well she can't be trusted," Andrei began.

Caroline's hand came up quickly, and she turned her wrist as she snapped her fingers. Without even speaking a word, she cast a spell paralyzing the odious man. Zoe was stunned. Only extremely powerful witches could do what she just witnessed.

"Caroline?" she rested her hand on her friend's arm. "What is it?"

The older witch placed a comforting hand over Zoe's, then gently steered her from the room, leaving the gasping and grunting Andrei on his own.

"Zoe, I cannot stand to see them treat you this way anymore. I promised your mother when she and your father left ten years ago that I'd watch over you, and that's what I'm doing." Reaching into her sleeve, she retrieved a wax-sealed scroll. "I wasn't lying. Éire Danu has requested the Fire Temple Head." She smiled. "I feel like my prayers have been answered." She passed her the scroll. "Go to Éire Danu, and don't come back to Storm Keep until either your brother or sister returns."

Zoe's mouth dropped. "I can't do that! I have responsibilities, the Temple and…"

"And all of your 'appointments'?" Caroline asked, making air quotes. "The council fills every moment of your day to control you."

Zoe looked down. "I know. I know that's what they're doing, but it's the only way to keep everyone safe around me."

"Bull hockey!"

Zoe's head snapped up.

Caroline grasped both of her upper arms and gave her a gentle shake. "That's a lazy solution. They haven't even tried to understand why your magic goes awry. Instead, they stack all their busy work in front of you so that you don't have any opportunity to do anything else."

"Like burn the city down?" Zoe asked sarcastically.

Caroline released her arms and pinched the bridge of her nose.

"You look like Kendrick when you do that," Zoe teased.

Caroline shook her head. "I'll take that as a compliment." She sighed. "If he were still in the city, I'd send you to him. The council avoids him like the plague."

"Where is he?"

Caroline shrugged. "I lost track of him after he left Noctem Falls. Knowing him, he's where his brother is in Lycaonia."

Zoe nodded. That made sense. No one loved their brother more than Kendrick loved Keelan, well, except maybe her. She desperately missed Mikel. Thinking of both her brother and the afflicted Keelan had her sniffling.

"I know, darling. I miss Keelan too."

Zoe scrubbed at her eyes. "What if I burn

something in Éire Danu," she swallowed hard. "Don't they have sacred trees there?"

"I have every faith that, actually given the opportunity, you can gain control of your power. Unfortunately, up until now, the council has been afraid of that power and have made every effort to keep you locked inside your childhood home and now to your desk here in the Temple."

Zoe looked down at the scroll, her hands trembling. "I can actually leave?" she whispered.

"Yes, and the sooner, the better." Caroline glanced back at the office door. "That spell won't hold forever."

"Won't you get in trouble with the council?" Zoe asked, afraid for her friend.

Caroline snorted. "I've been dancing around the council for close to a hundred and fifty years. Leave those busybodies to me." She shrugged. "Besides, if they try anything, like assigning me to some remote location, as they are wont to do, I'll simply go to Noctem Falls. I have a standing job offer there from the Prince himself."

"Wow." Zoe blinked. "You know an actual prince?"

"Oh, youngling, I wish I could go with you. I feel like I'm sending a lamb into a forest of wolves." Caroline fretted. "You haven't seen much of Storm Keep, much less the outside world."

Zoe straightened. "I can do this. I've always wanted to travel, now is my chance."

Caroline smiled. "That's the spirit. You help the queen in Éire Danu, and I'll try to call your family home. Neither your parents, nor your siblings would stand for the council's treatment of you."

Zoe grinned. Her brother would probably destroy the council building. "Do you know where they are?" She had been trying to find them for years.

Caroline shook her head, looking sad. "The assignment your parents are on must be top secret. Despite having access to more than most, I haven't been able to find out where they are." She then snort laughed. "And no one tells your siblings what to do. They could be anywhere."

Zoe grinned. "What do I pack?"

"Some clothes and toiletries." She paused. "And probably anything of value to you personally, no telling when you'll actually return."

"Where do I get a suitcase? How does one pack it?"

Caroline blinked. "Oh, dear."

"I can do this. I can. I just need to know how."

Caroline exhaled. "You're right. How would you know unless you've been told? Come along, witchling, I'll show you how to pack."

Zoe looped her arm through Caroline's, and they both hurried toward her quarters.

❧

Clutching her suitcase to her chest, she stared at the large golden fae in front of her. "I..I'm the Fire Temple Head. The queen sent for me?"

The large fae's mouth twitched as he tried to hide a smile. "Are you asking?"

"Yes, I mean no."

"Cut the poor girl some slack. You can clearly see she's nervous." A handsome warrior rebuffed his friend. "My name is Ramsey Lionhart. Welcome to Éire Danu, Lady…"

Zoe beamed at his kindness. "My name is Zoe. Thank you for being so nice. This is my first time leaving Storm Keep," she paused. "Actually, this is kinda my first time leaving my house too."

Both men blinked.

"I'm sorry?" she said, afraid she might have misspoken.

Ramsey recovered first. Stepping forward, he took her luggage and handed her suitcase off to the fae behind him before tucking her hand into his elbow. "That's perfectly fine. That just means we have that much more to show you whilst you are here."

The fae holding her suitcase turned to the two warriors standing against the wall. "You two have portal duty so we can escort this lovely lady to the palace."

They nodded, and the taller fae placed a hand over his heart and bowed. "Forgive my lapse in manners. My name is Aeson Vi'Liordon. I am leader of the Chi Unit, and we will happily escort you to our queen."

Blushing at their attentiveness, she could only nod. No one in Storm Keep had ever treated her like this.

As they walked, Ramsey pointed out different shops and made recommendations on where to eat. "Now, if you're looking for a good beer, no place is better than Dav's pub."

"Does she look like the type of lady that drinks beer? She's delicate. I bet she enjoys wine more," Aeson interrupted.

"I've never had either, though, I'd like to try them someday."

Ramsey smiled down at her. "Then you shall."

Zoe stopped walking, and both men turned to look at her with questioning expressions. "What is it? Do you need to rest?" Ramsey asked.

"Why are you being so nice to me!" she blurted out, unable to take not knowing. The only ones that had ever treated her like this was her family, and they weren't her family.

Ramsey looked a bit shocked. "How else are we to treat you?"

Zoe made a sneering expression. "Know your place and do your work," she said, repeating Andrei's most used phase. She scrunched up her nose. "Like that."

Ramsey's smile seemed locked in place, but his eyes hardened. "And who, exactly, speaks to you like that?"

"Andrei, he's the assistant the council assigned to me when I became the Temple Head, but I think he's just there to spy on me. His beady little eyes follow me everywhere."

"Is that so," Aeson muttered under his breath. "Well, unlike that basta... I mean fellow. We know how to treat a lady. Not only are you a guest in our city, given that you are the Fire Temple Head, you are afforded a certain amount of respect and deference," he said, pointing to her robes and rank emblem. "You have also been asked to come here by our queen. With our current problem with the city's lighting, we assume you're here to help us. All of these reasons and common courtesy have guided our actions," he explained.

Zoe felt foolish. When he explained it like that, it made perfect sense to treat her courteously. But, if that were true, then how could it be such a stark difference to home?

"And you're a very pretty woman, and it's a delightful change of pace to spend time with you, rather than stinky warriors," Ramsey teased.

Zoe giggled at his levity. She playfully punched him in the arm. "My brother is a warrior or was. He isn't stinky."

Both men now leaned forward. Aeson smiling. "Who is your brother?"

"Mikel Appleblossom," she replied proudly, puffing out her chest.

"Holy shit," Ramsey whispered.

"My dear, dear, lady, you are thrice welcome. Mikel Appleblossom is one of the best warriors to ever serve. He helped shape the Alpha Unit when Aiden McKenzie became Unit Commander. It is an honor to be able to escort his beloved baby sister," Aeson said, sweeping down into an elegant bow.

She stepped forward and placed both hands on his forearm. "Do you know where he is? I've been looking for him for years. Things at home are…" she trailed off.

Aeson passed her suitcase to Ramsey and placed a large, warm hand over hers. "I will find him and bring him to you, this I do swear."

"I do swear," Ramsey echoed.

Zoe couldn't stop her tears. They reminded her so much of Mikel, and it was a relief to finally feel safe again.

"What in the hell have you done to that poor girl!" an angry voice demanded.

"Nothing, Dav, I swear," Ramsey said, looking frazzled at her tears.

A rough, calloused hand wiped away her tears. "There, there, honey, you tell ole Dav what these two idiots have done, and I'll right it for you."

"They aren't idiots, they're very nice. And you're nice for asking. It's just, I feel so safe that I've suddenly become tired," she admitted, sniffling loudly.

She looked up into Dav's eyes, and his kindness reminded her of Caroline. "I'm sorry."

He wrapped an arm around her shoulders. "You don't have a thing to be sorry for." He looked down at her. "Been having to be strong for a while, huh?"

She sniffled again and nodded.

"Well, you're here now, and we'll take care of our girl." He looked at Aeson. "Where are you two brats taking her?"

Aeson rolled his eyes at the 'brat' comment and answered. "Queen Aleksandra summoned her as the Fire Temple Head, we think she's here to investigate the dimming of the lights, and she's Mikel Appleblossom's baby sister."

Dav sucked in a breath. "All that, huh." He looked down at her. "Whose ass do I need to beat that you only feel safe with three ugly warriors you just met?"

"You mean two ugly warriors," Ramsey corrected. "I'm fabulous."

She shrugged and looked down at the street. She didn't want to cause any trouble.

"Ramsey and I will be heading to Storm Keep to beat some bastard named Andrei and any council member that was a party in assigning him as her assistant," Aeson announced.

She looked up quickly, and seeing that they were serious, her mouth dropped. "You... you can't do that!" she stuttered.

Ramsey tilted his head. "Why?"

"They're council members!"

Aeson tilted his head in the other direction. "And?"

She looked to the third, older and hopefully wiser warrior. He just grinned wickedly. "We would rather face the political fallout from beating down prissy, witch council members than your brother if he finds out we did nothing after seeing you so distressed."

She turned back to Aeson. "Are you really gonna hit them?"

He patted her on the head. "Don't you worry about that. Now, what would you like to do?"

Zoe felt her heart begin to race. Making choices was hard. "Ummm, uhh, meet the queen? It's why I'm here. Right?"

Ramsey nodded. "Sounds good."

She exhaled in relief. Then she frowned. "How do you greet a queen?" She began to rub her belly. Her stomach was in knots imagining all the ways she could mess up."

"Whoa!" Aeson exclaimed, moving them back a few steps. "That's the brightest I've seen them in a while."

Zoe looked around to identify what the men were looking at. To their left, about eight feet away, a city lamp shone brightly.

"It is?"

Ramsey nodded, smiling. "Looks like you're exactly what we need."

Zoe wanted to be happy, except for the fact that she hadn't meant to do anything to the lamp. She could only be grateful nothing was on fire.

"After your visit with the queen, you have to swing by my pub. I'll serve you the best fish and beer you've ever had," Dav offered.

She smiled up at him. "Thank you. I can't wait to have my first beer."

Dav blinked, then broke out in a broad smile. "Then I'll have to make sure it's extra cold for you." He turned to the other two warriors. "You both know what's been going on. Straight to the palace and stay by her side," he ordered.

"Yes, sir," both men responded before, once again, Ramsey offered her his elbow. "My lady."

She accepted his elbow, and they resumed their way toward the large looming palace above them.

❦

Aeson stepped away from the fae woman, who nodded and motioned for them to follow. Moments later, they were standing in front of a very imposing door.

The woman knocked, then opened the door. "Your Majesty, the Fire Temple Head from Storm Keep is here at your request." She stepped to one side, and with Ramsey on her left and Aeson on her right, they escorted her into what looked like an elegant set of living quarters.

They walked her up to an impressive table where a large group of people were sitting. Without looking at them, she focused on the only one who could possibly be the queen of the fae. Dropping into a curtsey, she greeted her. "Your Majesty."

"What in the hell are you doing here, Zoe?" a familiar, grouchy voice demanded.

She looked up and smiled. "Kendrick! Why are you here? Caroline was certain you'd be in Lycaonia with Keelan. Is he okay?" Forgetting decorum, she raced around the table. "I've missed you so much. You've been gone such a long time." She looked down and saw a pretty woman looking at her, her brows furrowed. "Is this your mate? She's lovely." She smiled at the woman. "I'm sorry you got stuck with such a sourpuss, but he's really nice on the inside."

"Zoe!"

Turning to her right, she saw two redheads barreling toward her. Seconds later, she was swept up in a group hug. Nigel and Neil were her secret best friends. They were the only ones she knew that had red hair like her. Except theirs was straight whereas hers was a massive mess of corkscrew curls.

"No! No. You head right back to Storm Keep," Kendrick demanded, extricating her from the twins.

"But.."

"No buts. We summoned the Fire Temple Head…"

"I am the Fire Temple Head," she refuted.

He stopped mid-sentence. "What?"

She pointed at herself. "I am the Fire Temple Head."

"What! Where's Mikel?"

She shrugged. "I don't know, he disappeared a few years ago to do some sort of mission, and when I came of age, they locked me away in the temple."

"Locked?" Aeson growled.

"I mean, assigned me to the temple," she corrected, not wanting to incite more trouble.

"There, there, Aeson, we were already planning on going to Storm Keep to take care of those bastards," Ramsey said soothingly.

"Locked?" Nigel and Neil said in unison, with clenched jaws.

She looked down at their shoes. "They said it was for my own good, given my affliction."

"Affliction?" a melodious voice asked.

She turned to see that the queen had stood and was now at her side. "Yes, Your Majesty, I, um, I have the tendency to set things on fire when I lose control of myself."

"Kickass," a small female said, looking impressed.

"Meryn, we have to take care of her," Neil pleaded.

"She's one of our bestest friends. She can't go back to Storm Keep if they are locking her up!" Nigel protested.

The one that had proclaimed her to be 'kickass' nodded. "Of course. Besides, with that red hair, I'm surprised she isn't a cousin or something."

Zoe beamed at her. "Actually, my red hair comes from the Appleblossom family. We're said to be descended from the first cousin of the last Stormhart king," she announced proudly. "Appleblossoms always produce strong witches."

Meryn looked to Kendrick. "Isn't that interesting, Kendrick? Those descended from the Stormharts are always strong witches. Who woulda thunk it?"

"Quiet, Menace," Kendrick growled.

Neil looked over to Aeson. "When are you leaving?"

Aeson nodded approvingly. "As soon as I can get some leave approved by Ari," he looked around. "Where is he anyway? I thought the Tau Unit practically lived in the palace now."

"They'll be here shortly. After that portal closed, Ari and Brie stayed behind to show some of the Old Guard how to use the goggles, and Gage and Priest are disposing of the feral," replied one of the largest men Zoe had ever seen.

He wasn't just tall. He was also widely built. When the man stood and headed in her direction, she took a step back and collided with Neil, who smiled and leaned down. "That's the Unit Commander, Aiden McKenzie. He's Meryn's mate and kinda our adopted brother now," he whispered.

Seeing that his height made her nervous, he dropped down, so he was kneeling down on one knee. "Zoe, isn't it? The beautiful baby girl with emerald-colored eyes and a riot of red curls." He smiled gently up at her.

She frowned. "Have we met?"

He shook his head. "No, but I have heard all about you from your brother."

She felt her eyes widen. Aiden McKenzie, the Unit Commander, was also the unit leader of Alpha, her brother's old unit. "You're Mikel's Aiden, his unit leader," she whispered, covering her mouth with both hands.

He reached up and took her hands. "It's wonderful to finally meet you. I don't know if your brother ever told you this, but he had such a hard time picking your *athair*."

She nodded. She had heard that her whole life. Her brother had met so many amazing men in his travels he couldn't choose just one. "He couldn't pick one, so I ended up with none."

Aiden frowned. "That's half true. You're right that he couldn't choose one, but wrong that you ended up with none. He chose all of the Alpha Unit warriors to become your *athai*r." Aiden stood smiling. "When he was told that wasn't the way things were done, he simply said…"

"Deal with it," she said, finishing his sentence. She knew her brother's stubbornness all too well.

Aiden chuckled. "Mikel Appleblossom is famous for doing things his own way. So, you see, you have many unofficial *athairs*. We thought he would bring you to visit, when you came of age, to introduce us, but when that didn't happen, we assumed it was because he had changed his mind."

Another fae walked up to stand beside Aiden. "My name is Darian Vi'Alina. I am also one of your unofficial *athairs*, Zoe. I was hoping that I'd be able to convince Mikel to bring you to visit after he was done investigating the lights. It's such an amazing surprise to meet you instead." Still smiling, he looked over to Aeson. "Room for one more?"

"Two," Aiden corrected.

"I don't understand, why?" Zoe asked. For the second time in one day, she felt overwhelmed by her own emotions. Seconds later, she was terrified to feel sparks forming around her. Squeezing her eyes closed, she tensed her entire body, trying to shut down her magic.

No, no, no, no! Not now, not them, please don't hurt them! She prayed to anyone listening.

She felt a hand on her head, and the sparks died away and the heat in her body faded. Opening her eyes, she looked up to see Kendrick's concerned expression. "Are you okay, Zo?" he asked, gently steering her to one of the seats. Moments later, a glass of cold water was pressed into her hands. "Why was your magic threatening to break free?" he asked, as everyone sat back down.

She gulped down the ice water gratefully. "It's my affliction," she admitted.

"Excuse me?" he asked.

"Mother and father didn't want me discussing this outside the family, but I guess it's a moot point now, and technically *athairs* are family, so…" She exhaled. "I cause fires when I get overwhelmed. It's why the council advised my parents to keep me secluded as much as possible to prevent anyone from getting hurt. The times I snuck away from home to play with Nigel and Neil are the only times I was unsupervised." She looked at the twins. "I'm so sorry to have put you in danger, but I always had so much fun being with you."

"You don't ever have to be sorry for playing with us," Nigel protested.

"Yeah, you're one of the only ones that treated us like people. Everyone else called us urchins," Neil admitted.

"I don't understand. Every witch goes through phases where their magic goes haywire. Why would they seclude you?" Another warrior asked.

"Good question, Kincaid," Kendrick said approvingly. He took her hand. "Did Mikel agree to this?"

She shook her head. "No, he said I just needed

time to learn, but mother and father were afraid. When I lost control, it was always so violent. They were terrified I'd hurt myself, so they listened to the council, kept my life regimented, and it worked."

Kendrick shook his head. "Zoe, honey, your brother was right. You needed to learn how to control your magic. What your parents and the council did was simply put you in an environment where you didn't have to think, which limited the demand for your magic. I can understand why your parents, being worried for you, would listen to the council, but the council should have known better. What they did was similar to drugging an ornery toddler. Eventually, there will come a time when the child isn't drugged, and it's a thousand times worse because they haven't learned how to process their emotions."

"I was a drugged toddler?" she asked, incredulous.

He shook his head. "No, your magic is the ornery toddler. It acts out because you were never taught how to tame it."

"Why? Why would they do something like that? It's like they wanted her to explode or something," Neil exclaimed angrily.

Zoe closed her eyes, thinking back on how she grew up. Always taken care of. Every need anticipated, never put in a situation to think for herself. Simply managed so that her magic never flared.

"I'm a monster," she whispered.

"No, you're a weapon," Meryn corrected.

Silence filled the room as the weight of the truth from her words ricocheted from person to person.

CHAPTER THREE

ℭ

MERYN LOOKED AT THOSE STARING at her. "What? Why else would they deliberately not train her? I think Kari said something similar to Magnus regarding his incompetent secretary. 'I do believe there is a fine line between incompetency and sabotage. One is deliberate, but both can result in disaster.' For a group of witches that annoyingly brag about their training system, this feels planned," Meryn explained.

"Mikel would never stand for something like that," Kendrick argued.

Aiden nodded. "He is fanatically protective of his baby sister."

The word weapon bounced around Zoe's mind. She recalled the dozens of arguments her brother and sister had with their parents over her upbringing. "He may not have had a choice. My parents ultimately made most of the decisions about my schooling and lessons. I remember him arguing with them many times, but he didn't have any authority over me," Zoe said, looking from Kendrick to Aiden. "I think they were scared I'd hurt myself one day. I don't see them orchestrating a weapon scheme."

"What if it's nothing nefarious?" the woman at Darian's side suggested. She smiled in her direction. "My name is Amelia. I was raised in Storm Keep as well." She turned to Kendrick. "You know how lazy and self-serving the council can be. They may have told her parents to keep stress to a minimum and moved on to the next thing. That would be far easier than arranging for specialist tutors that could be better utilized elsewhere."

Kendrick eyed Meryn, then nodded his head slowly before turning back to look at Zoe. "I could see that as a possibility. It would take a very strong, seasoned witch to guide her. I don't see them wanting to lose one to a teaching position. Your parents and siblings are all fire witches, correct? Could they not help?"

Zoe flushed. "I always overrode them. There wasn't much they could do."

Kendrick cursed and muttered under his breath. "They should have come to me."

Zoe blinked. "That's right. You're a fire witch," she set her glass down excitedly. "Do you think you can help?"

Kendrick looked from her, to the puppy dog expression of the twins, then to Kincaid. "How? When did I start accumulating children?"

The queen began to laugh. "Your fun is only just starting," she said cryptically.

"Oh, please, Kendrick! I'll do what you say, honest. I'd give anything to be able to control my magic, so I don't have to stay inside all the time," Zoe pleaded.

Kendrick threw his arms up in the air. "Fine!" He rounded on her, then the twins. "If you want to join in, you'll have to do exactly as I say. My lessons are brutal," he warned.

Nigel smiled up at Kenrick's menacing figure. "Sure," he agreed happily.

"Man, if only Serenity and Keelan were here," Neil sighed sadly.

Zoe stood and hugged Neil tightly. "We'll all be together again someday. Then we can travel and do all the cool things we talked about growing up."

"We'll have to bring Micah along, he mated Serenity," Nigel reminded her.

She nodded. "Of course! I heard she had mated, but since the council banished her, I lost any opportunity to meet him. Do you think they'll come here to visit any time soon?"

Neil whipped out his phone. "Micah is gonna hate me," he said, chuckling. "Too bad," he added in a singsong voice.

Zoe giggled. "I still have work to do in fixing the lights and Kendrick's lessons, but other than that, I'm free."

Zoe watched as the one Kendrick called Kincaid edged forward. "Could I take some of those lessons too?"

"Arrrgh!" Kendrick groaned and rested his head on the table.

"Serves you right, old man. That's what you

get for hiding away amongst your books all these years," Thane teased.

Kendrick's head popped up, and he glared at Thane. "I'll have you know that I have been keeping an eye on these children for years." Sighing, he looked at Kincaid, and his eyes softened. "You, of course, are welcome to any additional lessons, especially as they will be fire in nature."

Zoe smiled at Kincaid. "You're a fire witch too?"

He shook his head sheepishly. "Not exactly."

Neil pointed to the abashed witch. "He's like a combination of you and us. He's fire and earth."

Kincaid nodded. "And my magic doesn't work quite right either, so you're not alone in that."

She felt her eyes widen. "You set fires too?"

He waved his hands in front of him, shaking his head. "No, worse. Most times, nothing happens, or if it does, it's not something I intended."

"Kendrick, besides a space to teach, do you require anything else for our young friends?" the queen asked.

"No, everything else I need, I have with me," he replied, holding up a small satchel.

"I want witch lessons too," Meryn announced.

"Me too!" an adorable, dark-headed young man beside Meryn said, chiming in.

"What? Why? Your innate empathy isn't at all like elemental magic," Kendrick asked, looking confused. He turned to the young man. "And Pip, you're a vampire, for gods' sake!"

"Cuz I wanna," Meryn replied.

"Yeah," Pip echoed.

"Meryn…" Aiden started.

Meryn glared up at her mate. "Why can't I expand my horizons? The twins are going," she said, looking in their direction.

"The twins are witches," Aiden pointed out, smiling.

Zoe recognized the determined look in Meryn's eyes and the set of her shoulders. Mikel always had the exact same look when he dug his heels in. "I don't think it would hurt anything if she wanted to sit in on the lessons."

"Yeah, she and Pip can stay with us if they want to," Neil added.

Kendrick simply stared at them.

"You know, it may not be a bad idea to open up the lessons to any unit witch that wishes to attend," Aiden said, rubbing his chin thoughtfully.

A tall man came up to stand behind Kendrick and slapped him on the back. "We were already going to be showing them defensive magic and how to set early detection spells."

Kendrick sat back, sighing. "Thane, for the unit warriors to learn such things, I understand and agree with it completely, but the children? They should be planting gardens, reading books, and having tea."

"That doesn't sound very efficient," Zoe said, scrunching up her nose.

"Or useful," Neil added.

"How does planting a garden help you get powerful," Nigel asked.

Kendrick cocked a brow. "And it's power you want?"

Nigel, Neil, Zoe, and Kincaid all nodded emphatically.

Kendrick looked taken aback at their response.

Thane turned their way. "Tell him why," he said softly.

"To be safe," Zoe responded.

"To protect others," Nigel added.

"To carve out our own way," Neil answered.

Kincaid nodded. "To protect my unit brothers and our people."

"Kendrick, these kids are a product of their generation. They've grown up in uncertain times and within a system where results are everything. They have no use for gardens."

Kendrick's expression turned tragic. "Then we have failed them more than I realized."

Neil snorted and shrugged. "I'll take tracking ferals and cyber mayhem over tea parties any day."

Kincaid laughed out loud. "It does sound like we're having more fun when you put it that way, doesn't it."

Zoe walked over and placed a hand on Kendrick's arm. "Maybe we're exactly as we are and where we are because that's how it's supposed to be."

"There is something to be said for a generation of witches that value protecting others over money and assignment placements, Kendrick. Don't sell yourself or them short," the queen admonished gently.

Pip looked at Kendrick. "Will you be serving snacks? Maybe, some tea?"

Zoe recognized that Pip was trying to soothe Kendrick, and her heart melted. He was so cute! "Tea would help keep us focused," she said.

"And we'll be doing lots and lots of reading," Nigel added, catching on.

Kendrick looked around the room. A slight sheen glinted from his eyes. "I suppose you'll want to tour the gardens here in Éire Danu too," he asked, his mouth quirked up in a smile.

"When in Rome and all that jazz," Meryn answered.

"Kendrick Ashwood, consider yourself truly blessed," the queen said as she lifted her teacup to her lips.

"Blessings won't help them during lessons. I will make sure they learn," he grumbled good-naturedly.

Zoe turned to the queen and gave a small curtsey. "I apologize for disrupting your lunch," she said, realizing that there was still food on the table.

The queen smiled. "It was a delightful interruption, my dear. Please, sit and join us. We had only just started when you arrived."

"We see you're in good hands, Zoe, though, I hope you'll swing by the pub later," Ramsey said as he and Aeson bowed to make their exit.

She looked to Aiden. "May I?"

Aiden blinked. "Huh?"

"May I go later?"

Meryn nodded. "You're a free chick now and of age, so do whatcha want."

Aiden frowned down at his mate. "Maybe not everything she wants." He then turned to Aeson. "Dav's?"

"Yes, sir. She made an impression on the old timer, so he wants to serve her her first beer."

Aiden nodded. "Sounds important, not something one should miss out on." He looked down at his mate. "Would you like to go try that fish you've been hounding me about tonight for dinner?"

Meryn's eyes brightened. "Hell yeah!"

"Party at Dav's?" Neil asked.

"We gonna get funky!" Pip announced.

The queen snort laughed into her tea cup.

Ramsey rubbed his hands together. "It can be Zoe's welcome party."

Aeson grinned. "We'll bring snacks."

Ramsey gave a small salute, and he and Aeson left arguing over which snacks would go best with beer.

Zoe sat down and looked around the table. Even knowing the twins, there were still a lot of names she didn't know. "Hello!" She started in a bright voice. "My name is Zoe Appleblossom. I look forward to working with all of you."

Meryn grinned. "Appleblossom jeans…" she sung.

"Boots with the fur…" Three others in the room responded at the same time.

The tall cocoa-skinned man turned to Meryn, a look of disgust on his face. "Thank you, ever so much. Now that song will be stuck in my head for days."

Meryn cackled in her chair. "Watch out, Pierce, earworm attack."

Kincaid and the young woman sitting next to the queen also glared at Meryn.

The queen tilted her head. "I'm afraid I don't understand."

Kincaid sighed. "It is, or was, a popular song in the human world. It has a very catchy tune, so it stays with you once you're reminded of it. That's what Meryn meant by earworm. It's a song that sort of plays on repeat in your mind."

The queen looked at Meryn aghast. "That sounds dreadful."

"He he he he," Meryn chuckled to herself.

"I think some introductions are in order since Zoe greeted us so politely," a woman said, standing. "My name is Kari Lionhart. I am mated to Declan," she pointed to the man next to her.

For the next twenty minutes, they went around the room, slowly introducing those present and explaining any familial or political connections.

Zoe sat there, trying her best to keep up. A light tap on her shoulder had her looking up. "Cord, right?"

"Yes, Lady Zoe. You're doing very well in remembering everyone. What can I prepare for you for lunch?" he asked.

She just blinked up at him. She had never had to pick her lunch before. It was always prepared and served to her. "I don't know."

His eyes widened, and he tried a different tactic. "What is a favorite from home? I can try to make it for you."

"I…I…I don't know. I have never picked my lunch before," she admitted.

"Serious-fuck-ing-ly?" Meryn asked, her eyes wide.

Zoe tried to ignore the incredulous looks she was getting from around the table. "Lunch is always at two o'clock. On the weekdays, it was soup, and on the weekends, it was roast."

"No pizza? No sushi? No *Hot Pockets*??" Meryn asked.

"I know what pizza and sushi are from books I've read, but I've never had them." She frowned. "What is a *Hot Pocket*?"

Meryn spun in her chair toward her squire. "Ryuu!"

Ryuu placed a hand on his charge's head. "I will work with Cord, Meryn, don't stress yourself. We'll make sure Lady Zoe gets to experience all your favorite foods."

Meryn exhaled in relief and turned back to her. "You are my brothers' bestest friend, so that makes you my bestest friend. And in our bat cave, we eat pizza and *Cheetos*, with coffee and sugar-free *Red Bull*. I would be a bad bestest friend if I did not introduce you to the finer things in life. Consider yourself mine now."

"Here we go again," Aiden said, chuckling. "I don't mind this time. She's technically my gods-daughter, so she was already family."

Meryn flicked a pea at him. "How come you never mentioned that?"

He shrugged. "I haven't heard from Mikel in nearly a decade, so I wasn't sure if he still considered the Alpha Unit her *athairs*."

"How come she didn't know?" Meryn asked.

Zoe looked to Aiden. "Yes, why do you think Mikel never told me?"

"Probably to keep you safe," Kendrick replied. "If you had known you had four unit warriors as *athairs*, would you have complied as much as you did once your parents and siblings left?"

Zoe shook her head. "I would have gone to Lycaonia the day I came of age." She smiled. "I probably would have written to them all the time about how bored I was too."

"He knew you well. I'm willing to bet he planned on being with you up until your one-hundredth birthday, and then he would have brought you to Lycaonia for safekeeping. Something must have changed his plans." Kendrick looked over at Aiden. "Do you have a way of getting ahold of him?"

Aiden's face became thoughtful. "Maybe, if he still uses his unit-issued cell. Nearly all unit warriors past and present carry one." He frowned. "It's not a sure-fire method of reaching warriors. We never heard back from the missing Vanguard."

Zoe's mouth dropped. "Caroline and I have been looking for him for years and it's because we didn't have his number?"

Aiden winced. "It's only used amongst unit warriors. Did he leave you no way of contacting him?"

She shook her head. "When he left, he said he wouldn't be gone long." She felt her eyes fill. "What if something's happened to him?"

"What about your parents?" Anne asked gently.

She felt her curls sway as she shook her head again. "The council assigned them out ten years ago. Caroline said it must be important because she has access to most of the council's records and couldn't find anything on them."

"When did you come of age?" the queen asked.

"About a month ago," she answered. "That was when the council moved me out of our family home and into the Fire Temple to act as the Fire Temple Head."

"Why you, if you're so young?" Meryn asked.

"An Appleblossom has always led the Fire Temple. With my parents on assignment and both my brother and sister having served and gone, it fell to me once I came of age," she explained.

Pip stood and walked over to sit beside her, then pulled her in for a hug. "Meryn said I am in charge of cuddles, and since you were raised kinda like me, I know you need cuddles."

Zoe returned his hug and relaxed against him. "Were you kept secluded too?"

He nodded. "Yes, my father did not care for me much, so those in our household followed his example in their treatment of me."

She looked at him. "What's there not to care for? You're amazing."

He smiled brightly. "I can believe you now

because Meryn tells me that all the time. I think you're amazing too since you stayed true to yourself."

"You aren't afraid I'll set you on fire?" she asked.

He shook his head. "Nope, but even if you do, I will not blame you because I know you would not do it on purpose." He flexed his opposite arm. "Besides, I am a vampire, and Aiden has been showing me exercises so I can be strong. I bet I would heal really, really fast."

"You have?" Meryn asked in a soft voice, looking up at her mate.

A flush worked up the back of Aiden's neck. "He said he wanted to be able to protect you, and I want him able to defend himself so no one mistreats him again."

Meryn simply climbed over his thigh, under his arm, and settled into his lap. "I love you, babe."

Smiling, Aiden rested his cheek on the top of her head. "I love you, too."

"That's so sweet," Zoe observed.

"They are the best brother and sister a guy could ask for," Pip added.

"Since Meryn said I belong to her now, I'll share my brother and sister with you, Pip," she offered.

His eyes widened. "Really?" he squeaked.

"Yup, they are going to love you to pieces." Zoe was certain they would spoil the vampire rotten. He was too cute not to.

Pip frowned. "Meryn, we need to find our new brother," he said in a serious tone.

Meryn gave a short nod. "Babe, call your secret number or whatever and tell Mikel to come here."

Aiden was already pulling out his phone. "I was going to reach out to him anyway. It's not like him to miss her birthday, especially her coming of age." He tapped the screen of his phone then held it up to his ear.

"Mikel, it's Aiden. Where in the hell are you?"

Zoe felt her breath catch. Her brother was really on the other end of the phone?

"Why am I asking? Because I have a very distraught Zoe in front of me, who is worried sick over you. What? No, I'm not in Storm Keep. I'm in Éire Danu. Why? Long story, but I'm glad I'm here since ferals started appearing. Yes, Zoe is here." Aiden pulled the phone away and scowled at it before returning it to his ear. "I'll have you know my mate is also here, and I would never let anything happen to either of them. Hmm. So, when are you getting here? Why? Do you need an extraction?" Aiden paused. "Then why?" Aiden listened some more. "You know what, you tell her." Aiden tossed the phone to Cord, who was still standing behind her. He easily caught it and presented it to her by laying it on his forearm. "Lady Zoe."

She brought the phone up. "Mikel?"

"Baby girl, what are you doing in Éire Danu?"

"The queen requested the Fire Temple Head

since they're having problems with their lights, so Caroline made sure I was able to leave."

"Fire Temple Head? You?"

"Yes, I had my coming of age last month... alone," she added for good measure.

"Oh, honey, I would have been there if I could have, but what I'm working on, it's for both of us, okay?"

"Can't you come home? Caroline said I shouldn't return to Storm Keep unless you or Morrigan were there."

"Why on earth would she say that?"

Zoe hesitated. If he was truly working on something important, then she didn't want to upset him.

Pip nudged her. "Tell him."

"Tell me what, who is that?" Mikel demanded.

"The council came to the manor and packed up my things and moved me into the Fire Temple. Then they assigned me an assistant that tracked my every move. He wasn't very nice," she admitted, her voice cracking. Under the table, Pip took her other hand.

There was a long silence before her brother spoke again. "Zoe, baby, you never have to return to Storm Keep if you don't want to. You are with people now that will protect you until I can return to your side. Know that I love you very, very much, and I'm doing everything I can to come back."

She wiped her tears. "I know, I've just missed you so much."

"I know. Now, you help out if you want to, but

you don't have to. Aiden will take good care of
you in my stead. He's sort of your *athair*," he
said, stumbling over the word.

She laughed. "I know, he told me to help
explain why he wanted to join Aeson and Ramsey in going to beat up the council."

Mikel exhaled, then gave a short laugh.
"Thank the gods for my commander. Don't forget you are an Appleblossom. You have access
to our accounts, so you aren't without means."

"The council took control of the accounts after
you left since I wasn't of age," she explained.

"They can't do that," Mikel exploded. "Those
accounts and funds are tied to the entire estate."

"Most of our relatives were assigned out to
other houses and out-of-state companies. There
wasn't anyone to protest."

"Gods above, you really were alone, weren't
you? I am so sorry, baby. If I had thought for a
moment they would go that far. I never would
have left."

"I know."

Mikel took a steadying breath. "I love you Zo,
I'm coming home as soon as I can. Can you pass
the phone to Aiden again?"

"I love you too, and please hurry." Looking
up, she passed the phone to Cord, who walked it
back over to Aiden.

Aiden, frowning fiercely, took the phone. "I
heard. You don't even have to ask. We'll wait for
you to act. Just get your ass back here. No one
fucks with a warrior's family and walks away
unscathed."

Zoe felt as if a huge weight had been lifted from her shoulders. Her brother was safe and coming home.

Hearing voices at the door she looked up to see who was entering. Three men and a woman walked in and stopped when they caught the tail end of what Aiden was saying.

The tall blond frowned. "Are we kicking someone's ass?" he growled.

"Ari, what did you hear?" the woman asked.

"We're gonna fuck some people up," one of the other two men replied.

When her eyes met the crystalline blue ones of her dreams, she gasped aloud. "You?"

"That call is about you, isn't it?" he demanded, the blue bleeding to a dark crimson. "Who hurt my mate?" he growled.

"Mate?" Meryn asked, her eyes going wide. "No shit?"

Zoe nodded. "He's the one from my dreams, the eye of the firestorm, my safe harbor," she whispered.

Aiden stared, then began laughing. "You heard right, her mate just walked through the door. Maybe she won't need you after all," he teased.

Whatever Mikel said in response had Aiden paling, but he was still smiling. "Then you better get here fast." He tapped his phone and set it down. Rolling his eyes, he winked at her. "Brothers, am I right?"

The dark-haired man strode forward and knelt down on her other side. Very gently, he wiped away her tears. "Tell me what needs to be done to make you smile again."

She pulled her hand from Pip, and he patted her encouragingly. "I'm not sure, but maybe we can figure it out together." Straightening her back, she thrust out her hand. "My name is Zoe Appleblossom, it's wonderful to finally meet the man of my dreams."

With the crimson fading, his blue eyes smiled up at her. Taking her hand, he turned it over so he could kiss it. "My name is Gage Fabre, and it is an honor to meet the keeper of my heart and soul."

Where his lips touched her skin, a flush of heat began. Within her body, a blaze erupted in her core and spread. "My mate," she whispered, feeling her cheeks burn.

"Holy shit!" Meryn exclaimed.

Seconds later, Gage was pulling her out of her chair and away from where the drapes had suddenly caught fire.

Cord, in one fluid movement, pushed Pip to safety and yanked the drapes down to stomp out the flames. Without breaking a sweat, nor with a hair out of place, he turned to Zoe. "Now, Lady Zoe, would you like to try pizza for lunch?"

CHAPTER FOUR

"I'VE SAID IT BEFORE, AND I'll say it again, squires are some badass mother-fuckers," Meryn said, still a bit wide-eyed.

Zoe covered her face with both hands, mortified at what she had done.

"Lady Zoe, do not worry about the drapes. I was planning on replacing them soon anyway. What's more important is that you eat to keep up your strength," Cord said in a soothing manner.

"Zoe, are you alright?" Gage asked, pulling her against him as they stood next to the table.

She moved her hands and looked up at him. "I'm going to incinerate you!"

Gage's mouth twitched as he clearly struggled not to smile. "What a way to go," he teased.

She felt her mouth drop open and his meaning sunk in. Blushing furiously, she pushed him away and looked around for a way to escape.

Cord simply steered her back to her chair and helped her to sit. "Master Gage, maybe refraining from such emotion-inducing comments for the moment might be wise? Calmer seems to be the wiser course of action," he suggested.

Gage nodded before placing his hand over his heart and giving a half bow. "My apologies, Zoe, I did not mean to make light of your fears."

She looked up at him and saw concern for her and sincerity in his eyes. "I don't want to hurt anyone, especially a mate I've dreamt of."

He sat down next to her and took her hand. "Kincaid has some issues with his magic, so I am aware of how frustrating it can be. Whatever you need, I will help you see it through."

The queen took another sip of her tea. "Maybe we could switch the color scheme to blue? What do you think, Cord?"

Cord winked down at her before looking over at his queen. "I was of the same mind myself. We've had gold and amber tones for centuries. It might be refreshing to see something different."

"Mo-o-t-t-h-h-her…" Darian drew out the word.

She gave him an innocent expression that made her look as young as Meryn. "What?"

When Zoe looked around, she realized from the other's confused expression that they were as in the dark about the banter as she was.

"What'd I miss?" Meryn demanded.

"Blue is the primary color of the Alina coat of arms," Brennus explained, smiling. "I think that would be perfect."

"Excellent, I'll start ordering fabrics immediately," Cord said, then looked down at them. "And for Lady Zoe, I will bring out one of Meryn's favorites. From what Ryuu explained to me, this is a Japanese version of her favored *Hot*

Pockets. They are baked with cheese, seasoned tomato sauce, and pepperoni. In a way, it's like a pizza and a *Hot Pocket*, you can try both."

Taking a deep breath, she smiled. "Thank you, that sounds wonderful."

Meryn licked her lips. "Cord…"

"Yes, Meryn, I'll make some for you as well."

"Ahh, Cord…" Aiden started blushing.

Cord looked around the table at the varying degrees of interest. "Understood. Since so many seem to be craving pizza, I'll put some prepared pizzas in the oven and bring those out for larger appetites. The *taiyaki* pockets will come out as soon as they are done for little Meryn and Lady Zoe."

Aiden looked relieved. "Thank you, Cord. I didn't mean to add to your already packed daily schedule, but when you mentioned pizza…"

Cord chuckled. "You weren't the only one," he said, pointing to where Darian and Oron were grinning ruefully. "It has been a long time since I had to cook for such grateful appetites. Let me worry about my schedule." He gave a half bow and walked back toward the kitchen.

Zoe looked around. No one, not one person, was staring aghast at the scorched wall. "Is no one scared of me?" she whispered to herself.

Meryn tilted her head. "Why would we be scared?"

Zoe just stared. "I could set you on fire!" she exclaimed.

Meryn shrugged. "And Ryuu would put it out,

and one of the witches would heal me, no worries."

Zoe blinked and looked around the table, and everyone was nodding. "It's that simple?"

Meryn picked up her coffee cup. "Well, yeah. You're a fire witch, so wouldn't the easiest solution be to have a water witch with you while you're learning?" She pointed back to Ryuu. "That's why I said he'd put out the fire, he can use water." She frowned. "Coming from Storm Keep, I thought for sure you'd have like a water witch squire or something by now."

"Meryn, I know you hear it often, but you're a genius," Kendrick said, admiration in his voice.

Zoe collapsed back in her chair. Meryn was right, it was a simple solution, but none of the older witches had thought of it. Meryn's earlier comment about her becoming a weapon didn't seem that far-fetched anymore. "I don't understand why they did the things they did. What would they have to gain?" she questioned, shaking her head.

Gage wrapped his arm around her shoulders and pulled her close to his body. "And we probably won't until we go to Storm Keep to pummel those involved."

Zoe looked up at her mate. His handsome face looked grim as he clenched his jaw, thinking about her plight. She reached up and touched his cheek.

Looking down, he smiled, and her heart was lost. Every ounce of emotion was there in his eyes. From the depth of affection she could see, he wasn't fighting the mating pull at all. "Thank you."

He leaned down and kissed her forehead. "It is my pleasure to ensure your happiness." He looked back up and over to Kendrick. "Any suggestions for a squire?"

Zoe couldn't help the thrill of excitement. If she had a squire at her side who could use water, she'd be able to go anywhere. She wouldn't have to worry about hurting anyone.

Kendrick sat back, rubbing his chin. "The only ones I'd trust aren't squires and are unfortunately too busy to act as one."

Behind Meryn, Ryuu brought up his fist to his mouth and coughed. "I may have a suggestion."

Kendrick looked intrigued. "You know of a squire who can use water magic? Have I met them?"

Ryuu shook his head. "They aren't a squire and are currently in service with another family, but..." he hesitated, turning to the queen. "I believe if the request came from the fae queen, compensation could be arranged."

The queen smiled. "If this person has your recommendation, they are more than welcome here."

"Compensation? I don't have access to my family's accounts," Zoe clutched at her chest.

The queen smiled at her gently. "You are here to serve my city and help my people. It would be remiss of me to deny you something that would help you." She looked over to Gage. "You are also mated to one of my city's warriors, who has served faithfully for centuries. For that alone, I would lend my assistance."

And in that moment, Zoe saw the difference between a ruler who cared for her people and a council of selfish individuals.

Kendrick humphed. "I can assist too."

Zoe turned to him. "I know you care, but it's not like you're a leader in Storm Keep. I wouldn't put this burden on you since you don't share in the responsibility. The queen seems to have the clout and resources needed that you simply don't." She turned to the queen. "Queen Aleksandra, I thank you for your kindness and swear to do everything in my power to ensure that your city returns to its full glory."

Kendrick's mouth dropped, and around the table, muffled laughter was heard from nearly everyone. "I....I...," he stuttered.

The queen reached over to pat his hand. "Be at ease. There is no shame in not having the clout or resources one would acquire from being born into a royal family and living for thousands upon thousands of years," she said, her mouth twitching horribly.

Zoe nodded. "She's right. I know you mean well, but I wouldn't take from you, Kendrick. Many here may not know the significance of living in the Lower City, but I do. You keep your money for you and Keelan." When she looked over, she saw that Kendrick was now an unhealthy shade of red. "Are you okay?"

Across from here, Meryn was laughing so hard, she was beginning to slide under the table.

Her squire, holding her up by the armpits was the only thing preventing her from disappearing from sight. "He's just a poor boy, from a poor family…" she sang, between fits of laughter.

"Dammit, Meryn! I had just gotten that other song out of my head. That one is a thousand times worse," Pierce complained.

Zoe looked up at Gage, who was also laughing. "What?"

He kissed the tip of her nose. "Nothing, my darling. I have a feeling Kendrick was due this."

She shrugged. "He's a bit grouchy, but he cares."

Aiden, shaking his head, turned to the queen. "Alpha will also help to defray the cost. We are, collectively, her *athair*, after all."

Ryuu made sure Meryn was securely in her chair before straightening. "As Storm Keep is currently without a king or queen, Queen Aleksandra as Zoe's current employer would be the only way to make such a request," he shared, looking over to Kendrick. "We all know you would help if you could."

Kendrick growled, shocking Zoe. "You too?"

Ryuu gave a half-shrug. "These opportunities are so few and far between, let us enjoy them when they do arise."

The queen chuckled. "He's right, Kendrick, let us enjoy this for the time being. You can go back to being amazing later."

"Yeah, it's really too bad we don't have a king," Thane added, heaving a great sigh. "If we had, then that person would have more than enough clout to handle this situation and take care of a daughter of Storm Keep."

Kendrick raised his hand, and a moment later, Thane shouted and began thrashing around, trying to put out the flames climbing his pant legs. "See, Zoe, even when you do it on purpose, there's little harm done."

"Little harm done! That had almost reached my…" Thane shut his mouth and blushed.

"Reached what?" Anne asked innocently.

"Never you mind," he replied, trying to adjust his clothing.

"I'm impressed, the scorch marks barely hit your knees," Meryn said before giving a whistle. "This will definitely change your ranking."

Thane stopped his movements and looked over to Meryn, smiling. "Really?"

"Oh, yeah."

Aiden growled before he nipped her shoulder. "I thought I told you to delete that database."

Meryn nodded. "You did."

"So, why are you still ranking warriors?"

She frowned up at her mate. "Was I supposed to listen to you?"

Zoe watched the entire scene enthralled. She had never seen this many people tease one another and share open affection before. "You all are a beautiful family," she said, feeling a bit jealous.

Meryn immediately turned to her before breaking out into a huge smile. "We are, aren't we?" She pointed in her direction. "You're part of this craziness now. You're Aiden's goddaughter, so that makes you family too."

The queen clapped her hands. "You're right, Meryn. I can also assist based on familial ties. She is my son's goddaughter" She turned to Ryuu. "Would that help?"

Ryuu nodded. "Zoe's direct ties to the throne will help immensely."

"Why are ties to the throne important?" Zoe asked, feeling nervous.

Kendrick sighed. "Because in Japan, those with any magic are aligned with those in power. They maintain a more elitist way of life than we do."

Ryuu exhaled, looking sad. "Kendrick is correct. The individual I'm thinking of belongs to one of the four main royal houses, the Fujiwara clan. They would not accept a request from just anyone."

The queen looked to the fae woman that had escorted her to the room. "Portia, can you get the contact information from Ryuu and let them know we are interested in hiring one of their people."

Before Portia could nod, Ryuu stepped forward, grimacing. "I may have to explain things a bit further before we proceed." He looked over to Zoe. "The person I have in mind just finished their training, so their accomplishments and skills will be marketed to the other three clans and, of course, to any outside interest, of which there are usually none," he added. He quieted and frowned to himself as if debating on how to continue.

Kendrick picked up his glass and swirled the liquid. "They are, for lack of a better term, auctioned off."

The queen's expression wasn't the only one that turned frosty. "Explain." Was the single word command.

Ryuu inclined his head and continued. "Two to three auctions take place per year as candidates finish training. What they can do is listed, and anyone interested can approach the clan and make an offer. The best offer for the clan and the individual is accepted."

"Why would the clan receive anything? Are they slaves to be bought and sold?" Anne demanded.

Ryuu shook his head. "No, they aren't slaves. The reason why the clan receives payment or goods in exchange is to compensate them for the loss of their clan member."

"Wouldn't they want to keep the good ones?" Zoe asked.

Ryuu nodded. "Of course. Those that are available did not receive an offer from their birth clan."

Zoe shrugged. "Sounds about right to me."

Kendrick turned to face her. "How so?"

Zoe looked around the room, confused. "Isn't that how the Magical Academy assigns out witches? They are given a test score, and then they see who is willing to pay the most for the contract." She felt her stomach begin to churn as each person regarding her looked horrified. "That's normal, right?"

Thane spoke first. "I never questioned it until she described it aligning so much with Japan's system," he said quietly. "I always believed the auctions were barbaric, but we hardly do any better."

Portia lifted her pen. "So, I take it that the offer should compensate the clan heavily to be favored?"

Ryuu held up a finger. "Exactly."

Portia turned to the queen. "We could easily offer a portal. Only the fae can create them, so it isn't something they have ever had access to."

The queen nodded slowly. "If they will allow the normal stipulations of having it maintained by our people, I would allow it." She tapped her finger on the table absently. "It would cost us nothing but could elevate the status of the clan we offer to."

Ryuu smiled. "That is the mindset needed when dealing with the clans."

Meryn scowled up at Ryuu. "Were you auctioned off?"

His expression softened when he looked down at her. "No, Meryn, I wasn't. I am a squire. The person that we will be offering for is not."

Meryn frowned. "What are they then?"

"An attendant, or type of servant," Ryuu explained.

"They don't cook or take care of the house?" Meryn asked.

He shook his head. "No, they answer only to

their master or mistress. If the one they serve gets hungry, they go to the cook and arrange for a meal. Their sole responsibilities are centered around their master."

Meryn's eyes narrowed. "And you just so happen to know of someone that is finishing their training?"

Ryuu winked at his charge. "Like Kendrick, I have kept tabs on a few youngsters as they grew. The ones I have in mind are unfortunately predicted to serve my old house."

Meryn growled. "That douchebag that tried to hurt you?"

He nodded. "I would prefer that they do not go to that family."

Zoe looked from Kendrick to Ryuu, then to Meryn. "If he has been looking out for them, then we have to help."

Though she hadn't been very close to Kendrick growing up, she knew that he had helped her on many occasions when she was young. If the ones that needed help were now alone because Ryuu was here, she could understand how lonely that could be.

"If you wished to help them, you, of course, would have our support, but I have to ask. Will they truly be able to help?" the queen asked.

Ryuu placed a hand over his heart. "Despite my worry, I would not have suggested them otherwise. I believe the saying is 'two birds, one stone'."

Portia tucked her quill into her scroll. "Ryuu, who should I contact?"

"The home of Akihiko Fujiwara. His squire is Goro Sato."

She gave a curt nod. "I will reach out to them immediately. Should I mention you or no?"

Ryuu nodded. "I believe knowing that I am involved will help." He grinned wickedly. "The head of the Fujiwara clan isn't on the best of terms with my old family, and due to that, relations with the Tiara clan, to whom they serve, have been strained."

"I will see it done." Portia dipped into a small curtsey and left to get started.

Zoe sat back, feeling exhausted. She had only left Storm Keep a couple hours ago, yet so much had changed.

Gage rubbed her back. "It will be okay," he reassured her. "What would you like to do next?"

"I really want to get out into the city and examine the lights."

"Zoe, please don't take this the wrong way, but do you really think you can help?" Kendrick asked.

She fought the urge to roll her eyes. "Oh Kendrick, that's so funny! It's just a little light, silly." She giggled inanely to add to the ridiculousness of his question.

Kendrick flushed while Anne, at his side, laughed. "You deserved that," she said, tossing a scone at him.

Thane rubbed the back of his neck. "I understand what he means. He, along with my brothers and I, have examined the lamps thoroughly and haven't been able to see anything wrong."

Zoe just looked from one man to the other. "Why would you think you'd know one way or another if it was working properly?"

Both men looked stumped.

Meryn snickered. "Because they are older, strong males, why wouldn't they?"

Kendrick raised an eyebrow. "We have had more time to learn about magic," he added dryly.

"Do you know the design of the power grid that was created and installed here in the city by the Appleblossoms?" Zoe asked, crossing her arms over her chest.

Kendrick's eyes widened. "The what?"

Zoe sighed. "There is a reason why Appleblossoms always lead the Fire Temple. We only teach those within our family trade secrets."

Thane scowled. "If it's only a matter of learning the way fire magic was used…"

She cut him off. "Do you have a degree in engineering?"

He swallowed. "No, but I take it you do?"

She did roll her eyes this time. "I wasn't allowed to leave the house, all I could do was study. Yes, I have a degree in engineering and electrical engineering. I have written entire journals on blending human technology and fire magic to create sustainable power sources, amongst other things. Even with my magic as unstable as it is, I could run circles around both of you when it comes to fire tech."

"Boom! Mic drop!" Meryn exclaimed, laughing. "She told y'all."

Zoe shrugged, smiling. "I don't know, Thane,

but Kendrick has to be reminded he doesn't know everything every once in a while."

"Brat," Kendrick said, smiling softly.

When she looked at him, she was surprised to see the pride in his eyes. "I can really do this," she said, meeting his eyes.

"Forgive me, Zoe, I never meant to belittle you. When I look at you, all I see is the tiny girl running around behind Nigel and Neil, getting into mischief and nagging me for food."

Now it was her turn to blush. "Your house always felt safe," she said by way of explanation.

"You always grumbled and complained, but you never turned us away," Nigel added.

"So, you didn't turn people into animals like Serenity said?" Meryn asked.

Neil laughed out loud. "Oh, no. He did. But it was usually a self-serving jerk looking for an easy handout. Kendrick never helped anyone that wasn't willing to put in the work."

Anne stared up at her mate. "You were the neighborhood mom?"

"What? No!" Kendrick sputtered.

Nigel and Neil looked to her, and they all nodded. Zoe spoke first. "Why does that feel right?"

"Why, mom? Why not neighborhood dad?" Kendrick asked his mate.

"It's a thing," Anne said, trying to explain. "The neighborhood mom ran the house everyone went to. It may not have been the cleanest or even had the best toys, but it was always wel coming, and there were always seconds when it came to food."

"Oh, gods. That was him," Amelia whispered, covering her mouth with her hand in disbelief. "He'd fuss about taking your shoes off, made sure you had done your lessons, always had something on the stove, and was always there if you needed help."

Nigel and Neil sniffed dramatically. "Mom!"

Kendrick whirled on them. "Now, don't you two start."

Ryuu smiled. "It's nothing to be ashamed of. You've come a long way from the bitter vagabond I met so many years ago."

"I must say, I like seeing this side of you, Kendrick. I knew raising Keelan had changed you, but it's wonderful to see the proof," the queen added.

Thane smiled. "Caiden is the same. We'd visit, and there'd be kids everywhere playing with Amelia. I think he even owns an apron he wears."

Amelia giggled. "I got that for him when I was three. I overheard him complaining that he kept getting stains on his uniform when cooking for me, so I asked Tristan to get it for him for Winter Solstice."

Thane grinned. "Oh, we know."

Kendrick sat back. "I can admit, that description doesn't sound too bad."

Meryn looked a bit sad. "I wish I coulda been raised with Amelia, then I coulda played with you all too."

Brennus sat forward. "You would have been raised here in Éire Danu Meryn," he reminded her gently.

"True, but I woulda at least spent summers there or something, to visit my aunt and uncle," she said, pointing to Amelia. "We could have tortured Kendrick together."

Kendrick shook his head. "Gods above."

Nigel grinned at Meryn. "Us, Amelia, Serenity, Zoe, Laelia, and Radclyffe. That would have been amazing."

"No. Just no." Kendrick frowned fiercely. "There's no way I could handle the lot of you."

Meryn pointed around the table. "Aren't you doing it now? Except we're older, their magic is stronger, and we have access to *Amazon* and alcohol. If Keelan were here, then we'd have like all four elements covered."

Kendrick paled.

The queen inhaled sharply.

Thane's eyes widened.

Ryuu tapped his finger to his lips. "Interesting observation, *denka*."

"Meryn, are we taking over the world?" Pip asked, in a whisper heard by everyone.

"Yup," she answered.

"Can I play too?" Kincaid asked, looking excited.

"Sure, I think your magic is neat," Meryn answered.

Pip looked sad. "But, I don't have magic."

Meryn took his hand. "You have the best magic of all Pip, you make people feel better."

"I do?" he squeaked.

"Every day, buddy," Neil answered.

"It is a superpower?"

"Absolutely!" Amelia said, nodding.

"We have to include our other brothers, Noah and Jaxon," Pip reminded Meryn.

"The Mischievous Misfits," Meryn said, pulling out her laptop. "I'm ordering tee-shirts."

"Gods above help us all," Aiden said, looking around the table.

"Do I get a flamethrower too?" Pip asked in a serious tone.

Meryn grinned and pointed in her direction. "We don't need one anymore. We have Zoe now."

Zoe couldn't hold back her smile as she took another bite from the flaky fish-shaped meal Cord had made for her to try. For the first time in her life, with her mate at her side, she felt like she finally had a place where she belonged, and she wouldn't let any council members or her own erratic magic take that away from her.

Chapter Five

G AGE TURNED TO HIS MATE and smiled. He had a mate. This morning she was only a dream. Now she was at his side and everything he had ever wanted. Her chaotic innocence intrigued him since she held nothing back when it came to her emotions. She was fierce one moment and crying the next. He wondered if she knew how amazing that was.

"Darling, when did you want to leave to investigate the grid?" he asked. He was peripherally interested since it was affecting the city, but he mostly wanted to see what his mate could do. He was quickly becoming addicted to the stream of expressions that flitted across her face.

When she beamed up at him, he felt his heart stutter. Gods, she was beautiful!

"Anytime, really. I'm just as curious about the city as I am about the power grid," she paused. "I haven't been many places," she admitted shyly.

He took her hand and brought it to his lips. Immediately, she began to blush. He could almost smell the blood in her cheeks. "Then I will ensure you see all of Éire Danu, wherever you wish to go, whatever you wish to do, I will make it happen," he promised.

"I...I...I'm not sure. Maybe my first beer?" she stuttered.

He kept her hand and gave it a gentle squeeze. "Of course, Dav's is a wonderful place to visit. I think you'll appreciate the more laid-back atmosphere."

"Zoe, we had rooms prepared for you here, but seeing how you have met your mate, would you prefer to stay with him?" Brennus asked.

The queen slapped his shoulder. "She may want her own room whilst they get to know one another. She shouldn't be rushed."

Brennus looked down at his mate and raised an eyebrow. "I seem to remember a certain queen ordering my things to be taken to the royal quarters not an hour after my arrival."

The queen flushed. "That's different."

Gage chuckled at the interaction. "Zoe may choose whichever place she wants. If she'd feel more comfortable here, I'll just have to visit more often."

Zoe frowned for a second before she shook her head. "I think we'll get to know one another faster if I were to stay with you."

Gage's heart soared. "I'd like nothing more."

"I'll let Aeson know to organize the guys. We'll have a welcome party later at the villa so she can meet everyone. We're heading there next, so I can take her luggage if she's okay with it." Ari offered.

Brie turned to Zoe. "Ari and I stay there

throughout the week, so you won't be the only female there."

Zoe smiled at Ari. "I'd really appreciate you taking my suitcase to the villa." She then turned to Brie. "It makes sense that you live there since you're a warrior too. Do you think the men will mind if I suddenly move in?"

Gage could tell that Brie was flattered to be considered a warrior.

Ari chuckled as he wrapped an arm around his mate. "I think the guys will absolutely adore you."

Gage looked over to his unit leader. "Ari, if we're all getting mates, won't the villa become too small? Is there a way to build on?"

Ari's easy-going smile turned into a frown. "You're right. Unlike other pillar cities, we all live together. We need more space, but I love where we're located. We're central to just about everything."

"Go up," Meryn suggested before taking a bite of her scone.

"Excuse me?" Ari asked, looking confused.

Meryn took a sip of her coffee, then swallowed. "In most major cities, when you run outta ground space, you build vertically. Since y'all have trees and stuff, couldn't you just make like a warrior treehouse city or something?"

Ari, Priest, Kincaid, and even Brennus looked around with eager expressions.

Brennus turned to his mate. "Is that something that can be done?"

The queen nodded. "Of course, I'll even

donate an oak sapling to act as a corner anchor if need be. The holly that Darian donated isn't exactly the best for tree houses."

Gage looked to the prince. "Could we build in a circular fashion around the holly? She has been good to us and should be included."

Darian nodded slowly. "I think she'd like that."

"I'll schedule a meeting with Portia and Molvan to get the plans started for expansion," the queen offered. "In the meantime, Gage, why don't you show this young lady around? I think you'd both like some time together."

Gage stood and assisted Zoe in rising. "Your Majesty, your wisdom is surpassed only by your beauty."

The queen shook her head smiling. "As a mating present, please visit Baba's and get fireproof robes for Zoe. I have a standing account with her as she has proved to be one of the best merchants we have."

Gage inclined his head. "Many thanks, Your Majesty."

"I get a new dress?" Zoe asked.

"You get whatever you want," he replied.

She looked him up and down. "Good."

Gage felt his mouth drop.

Zoe curtsied. "Thank you for all your kindness, Your Majesty. I'll report back my findings regarding the lights as soon as I can."

The queen waved her hand, grinning openly. "I have every faith in you."

Zoe let go of his hand and started toward the

door. "Coming…?" She raised an eyebrow, then walked out.

"Gods above," Gage managed to choke out the words.

Around the table, his unit brothers were laughing at his circumstances.

"Better get fire-proof sheets while you're at it," Meryn teased, then she added. "Maybe a fire extinguisher by the bed?"

"If you will excuse me," Gage managed to say before he swiftly walked toward the door himself.

As usual, Meryn's suggestion was a good one.

C

Zoe pressed her hands to her cheeks and could feel the heat. What had possessed her to do such a thing? And in front of the queen? Taking a deep breath, she straightened when she heard her mate walk up behind her. Smiling brightly, she held out her hand. "I'm all yours. Show me your city."

His hand trembled slightly when he took hers before he gave it a quick squeeze. "Let us examine the lights first. That way, you can enjoy the evening without anything hanging over your head."

"Sounds perfect."

They walked leisurely, taking nearly the same streets she had seen when walking to the palace. With Gage at her side, he took slight detours to show her certain gardens or a shop that they'd visit later. The promise of more things to come excited her.

When they reached the center of Merchant Square, Gage walked her over to a tall street lamp shaped like a tree with hanging bulbs. It was unlike the others she had seen as they walked.

"This is gorgeous," she breathed, looking at the craftsmanship. The fae had guided and nurtured the tree to grow around the crystals needed to power the lights.

"I figured we could start here. I'm no engineer, but from what I've observed, I think the other lights all feed back to this one," Gage explained.

Zoe exhaled and called on a small portion of her magic. Very gently, she sent it into the tree to check the crystals. Each line was still intact and, to her surprise, well maintained. She expected, at the very least, some fractures, but they were in pristine condition. "There's no damage at all." She turned to him. "Have they been serviced?"

Grinning, Gage nodded. "The Eirlindol family was asked by the queen to maintain the lights after they were installed when the city was being formed and built. They have been fulfilling that role ever since. Amongst the fae, they are called the Lightbearers."

"That will make things so much easier. Can I meet them?" she asked.

Gage hesitated for a moment. "I can take you to House Eirlindol, but you may not receive much help from them," he admitted, his eyes sad.

"And why not?"

"That family recently lost one of their sons.

The older fae who resides there was always a bit crotchety, but now, he's downright antagonistic."

Zoe felt tears form in her eyes. "That poor man."

"The rest of his family live in a separate estate from the main house, so he's been alone for quite some time," he warned.

"We have to go see him now." Zoe pulled her magic from the tree and set her shoulders. If this family had diligently maintained the grid for thousands of years, she needed to speak with them.

"Are you sure?" Gage asked, rubbing the back of his neck.

"Yes. Oh, and can we stop somewhere to purchase some pastries?"

She looked around the glittering market area for a shop that sold sweets.

"If you're hungry, we can go to Dav's first," Gage started.

She shook her head. "No, it's for the head of House Eirlindol. I can't just show up empty-handed when meeting for the first time."

Gage shook his head, smiling. "I know of just the place." He held out his hand.

She took it, and he guided them through the throng of people shopping and eating their midday meals. When he stopped, she looked up and blinked. "It looks like a brick oven," she exclaimed.

Gage chuckled. "It's supposed to. The owner wanted something different. It caused quite a stir when it was first built as it didn't go with the elegance of the city at all, but it quickly became an iconic landmark." He opened the door and held it for her. "After you, my lady."

Smiling, she stepped quickly inside and inhaled deeply. The scents of cinnamon, vanilla, and chocolate washed over her. "Gods, I could live here," she said before taking another deep breath.

"If I had a dollar for every time I heard that, I'd be able to afford the espresso machines I want," a deep voice said.

When she looked up, she blinked. Then blinked again. "You're quite an imposing fellow," she said, still staring.

The man looked down at her before erupting into peals of belly laughter. "And you, my dear, are right. I'm Peter Lindon, owner of the Brick Oven. Now, what can I do for you?"

She stepped up to the large glass case. "I was purchasing for someone else, but I may have to get a few things for myself too." She looked back to Gage to see if that was okay.

He rolled his eyes and nodded.

She took that to mean she was being silly for asking, but, to her, it would have been rude to assume he'd pay.

"Have a hankering for something?" Peter asked.

She took in all the colors and glazes. The sprinkles and the bits of fruit shined like jewels. "I'm not sure. I've never had sweets like this before."

Peter frowned. "They're not exactly exotic."

"At home, cook only ever made vanilla cake."

He stared. "That's it?"

She nodded, distracted by the dark brown squares. "That's chocolate, isn't it? I read that it was brown, but that really does it a disservice. I think it should have its own color name."

"Young lady, do you mean to tell me you've never had chocolate before?" Peter asked, looking baffled.

She nodded. "Mother and father were afraid it would stimulate me too much."

"Peter, we'll take a half dozen of everything you have. Whatever she doesn't want to try now can be sent to the warrior villa, and add a note that it's for her, so the greedy bastards don't eat it before we get there," Gage said, looking a bit angry.

"I'm sorry, Gage, I didn't mean to..." Zoe didn't mean to upset him. She wasn't angling for sweets.

He stepped forward and pulled her into his arms. "My ire, dear one, is not directed at you. I hate how little you have experienced. I would give you the world if I could."

Zoe swallowed hard. "It wasn't so bad, and look at it this way. I get to try so many new things with you because of how I was raised."

"Lil lady, you just pick which ones you'd like to try now and which will be your gift, and I will personally deliver these to the warrior villa," Peter promised, already pulling out cardboard boxes designed to look like bricks.

Zoe looked up at her mate. "I'd really like to

try those chocolate squares, whatever is your favorite, and a dessert that would go well with a soothing tea."

"Peter, a half a dozen brownies, two apple fritters, and a box of chamomile shortbread," Gage ordered.

"Chamomile shortbread?" Peter sighed. "Been selling too much of that one lately."

"It's for Dirk Vi'Eirlindol," Gage admitted.

Peter sucked in his breath, then exhaled. "I'll add in a packet of Blessed Chamomile to go along with the shortbread."

"Thank you so much, Peter," Zoe said, looking back at the huge baker.

He shrugged. "Despite my size, I'm not a warrior. If my baking can help these poor people in any small way, I'll be more than satisfied."

"You're a good man Peter Lindon," she said, causing his cheeks to flame.

He shook his head. "He's a great uncle, after all." He looked at them. "He wasn't always a mean old bastard. Tell him I'm thinking of him."

"We will," she promised.

Peter smiled and handed her the smaller of the three boxes. "Try that and see if it's to your liking."

Zoe took the box and opened it quickly. Without wasting a second, she reached in, lifted out one of the brownies, and popped it in her mouth. Within seconds the decadent, rich flavor coated her tongue, and the bittersweetness caused her to tear up. "Gods above," she managed to say, her mouth still full.

Peter laughed again, deep reverberating chuckles that seemed to echo around his midsection before erupting. "No charge for the brownies. It was worth it to see her reaction."

Zoe barely heard him. Her world had shrunk to include her and her box of treasures. With no thought of decorum, she simply sat on the floor where she had been standing and popped another brownie in her mouth. "Peter, if I hadn't already met my mate..." she sighed happily as she chewed.

"I've heard that one quite a bit too. Maybe someday I'll get those espresso machines," he lamented playfully.

"If I were to introduce you to an exceptional barista who could help you plan your machine purchases using wholesaler and distribution vendors, would you be willing to give my mate a treat whenever she visits?" Gage asked shrewdly.

Peter blinked. "You mean that wonderful woman that set up the coffee bar at Dav's?"

Gage nodded slowly.

"Deal! I heard she was mated to Prince Oron, so I dare not approach her over such a thing, but you can, as she is mated to a fellow unit warrior," Peter said, rubbing his hands together.

"Would coffee go with brownies?" she asked, looking up at her mate.

"Gods above, she hasn't had coffee either?" Peter asked.

She shook her head. "My magic is a bit wonky. I don't think my parents wanted to give me anything that would overstimulate me or cause me to lose focus."

"Wonky?" Peter asked.

"I set fires a lot," she admitted and ate another brownie.

"Fires?" Peter swallowed hard. "How many brownies have you had?"

She shook the empty box. "All of them." She looked between the two. "Was I not supposed to?"

Gage just smiled. "Visiting Dirk Vi'Eirlindol should be very entertaining."

Peter handed the other two boxes and a small sachet to Gage. "It might be just what he needs."

Gage accepted the boxes, then held a hand down for her, helping her to stand.

"Peter, thank you so very much for the brownies. I hope you get your espresso machines soon," Zoe said, looping her arm through her mate's.

"Enjoy the fritters," he said, waving goodbye.

As they emerged into the afternoon sun, Zoe sighed happily. "Those were amazing! I can't wait to try other things. The cheesy things from lunch were to die for." She swung their hands back and forth between them.

"You radiate joy," Gage said softly.

"I'm happy."

"It's more than that," he indicated to the people who were shopping around them and the merchants at their stalls. They were watching her and also smiling. "I think they need someone like you right now. You remind them that there is joy in this world."

Zoe realized that he was referring to the murders, and it dawned on her that many of the people around her were actually grieving. "Gage," she said, feeling panicked.

"You've done nothing wrong. In fact, you've done something wonderful. Don't let worry dim your smile, my darling. You may be smiling for others and not even know it."

"I wish I could help them," she fretted.

"You are. Fixing the lights and taking away that worry will do wonders for the people," he said and pulled her close enough to wrap his arm around her shoulders. "After we visit Vi'Eirlindol, we can go to Dav's, and you can relax for a bit. How's that?"

"That sounds perfect," she admitted. She thought of the trip to the warrior villa yet to come. "Gage, the warriors won't eat my brownies, will they?"

"Not if they wish to continue breathing, they won't," Gage promised, smiling brightly.

"Good." Because now that she knew how delicious it was, she wasn't going to give it up.

᪥

Zoe watched as Gage knocked on a very impressive-looking dark oak door. Moments later, the door opened, and a tall, blond man nodded and greeted them. "Welcome to House Eirlindol. I am Nevan Anders. How may I be of service?"

"My name is Gage Fabre, warrior of the Tau

Unit. This is my mate, Zoe Appleblossom, Head of the Fire Temple of Storm Keep. She is investigating the lights dimming and wishes to speak to Dirk Vi'Eirlindol, as he represents the city's leading expert in regards to the lights."

The squire's eyes widened. "Lady Appleblossom, welcome, please, please come in. I know my lord will wish to speak to you," he said, ushering them inside.

Zoe felt some of her nervousness slip away at his kindness and welcoming nature. He led them to a simple but elegantly decorated sitting room. Like the front door, most of the furniture was dark oak. The fabrics around the room provided pops of color in varying shades of green in the form of curtains, tablecloths, and pillows.

Moments later, she heard a gruff voice. "Why should I meet with them? They'll just blame me like the others."

"My Lord, please, the young lady looks to have come here directly from Storm Keep. I implore you to speak with her," the squire practically begged.

Zoe turned to Gage. He looked as confused as she felt. She had never heard a squire beg before.

A tall blond man with silver at the temples stepped into the room. "That girl? That child is the Fire Temple Head? Fah! Get out of here with your lies!"

Zoe shrunk back in her chair, unsure of what to say.

Gage, on the other hand, stood and stepped between the angry man and her chair. "I kindly

ask that you keep a civil tongue in your head
when you address my mate Dirk Vi'Eirlindol.
Your squire is correct, she has only arrived this
morning, and aside from seeing the queen, she
insisted on meeting you."

"Another one too young to be taken seriously," the older man muttered before sitting
down. "Well? Sit. Let us see what she has to
say," he ordered Gage, pointing to the chair he
had vacated just moments ago.

Gage exhaled slowly and sat back down. Turning to her, his expression softened. "Ask him
your questions now, my darling. He'll be civil if
he knows what's good for him."

The older man harrumphed. "Go on."

"Sir, I have only been able to check one of the
lighting systems so far, but it was in such amazingly good condition that I insisted on speaking
with you before going any further. When my
mate told me your family has been protecting and
maintaining the lights since the birth of the city,
I knew I had to meet you," she gushed without
preamble. "I know I'm young. In fact, I only just
came of age last month, but my family were the
ones to design the grid, and I've been taught all
the spells used to create and strengthen the system." She inhaled and kept going. "The crystals
in the main tree were in near perfect condition!"
she leaned forward toward the older man. "Were
they replaced, or did you fix any fractures that
occurred?"

The older fae's eyebrows were nearly to his
hairline as he took in her jumble of rushed

words. Slowly, he turned to Gage. "Is she always like this?" he asked, his former bite of hostility diminished.

Gage cleared his throat. "We only met about an hour ago, sir. But, she did just experience eating chocolate for the first time by eating half a dozen brownies," he explained ruefully.

The older man shook his head. "Nevan, a pot of sugared tea for the young lady. If she doesn't have a steadily decreasing intake of sugar, she will crash later."

"Of course, my lord," Nevan said, looking surprised yet pleased.

"Oh! We brought these," Zoe said, holding up the box and sachet. "It's chamomile shortbread and Blessed Chamomile tea. I've never had that before either, though my good friend would try to get me to drink it from time to time back in Storm Keep."

Dirk's expression went from indignation, to anger before settling on begrudged concern. "Why would a youngster like you need this?" he asked, then waved Nevan over to collect the tea and cakes.

Nevan nodded to her and took the gift away to prepare the tea.

"I was alone all the time after my parents and brother left. Some days," she swallowed hard. "Some days, it was like the weight of everything was just too much. She'd offer the tea, but I remembered that my parents didn't approve, so I'd just nap until I felt better."

"All alone? At the Fire Temple?" Dirk asked.

She nodded. "The council assigned out most of my family to contracts outside of Storm Keep. The temple estate was huge and empty."

"When was the last time you saw your parents?" Dirk asked.

"Over ten years ago. They weren't even able to make it home for my coming of age," she admitted and sighed. "It was a sad little affair."

"The being alone part, that's the hardest," the older fae admitted.

She nodded. "I heard about your family's loss. I wish I could do more to help, but all I can do is inspect the lights."

Dirk's face turned stony for a moment. Then he relaxed when he looked into her eyes. "People need light, my dear. Light can be a source of warmth and hope. I think that's exactly what the people need most right now. I know it would help me confirm that I didn't miss something in grieving my nephew."

Zoe stood and squeezed herself between the older fae and the arm of the sofa where he sat. She took his hand. "You didn't miss anything! I sent my magic through the central tree, and each crystal was perfectly intact to the point that I thought they were new. You and your family have taken such wonderful care of the grid I feel like I won't be able to do much."

Still looking a bit shocked at her actions, he patted her hand where it rested over his. "Our family has an affinity for crystal. It's why the queen tasked us with maintaining the lights. You, on the other hand, know the magic that gives it life, light, and warmth. Don't sell yourself short. Others will do that for you, trust you me."

Nevan came in and nearly tripped when he saw his charge cozied up with their visitor. He quickly schooled his features, though he smiled the entire time. "My Lord, they have brought over treats from the Brick Oven. I know you've wanted to try some, as young Master Peter owns the establishment." He placed the tray down on the table before handing a poured cup to Dirk.

The older fae scowled and jerked his head toward her, indicating that she was to be served first. Nevan immediately switched to serve her.

"Peter, huh?"

Zoe accepted the cup from the squire and looked up at Dirk. "He gave us the tea for you and told us to tell you that he was thinking of you and that you weren't always a mean old bastard," she explained before lifting the shortbread off the plate.

Gage covered his mouth with his hand, his eyes dancing.

Nevan froze in handing the second cup of tea to his charge, and Dirk himself barked a short laugh. "Lies. I've always been a mean bastard."

"I think you're quite lovely," she admitted.

"Then you better keep that to yourself, missy."

She smiled, then took a bite of the shortbread. "This is good, but not as good as the brownies."

The older man shook his head. "You'll find as you get older, you appreciate less sugar."

She chewed. "Can I expect all the system crystals to be in the same state as the central one?"

He nodded. "I go out after the dim to avoid people and check them myself."

She took another bite, then sipped her tea. "It has to be the magic then, somewhere there has been a breakdown in one of the spells."

The older fae set his cup down. "I think that it is important to fix what is broken, but I think the bigger issue is to determine what caused it to break down in the first place."

She froze, the shortbread halfway to her mouth. He was right. Fixing it would mean nothing if it broke again. Setting the shortbread back down on her plate, she beamed up at him. "This is why I knew I had to speak to you. Someone who has been maintaining the system for so long would think of things I wouldn't. I hope you won't mind if I stop in from time to time to run things past you. As you said, I am young, so I'll be leaning on your wisdom whilst I try and figure things out."

Dirk grunted, then looked up at his squire. "This young lady can request to see me at any time, night or day. Together I'm sure we can get to the root of the problem," he grinned slyly. "That way she can then concentrate on her mating."

Nevan placed his hand over his heart. "Yes, My Lord," he said, nearly choking on the words.

Zoe blushed furiously, then batted at the older man's shoulder playfully. "You're going to tease me horribly, aren't you?"

The older man just grunted again, only this

time there was the faintest of smiles hovering around his lips.

Satisfied that the older fae was feeling a bit better and was willing to help her, Zoe took a bite of another piece of shortbread.

"Lord Vi'Eirlindol…"

He waved his hand. "Might as well call me Dirk."

"Dirk, may I ask you an important question?"

He frowned. "Of course."

"Does shortbread come with chocolate?" she asked very seriously.

To her utter surprise, the man gave another barked laugh and nodded.

"That it does, young Appleblossom, that it does."

"How remarkable," she observed and sipped her tea.

CHAPTER SIX

(

"YOU ABSOLUTELY CHARMED THAT OLD goat," Gage marveled as they walked away from the Eirlindol estate.

"He wasn't so bad. I grew up visiting Kendrick here and there. I guess I just learned how to tell when the bark is worse than the bite."

"So, you think it's the magic?"

She shrugged. "It has to be. The crystals are intact."

"What do you have to do to check on the spells?"

"There should be central points in the grid that house the spell, kinda like the tree, but maybe not as decorative. I'll need to ensure that each one is working."

"That will have to wait until tomorrow."

"Why? I feel amazing like I'm full of energy," she said, bouncing up and down as she walked.

"And in about thirty minutes, unless you eat something, you'll crash like Dirk warned. Let's go to Dav's and eat something a bit more substantial than brownies," he suggested.

"Like what?"

"Personally, I love his beef stew, but Meryn and Izzy rave about the chicken tenders and fried fish."

She licked her lips. It all sounded good to her. "When did I become such a glutton? At home, I never thought of food like this."

Gage shook his head. "I bet you had the same set of meals on repeat. Why would you look forward to eating?"

"I know that the reason why I came to be here is concerning, but gods, I've never been so happy. I feel free!" she twirled, then stumbled. Gage's strong arms encircled her and pulled her close.

To her, he smelled like sandalwood. Leaning in, she scooted her nose between the buttons of his shirt and inhaled. "You smell good."

Gage's head dropped back, and he sighed, smiling. When he looked down, there was a wicked gleam in his eye. "Later, you can smell me all you want."

She took a quick step back, realizing how her actions must have looked. "May...maybe I will," she said, as she lifted her head, then continued walking. She had taken ten steps before she noticed he wasn't with her. Looking back, she saw he stood in the middle of the street with a smirk on his face. "Gage?"

He pointed to the left. "It's that way. We can keep going down this street, but it's mostly business services like accountants and whatnot," he teased.

"Oh, you!" she wheeled back around and took his hand. "Okay, guide dog, show me the way."

Shaking his head, he lifted her hand for a kiss and maneuvered them down the correct street. When he stopped, she knew they had reached their destination. The wooden framed windows gave the entire place a homey atmosphere. Gage held open the door, and they walked in.

Upon entering, she heard her name from multiple directions. She looked around, confused. She didn't know that many people in the city. To her left, she saw Meryn, Nigel, Neil, Aiden, and Pip at a table. Pip was waving enthusiastically.

To her right, Kendrick, Thane, and Anne, along with some of Gage's unit brothers and Brie, smiled at her.

"Welcome little lady!" Dav came from around the bar and gave her a half bow before plucking her away from her mate. "I've been waiting for you."

With her head spinning, she let him steer her toward a beautifully polished wooden bar. Where the wood met the wall, branches reached up to the high ceiling, and the roots plunged through the floor. "Wow."

Dav waved toward Meryn. "That happened after she received a blessing from her Guardian. He's the spirit of the Elder tree. We didn't know it would affect the bar."

"How remarkable," she said and settled in on a bar stool. Spinning, she giggled. "This is fun."

Pip walked up and sat beside her. Together, they spun on the bar stools.

"Meryn, I like this," Pip informed his sister.

Meryn nodded. "So do I. It helps me think."

"Did you discover anything?" Kendrick asked from his table.

She turned, so she faced the room. "Only that it isn't the crystals. The Eirlindols have taken meticulous care of them. I'll be looking into the spells tomorrow."

"I can escort you to House Eirlindol tomorrow if you'd like to speak with them," Ari volunteered. "He's a bit difficult, but I'm almost positive he won't turn us away."

She shook her head. "We've already been there. I thought he was lovely." Thinking back on the visit, she spun to face Meryn. "I tried chocolate!"

Meryn leaned forward. "Good, wasn't it? What'dja get?"

"Brownies from the Brick Oven, I wanted to cry. They were so good. It was like my heart was wrapped in a fuzzy blanket."

Meryn frowned. "Brick Oven?"

She nodded. "It was an amazing bakery, the owner's name is Peter, and he's huge! But, very sweet."

Ari was still staring at her. "You thought he was lovely?"

Priest nodded. "Peter made sure we all knew those sweets were for her. I'm a trained warrior, but damn, even I don't want to cross that man."

"Too full of chocolate for something to eat?" Dav asked, sliding over a frothing pint of amber liquid.

"She ate half a dozen brownies. Then short-bread, I'm thinking some chicken would do her some good," Gage advised.

"*She* is sitting right there," Meryn said, narrowing her eyes.

Zoe realized that Gage had been speaking for her. She didn't mind, but she also didn't notice it until Meryn said something.

Gage looked at her, contrition on his face. "I did not mean…"

She nodded. "I know." Looking to Dav, she smiled. "I'd like to try the chicken and the fish and the beef stew, please."

Dav's eyes widened then he began chuckling. "Give me a few minutes."

"And fries!" Meryn called out.

"Aye, she'll probably want some fries too," Dav said.

Meryn rolled her eyes. "No Dav, I'd like some fries," she clarified.

"Of course, hun, be right out," Dav said and disappeared behind a set of swinging double doors.

"Can I have a bite of your beef stew?" Meryn asked.

"Sure. I may need some help eating it all. I shouldn't have ordered so much, but I really wanted to try everything."

"We can help," Neil offered, pointing between himself and his brother.

"Thanks, guys."

Gage nuzzled her neck by way of an apology, then turned to Ari. "She charmed the old bastard.

He is actually cooperating with her investigation."

"He honestly wasn't that bad," she refuted.

"He probably liked you because you're so sweet," Meryn suggested.

"I am?"

"Yup. And you have a warm smile."

"Thank you, Meryn."

"No charge."

When the door opened, she looked over and edged closer to Gage as six warriors walked in. Gage smiled and wrapped his arm around her. "No need to be nervous around these numbskulls, my darling."

The tall blond of the group walked over and simply pulled Gage away from her, passing him to a grinning strawberry blond behind him. She remembered them from earlier.

"Ramsey, get your paws off me," Gage protested.

She shook her head as the one before her took her hand and kissed it. "As I said before, welcome to Éire Danu, Zoe. I don't know if you remember, I imagine you've had a lot of names thrown at you recently, but I'm Aeson Vi'Liordon, the unit leader for Chi. The warrior that looks like he's having entirely too much fun torturing your mate, is Ramsey Lionhart, Ari's cousin. He was with me when we accompanied you to the palace." He stepped to the right and introduced the others with him. "This is Matthieu Lucien, of Noctem Falls, Leon March..."

"Fox- shifter," Leon added. "Everyone always

thinks it's a lion because I was named Leon, but I'm a fox."

She grinned at the way his nose scrunched up when he explained his name.

"And last but certainly not least, Carson Elderberry, our witch."

"Fire witch," Carson clarified. "I heard your magic is a bit tricky, so I'll help out whenever I can."

Aeson looked like a proud father. "You're actually wanting to help someone," he pretended to wipe a tear.

"Ow!" Ramsey exclaimed as he began to hop around, holding his foot.

Gage straightened his clothes and resumed his place at her side. "Zoe, as you may have guessed, these idiots are my unit brothers." Though he called them idiots, his voice was full of warmth and affection.

"He broke my foot!" Ramsey whined.

"I did not. Stop being such a drama queen Ramsey. You're making Ari look bad," Gage chided.

Zoe looked around and realized they really were like brothers. "You have a much bigger family than I do, and I can claim most of the Fire Temple as relatives."

Aeson wasn't the only one that flushed at her observation.

"Did you all come here just to torture me?" Gage asked.

"Of course not. We're here to see our newest baby," Aeson explained, pointing to Zoe.

Gage frowned. "You didn't do this with Brie."

Aeson rolled his eyes. "Of course not. Brie is a warrior in her own right and, according to human aging, much older than Zoe."

As Gage went back and forth with Aeson, she lifted the pint to her lips and took a healthy sip. At first, the bitterness threatened to overwhelm her, but then, a surprising nutty flavor took over. "Oh my, that's really good." She took a few more gulps and was mortified when a small burp escaped.

Ramsey laughed. "That's the best way to drink Dav's pints. Just knock it back," he said.

She nodded, then lifted the drink once more, this time not stopping until it was empty. A warmth started in her stomach and spread through her midsection, causing her to smile. "This is nice."

"What did you tell her?" Gage demanded.

Ramsey frowned. "To kill it."

Gage's eyes bugged. "I think that is the first alcohol she's ever had."

"I quite like this." Sighing heavily, she went to lean back but forgot she was on a bar stool.

Laughing, Pip caught her. "Come on. You can sit with us." He escorted her to the table he shared with Meryn.

"Can I have another?" she asked.

Meryn shrugged. "I don't see why not."

"Dav!" Neil and Nigel called out.

"Aye, aye, I'm right here," he said, carrying out a large tray of food. Seeing that Zoe was now at a table, he changed direction and headed their way.

"Don't eat too much," Aeson advised. "We're planning a welcome party for you."

"Snack party?" Priest asked.

Aeson shook his head. "Tapas party."

Gage sat down next to her and took her hand. "Feeling okay?"

"I feel great. What's tapas?" she asked.

Gage eyed his warrior brothers, then smiled. "Tapas are smaller portion meals, mostly comprised of appetizers. It's a perfect way to introduce someone to a multitude of different foods without filling up."

Zoe hopped up and hugged Aeson. "You're doing this for me?" she asked, then switched to Leon. She didn't stop until each one got their own hug, and when she was done, they were blushing terribly.

"We heard Gage was a bit upset over your lack of exposure, so we decided on the way to share with you all our favorite foods," Ramsey explained.

She looked to Gage and smiled. "I bet it was Peter."

Gage stood and grabbed Aeson's forearm, then pulled him in for his own hug. "I have the best warrior brothers in all the pillar cities."

"Considering I get electrocuted and glued to bell towers in Lycaonia, I'm inclined to agree," a white-haired warrior said from an adjacent table.

"Sascha, I shock you because I love you,"

Meryn quipped, causing her mate to growl and the white-haired warrior to sputter.

Moments later, Dav handed her another pint. "Enjoy!"

Throughout the rest of the afternoon, warriors came and went. The men joked that with them getting mates, they should get more name tags. The ones they wore were peeling on most of the corners.

She was on her third beer when a runner came through the door and looked around. She was surprised when he hurried over to her. "Urgent message from Storm Keep, for Lady Appleblossom," he said, before handing her a scroll, and then he jogged away.

Storm Keep? Caroline?

She unrolled the scroll and read the contents. Standing abruptly, waves of anger coursed through her. *How dare they!*

"Zoe!"

She heard Kendrick call her name before flames erupted around her. Instead of moving back, Kendrick, Kincaid, and Carson all ran to her side. Carson took her free hand while Kincaid placed a hand on her back. Kendrick reached out and rested his hand on her head.

"All is well, be calm, *conquiescere*," Kendrick repeated, sending soothing magic through her.

"I'm here, Zoe." Gage's voice penetrated her anger.

Exhaling slowly through her nose, she managed to quell her anger. When her legs gave out, Carson supported her long enough for Gage to step forward and lift her into his arms. "Zoe, what happened?"

She buried her face in his chest. Everything was so perfect, and now the council was ruining it.

"May I?" Kendrick asked, gently tugging at the partially singed scroll.

She looked over at him, nodded, and released the scroll.

When he read the contents, he began to clench his jaw. "Those parasitic sycophants," he hissed.

Thane stepped up beside him. "Witches' Council?" he guessed.

Kendrick nodded. "They are ordering Zoe back to Storm Keep and have heavily implied she may be charged for abandoning her post."

"Can't she just tell them to fuck off like Serenity did?" Meryn asked.

Kendrick stared down at the scroll. "They haven't stripped her of her Temple Head status. They are using it as the reason why she needs to return."

"I won't go back. There's nothing there for me anymore except Caroline. I can't go back, Gage, I can't," Zoe began to have trouble breathing as she started to panic. It had been less than one day, but she had had a small taste of what she had been missing. She couldn't go back now.

Gage rubbed her back soothingly. "You aren't going anywhere. You're forgetting Zoe. You're mated now. Your place is with me, and if you want that place to be here in Éire Danu, then that's where we'll stay."

Aiden held out his hand to Kendrick for the scroll. Kendrick looked surprised but handed it over.

"Zoe, with your permission, will you let your *athairs* respond," he said through gritted teeth.

Zoe looked over at him. "Really?"

Aiden gave a short nod. "Technically, Darian has more political clout, but Gavriel is a close second. I outrank them both as Unit Commander, though that's a matter of opinion," he waved his hand in front of him as if it didn't matter. "What I'm getting at is between the three of us, no matter which one is officially recognized as your *athair*, the Witches' Council would do well not to get on our bad sides."

Meryn poked her mate's side. "What about Colton?"

Aiden shuddered. "Mikel was closest to Colton while he served in Alpha. Let's leave his violent ass in Lycaonia, torturing the warriors."

Zoe could only nod. It had been years since she felt like she had any measure of support and was safe. "Thank you, *athair*."

Aiden puffed up a bit at her, acknowledging him as her *athair*. "Don't give it a second thought. You should only be concerning yourself with the city's lights, getting to know your mate, and figuring out what new foods to try."

She nodded and steeled herself to look around. "What's the damage?" she asked.

Dav looked up from where he had been inspecting the bar closely. "Nothing. Not even a scorch mark." He ran his hands over the wood.

"I think that may be a benefit from the upgrade Meryn's bracelet caused."

"Wicked," Meryn said, grinning.

"Thank the gods," Zoe said, laying her head back on her mate's shoulder.

"Would you like to go home, my darling?"

She turned in his arms to look at him. "It is my home now, isn't it?" she asked, excitement overriding her stress.

"Leon..." Aeson murmured.

"Got it, boss," Leon said, then darted out the door.

Zoe watched the interaction. "Is he okay?"

Aeson smiled broadly. "He's fine. Now. I highly suggest securing a growler or two of Dav's finest. Then we can escort you home. Right men?"

"Yes, sir," Ramsey, Matthieu, and Carson answered.

"We'll carry the growlers," Priest and Kincaid volunteered.

Meryn sidled up to Aeson. "Can I come and eat the little foods too?" she asked plaintively.

Aeson looked taken aback. "Of course, you can! Commander, I insist that your mate also adjourns to the warrior villa for an evening of little foods," he said, using Meryn's term for tapas.

Aiden nodded. "I'll leave her in your care while I head to the palace to handle this situation. I won't be long," he said, holding up the scroll.

Aeson placed a hand over his heart and bowed.

"You honor me, sir. I'll protect our princess with my life."

Aiden blinked. "Oh yeah. She is your princess, isn't she?" He rubbed the back of his neck, then looked down at his tiny mate. "Be good."

"No kisses?"

Aiden smiled, then leaned down to kiss her before straightening back to his full height. He glanced to Ryuu, who nodded, then walked out.

"Whooo hoo, party time! Where's the strippers?" Meryn exclaimed before the door shut.

"I heard that!" Aiden yelled back.

Meryn just grinned. "Let's boogie!"

Gage set her on her feet, and en masse, they left Dav's to head to the warrior villa. The longer they walked, the more her stomach filled with butterflies. This was going to be her new home. She had only known Storm Keep, and even there, only her familial home and, recently, the Fire Temple.

Up ahead, she noticed the men had stopped and were milling around in front of a large estate. As they got closer, she could see a majestic holly emerging from the building's center. "Is that it?"

Gage nodded.

At the gate to the villa, the men bowed in unison. "Welcome home, Zoe."

"You guys can't keep doing these things," she fussed, wiping at her eyes.

Walking up, she and Gage entered the estate, and voices boomed all around her.

"Welcome!"

It seemed as if all the warriors that called the villa home were there to greet her. Leon waved.

"Is everything okay?" she asked.

He stared, then laughed. "Yes. I left early to tell the guys to start heating up the foods that are best served hot and to let them know you were on your way."

He looped his arm through hers, ignoring Gage scowling at him. "We were going to set up each room by country, but in the end, we voted to keep like foods together."

"Like foods?"

"Yeah, for example, all fried foods are in the kitchen. Sandwiches, wraps, and pasta are in the living room. Salads, fruits, and vegetables are in the dining hall, and we've scattered your desserts everywhere," he explained.

Zoe looked around and didn't know where to start. Behind her, Gage was laughing at something Ramsey said and already had a glass in hand.

Leon nudged her. "Now, my lady. This is a marathon, not a race."

She nodded.

"In my opinion, I think you should start with something light, like a salad, then move on to something heavier, like fried chicken. After that rest for a bit with a spritzer, I think Bastien made a strawberry champagne mix that smelled amazing. Then start over, but maybe change it up and go heavy to light," he said, then handed her an empty plate.

She took the plate. "You all take your food very seriously, don't you?"

Leon nodded solemnly. "You have no idea." He looked around and saw Meryn stacking up her plate. "I'm going to go help the commander's mate. You okay starting on your own?"

She held up her plate. "I'm good to go."

She watched as Leon walked over and handed Meryn a second plate. She could see him pointing to each dish and wondered if she was getting the same advice she had.

Over the next couple of hours, the warriors came up one by one to introduce themselves. They were very conscientious and spaced it, so she never became overwhelmed. With each dish she tried, there was a small card from the one that suggested it and why. In one day, she had sampled more food than she had in her previous one hundred years at Storm Keep.

When Aiden arrived, he winked at her, then immediately went to Meryn, who was proclaiming Broden's buffalo wings to be the best in the entire world.

"Hello, cousin," a new warrior greeted her.

"Cousin?" she asked, setting her plate down.

"My name is Bastien Géroux. Technically, my uncle is mated to Gage's mother's sister." He shrugged. "We just claim each other as cousins. It's easier."

"You're the one that made the strawberry spritzer! Gods, that was delicious!"

He smiled. "It's one of Gage's favorites. He's a fiend for anything strawberry flavored."

"Thank you for such a warm welcome."

"We realized how daunting it could be for a mate to move in with so many warriors. We wanted to make sure you felt like this could really be your home."

"For Gage's sake." It wasn't a question. She saw how much the men looked after one another.

"For all our sakes," he corrected. "You'll be the first full-time mate to live here. If it's true and we're all getting mates, then you living here has to work."

"I have no doubt in my mind it will work," she said, picking up her plate.

"Why is that?" he asked.

"Because you all want it to work. I've seen firsthand what you men are capable of when you set your minds to it. You all are some of the most amazing men I have ever met."

He cleared his throat. "We're not too bad," he agreed.

"And how's my mate?" Gage walked up and nuzzled her neck, causing goosebumps to explode down her arms.

"Good. I was just chatting with your cousin." She glared at him. "How could you not introduce us?"

Gage paused in lifting the flute of the strawberry champagne to his lips. "Because every other one of my idiot warrior brothers was constantly swarming you. I knew he'd approach once everything settled down."

"He knows me well," Bastien agreed, nodding.

Gage took a sip and looked for her around. "Where's your plate?"

She held it up. "Here. Why?"

"Good. Aeson is bringing out a fresh batch of goodies from the oven now. Since you're the guest of honor, you get to choose your goodies first."

"As do you as her mate," Bastien observed dryly.

Gage just gave him a shit-eating grin. "I have no shame tonight. Our brothers pulled out all the stops. I haven't seen so many of my favorite dishes together ever."

"We wanted to make sure Zoe got a wide selection. That way, she can request her favorites," Bastien said, taking a bite of a pickle.

"So far, the pinwheels with ham, the cheese bites, and of course, your spritzer are in the running for my top three."

Gage scrunched up his face. "The pinwheels? Really?"

She nodded. "Whatever they put in the cream cheese gave it a zing that I can't stay away from."

Bastien lifted his glass and winked. "I'll let Leon know his creation was a hit. Have fun, kids." He walked toward Leon, who was in the corner with the twins and Pip passing plates around in what looked like a musical chair, eating game.

Gage leaned in, brushing his lips against her ear, causing her to shiver again. "How about we retire after another plate or two? I don't know about you, but I think the day is catching up to me. It didn't help that they served spritzers and beer and not a single source of caffeine," he said, taking another sip of said spritzer.

"Would you really have had anything else even if they had? I heard that was your favorite," she pointed out.

He shrugged, smiling slyly. "Probably not, but then again, I wouldn't mind the extra energy the first night with my mate."

She raised her glass to that and took a long drink. Crap! It was their first night together. What was she going to do?

CHAPTER SEVEN

❧

GAGE LOOKED DOWN AT HIS mate, where she dozed in the oversized chair in the living room. One of his brothers had covered her with a blanket, and in her sleep, she looked even younger. He had only gone to thank everyone, and when he finally was able to break away again, she had succumbed to slumber.

He gently scooped her up and held her close to his body. His brothers quieted as he walked by, heading toward the stairs, so as not to wake her. When he got to his room, he bent slightly and opened the door. With his foot, he kicked it softly behind him. Walking over, he placed her on his bed and stood back.

Her red curls stood out in stark contrast to his black bedding. He didn't know how long he stood there, just watching her sleep, but when he found his eyes closing on their own, he determined it was time for him to rest as well.

As he undressed, he paused; he normally slept nude but didn't want to upset his mate in the morning. Sighing, he reached for a pair of pajama bottoms and pulled them on. When he walked over to the bed, he was faced with another dilemma. What should he do with his mate?

The high-collared temple robes didn't look comfortable. With trembling hands, he unbuttoned the starched robe and gently eased it off her. Breathing a sigh of relief, he discovered she wore a long, white, plain cotton gown under it. It would have to serve as a nightgown for tonight.

With great care, he pulled the covers down and then over her before sliding in behind her. Hopefully, tonight, if he dreamt of his mate engulfed in flames, he would now see his brothers beside him, helping them as they had all day.

C

When Zoe woke, she stretched her arms over her head before snuggling back down. With a start, she sat up and looked around. It was too dark to be her own room. Where in the hell was she?

She reached around, and her hand found a glow-crystal on the nightstand and tapped it. Glow-crystals were primarily used in Noctem Falls. Eyeing her surroundings, she wondered if she was still in Éire Danu. The walls looked like they were made of stone, and she could swear she could smell the hint of water from a pond. When the door opened, she covered her eyes from the glaring light.

"Good morning, darling," Gage said, carrying in a tray.

"Where are we?"

He chuckled and kicked the door closed behind him. "In the warrior villa in Éire Danu."

"You're lying."

"I'm not. My witch brothers had quite a bit of fun creating this sanctuary for me. Bastien liked it so much, he had his rooms redone in a similar fashion."

"It looks like we're in a freaking cave Gage."

"It's meant to look like a cave."

"Is this what Noctem Falls looks like?"

"To a certain degree." He placed the tray down on the nightstand, then sat on the bed beside her. "I brought you some breakfast. Today Jace was cooking, so it's a bit meat-heavy since that's what his wolf prefers."

Zoe eyed the platter of fried ham steaks, bacon, and sausage. On the other plate were slices of buttered toast, cut cheese, and a bowl of fruit.

She reached for the toast and made a ham and cheese sandwich. Taking a bite, she smiled. "This is really good."

"Making a sandwich was a good idea. I think I'll do the same." He chose bacon over ham and added a bit more cheese.

"I'm sorry I fell asleep last night," she admitted.

"I'm not. I got to carry you upstairs and put you to bed. It felt right to take care of my mate."

"But what about... you know."

"Sex?" he asked.

She blushed and nodded.

"Zoe, I'm in no rush. Through no fault of your own, you haven't been exposed to much, so I doubt you dated often. I'm enjoying getting to know you as we become more comfortable with one another. It's not that I don't desire you. I do. I just want you to know your own mind and want me as I want you."

"I do want you, I do. It's just…"

"You don't know me."

She nodded.

"Zoe, let's take our time and enjoy the mating pull. We're both young for paranormals. In a way, we've been blessed to find one another so young. We have the rest of our lives to live, but we won't get these precious first days again." He leaned in, so their foreheads were touching. "Let me enjoy making you blush while I can."

"I have a feeling no matter how long we've been mated, you will find ways to make me blush, Gage Fabre."

He sat back and winked. "Only if I'm lucky."

She ate the rest of her sandwich and was working her way through the fruit when he cleared his throat.

"How particular are you about your clothes?"

"Not very. I mean, I'm normally in temple robes most of the time anyway. Why?"

"I may have taken the liberty of heading out this morning to Baba's and picking out a robe for you for today. I figured you may want to try something new. Later, we can head to the shop, and you can pick out some more, but this way, you can see if you like the design," he admitted a bit sheepishly.

"This morning? What time did you get up?"

He shrugged. "I'm an early riser, so about dawn."

She looked around. "Did you hide it?"

Rolling his eyes, he reached under the bed and pulled out a long white box. "According to Baba, this one is considered a classic. Self-cleaning and fire-proof," he grinned, then continued. "The collar is higher than most but not up to the ears like your temple robes. It's not belted but hangs in a straight line. I felt like it'd be more comfortable."

She opened the box and gasped. "Gage, this is…" she ran her fingers over the fabric. Woven into the ombre of orange and burgundy material were golden threads that shimmered like silk.

"I normally don't wear much red because of my hair."

"Why? I think it would complement you perfectly."

"Really?" She got to her knees and hugged him. "Where can I get dressed?"

The tips of his ears turned pink. "If you don't wish to change in front of me, the bathroom is toward the door and to the left."

She sat back and realized she wasn't the only one who was muddling their way through this mating. "I want to surprise you with the final effect. Besides, I need to pee."

Laughing, he helped her to stand. Clutching the new robes to her, she hurried to the bathroom, dying to see how it would look. After taking care of her morning needs, she pulled the robe on. After a moment, the underthings slid into place, and the waist narrowed to give her some shape.

Looking in the mirror, she was astounded to see that Gage had been right. The colors brought out the shine in her hair and the green of her eyes. She looked like a walking, breathing flame.

She opened the door and found that he had been pacing in front of it, waiting for her. When he saw her, he stopped, and his mouth dropped. "Gods, Zo, you look ethereal."

She twirled. "Really? I love these colors! I would never have picked them for myself, so I'm really grateful that you decided to surprise me."

He bowed, then straightened before offering her his elbow. "When I catch my breath, I'll escort you downstairs so you can stun my brothers."

Laughing, she took his arm, and he walked them downstairs.

Gage cleared his throat when they entered the dining hall, and almost in unison, the men turned, and their mouths fell open the way Gage's had. Chairs scraped on the floor as the men hurried to stand.

"Lady Zoe, you look...." Leon ran out of words.

"She looks like a fire elemental come to life," Carson whispered, also staring.

"Good morning, gentlemen. Is there coffee? I'd like to try some," she asked as Gage pulled out her chair and helped her to sit. Once she was settled, he sat beside her.

Aeson and Leon turned and practically ran into

one another in an effort to get to the coffee bar.

"You pour. I'll get fresh cream," Leon said.

Aeson nodded and went to the bar to pull a hot cup for her. With cup and saucer in hand, he carefully placed it before her. Moments later, Leon returned with a small pitcher.

Zoe looked down at the swirling dark brown liquid. "What do I do with it?"

Ramsey pointed to the sugar bowl, then the small pitcher. "Personally, I like two to three teaspoons of sugar and then a bit of cream. I would start with less, then add to your liking."

Zoe went with his suggestion and added the sugar and a splash of cream. She took a sip and frowned. "People like this?"

"Too bitter?" Gage asked.

She nodded, reaching for more sugar.

Ramsey placed a hand over the bowl. "Is it too bitter, or is it the bite afterward?"

"The bite."

"Add more cream. There's an inherent sweetness to milk, so that may be enough without making it too sweet," he explained.

She added some cream, then stirred. Looking up to Ramsey, he held up pinched fingers. "Maybe a tiny bit more."

Carefully she added some more, stirred, then took another sip. This time she could appreciate the flavor without the bitterness taking over. "I'll have to remember how to do this. It's wonderful."

"Ramsey converted another," Carson grumbled.

"Converted?" she asked.

Jace laughed. "We have two teams in the morning, Team Black Coffee and Team Cream. Carson not only loves black coffee, but Izzy has him adding espresso shots to his now. I don't think his tongue has bitter receptors."

"Sorry, Carson, but I think black coffee in the morning would do me in," she admitted.

He grunted.

She turned to Gage, who shook his head. "Carson isn't a morning person. It's a testament to how excited he was to eat breakfast with you that he's downstairs and his eyes mostly open."

Carson yawned. "I promised to help."

"So, what are you two up to today?" Bastien asked.

"Maybe some shopping? Then I'd like to check some of the spell centers before reporting back to the queen," she looked to Gage to see if he was okay with that.

He took her hand and kissed it. "I am ever your most humble servant."

She eyed her mate. "How come you and Bastien's formal talk slips sometimes?"

Both men stared. "Huh?" Gage asked.

Aeson laughed. "I told you."

Leon pointed. "They don't acknowledge that their formal speech from Noctem Falls disappears when they've been around us too long."

Both Gage and Bastien grunted.

"I like hearing both. I think it makes the times they say something formally that much more dramatic," she observed.

"Really?" Gage asked, brightening.

She nodded. "It makes it more special. Then again, I don't have much to base it on. Your flowery speech is normally directed at me."

Gage poured his own cup of coffee. "I like the sentiment that our formal speech highlights our words instead of thinking that the casual way of speaking is lazy on our part."

"Cousin, let us roll with that explanation," Bastien said.

"Phi and Chi are on rest rotation for the day, so if you need anything, let us know," Nerius offered.

"Could..." she hesitated.

Gage, Bastien, Nerius, and Aeson responded. "What?"

"Could maybe some of the guys, if they want to, that is, maybe check some of the city's spell centers? If they could just do a preliminary check to see if there's any visible damage, that could save me some time," she said, rushing her words in an effort to explain.

Aeson and Nerius both nodded before Aeson spoke. "That won't be a problem at all. It shouldn't take us more than an hour or so. I'll send either Leon or Carson to Baba's to advise you before you get started."

"How'd you know we were going to Baba's?"

Aeson's smile turned frosty. "After the way the other tailors treated Prince Oron. That's the only place the warriors have been going."

"Why would they mistreat him, isn't he a prince?"

Nerius looked to Gage. "Maybe you can explain on the way over to Baba's?"

Gage nodded. "I'll get her caught up on everything as we walk." He turned to her, his eyes a bit sad. "There's much to tell you, so we'll walk slow."

She finished her coffee and stood. "Then we should get started."

𝕮

By the time they reached Baba's, she was a wreck.

"Just take a deep breath," Gage said, ushering her inside.

"Gage Fabre! What have you done to this poor child?" A deeper woman's voice demanded.

Gage looked panicked and remorseful. "Nothing, Baba! I just got her caught up to everything that has been going on in our world."

"When?" the woman asked, making her way around the counter to come to her side.

"On the walk over," he said, pointing back toward the door they just entered.

Baba turned an incredulous look his way and steered her over to a plush chaise lounge situated in front of a set of mirrors.

"Oh dear," a fae woman murmured and sat down next to her, wrapping an arm around her shoulder. "Men!"

"What can I do?" he asked, walking back and forth in front of her.

"Besides scrounging up some damn sense? Run over to the Brick Oven and get this baby girl a treat. Kyla, keep her warm while I start some tea." Baba ordered, then shuffled her way toward the back of her store.

Gage knelt down in front of her. "I'm so sorry, my love. What can I bring you to help?"

"Chocolate. Those brownies and anything Peter recommends," she said through chattering teeth. She couldn't stop shaking.

He kissed her forehead and ran for the door.

"Let me guess. He told you what was going on as if he were making a report to Ari Lionhart?" Kyla guessed.

She nodded. "Why am I shaking?"

"I think you're fighting off shock." Kyla reached toward the end of the chaise and picked up an emerald wrap. Gently she secured it around Zoe's body.

"There's invisible beings killing babies? They killed shifters in Lycaonia for abilities, and they started a virus in Noctem Falls?" she asked, not wanting it to be true.

Kyla's eyes filled. "And now they're killing the fae. I lost my sister in the first attack."

Gripping each other's hands, Zoe squeezed a bit. "I'm so sorry for your loss."

"Thank you. I came here to Baba's to order new robes. Somehow, bright colors don't feel right, and she's the only one who designs in darker shades."

"We came here to get me more fire-proof robes."

"Fire-proof?"

"I'm a fire witch," Zoe replied.

"Ahh, I see. The one you're wearing is lovely."

"Gage picked it out."

Babe emerged from the back carrying a tray. "The boy has an eye for fashion for all he lacks in common sense." She set the tray down, and between her and Kyla, soon all three women held cups.

Hers only shook slightly as she took a sip. "I know what this is. We took Blessed Chamomile to Dirk Vi'Eirlindol yesterday." She inhaled the soothing aroma and took another sip.

"Poor man. He was quite close with his nephew," Baba clucked her tongue.

Kyla turned to her. "He was found in the third warehouse. That one was the most tragic. According to reports, they missed saving them by hours."

"Why is this happening?" Zoe asked, wrapping her hands around the teacup trying to absorb its warmth.

"Evil doesn't need an excuse to be," Baba said.

"Brie, Ari's mate, is a human and leading the investigation. She's using techniques we've never heard of. But, if we haven't heard of them, then our enemy probably hasn't either. In times of darkness, I noticed that some people shine all the brighter, and they're the ones to help others," Kyla said softly.

"Speaking of shining brighter, I heard you're here to help with our lights," Baba said.

Zoe nodded. "I'll be checking with the spell stations today to make sure they're functioning properly."

"Well, that's…"

The door opened, and Carson stepped in. He took one look at her, saw that Gage was nowhere in sight, and snarled. "What happened?" he demanded, striding over to her. "Who hurt you?"

Zoe sniffled. Carson's growling reminded her of her brother. "Gage explained things to me. I just got a bit overwhelmed. I'm fine."

"What did he go over?" he asked.

"Everything."

He blinked. "Excuse me, what?"

"The babies, and reapers and murders and everything," Zoe rambled.

"Right. You're okay, though?" he looked from Kyla to Baba, who both nodded.

"I will be. Gage went to the Brick Oven to get me a treat."

"I came by to tell you we checked the stations, and there was no visible sign of damage. Now, if you'll excuse me, I have a warrior brother to find." He gave a half bow and stalked out.

"Poor Gage," Baba murmured, shaking her head.

"Why?" Zoe asked.

"The warriors look after one another like brothers. You mating with Gage makes you their baby sister. It's a new type of bond I feel they will cherish. That being said, like any older brother, Carson feels like it's his duty to point out exactly what his younger brother did wrong and ensure that it doesn't happen again," the older woman explained.

"But, he won't hurt him, will he?"

Kyla patted her leg. "I'm sure nothing will be permanent."

Zoe sighed and took another sip of tea. Brothers were like that, after all.

❦

Gage looked up from the dessert case when the doorbell behind him chimed. He groaned when he saw Carson striding toward him. "I know, I know. I fucked up."

"What possessed you to lay everything out on a stroll to a dress store? When you left, I thought you'd give her a highlight reel, not everything," Carson roared.

"One explanation led to another, and before I knew it, she was pale and shaking," Gage exploded, running a hand through his hair.

"You have to be more careful of her, Gage," Carson said, crossing his arms over his chest.

"Don't tell me how to be with my mate..." Gage started.

Carson uncrossed his arms, took two steps forward, and poked Gage in the chest. "I'm not telling you how to be with your mate, you idiot. I'm telling you how to be with an unstable fire witch experiencing the whole damn world for the first time!"

Gage felt like his brother sucker punched him. All the air flew from his lungs. "Is she okay? Is she safe?"

"Looked like Baba was serving her Blessed Chamomile when I left. That tea dulls our magic, so, for now, she should be fine."

"Ari made this mating thing look so damn easy," Gage admitted, feeling defeated.

Carson snorted. "His mate is practically one of us, not a walking flamethrower. Cut yourself some slack."

Behind the counter, Peter smiled and shook his head as he continued to box up his huge order.

"She's all innocence and excitement, holding nothing back. I can't hurt her again," Gage turned to his grumpiest brother.

Carson shrugged. "Statistically speaking, you're both young, so you're gonna fuck up again before you both move on from this world."

Peter cracked up. "Gods, he's really bad at this."

Carson scowled. "It's not complicated. Gage will love and adore his mate, he'll fuck up, and his brothers and I will help, end of story."

Gage stared. It really was that simple. He wasn't perfect, so he'd mess up in the future. Knowing his brothers had his back made it easier to breathe.

"See, you're getting it," Carson said, slapping him on the back. "I let your mate know that the spell centers looked to be in good condition. I don't know the actual spells used, but I was able to send my magic in a bit. Everything seemed to be working as intended." He grabbed a pre-packaged bag of cookies. "Peter, can you charge the account?" he asked.

Peter looked over his shoulder. "Sure thing."

Carson stretched. "I understand that a lot of what Zoe will be doing will involve spells learned from her family at the Fire Temple, but if she needs any help, count me in."

"Thanks, Carson, for everything."

Carson shrugged. "That's what brothers are for. Hurry back to your mate and grovel," he ordered, grinning.

Gage came to attention and saluted. "Sir, yes, sir!"

Chuckling, Carson walked out.

"Should I start an apology account for you, Gage?" Peter asked.

Gage went to shake his head, then stopped. "You may be joking, but that's not a bad idea."

"I was half joking."

"Let me pay for a standing order to be delivered weekly. That way, no matter what, I'm covered."

Peter nodded approvingly. "Kid, I like the way you think."

Gage exhaled. "Hopefully, so will my mate."

CHAPTER EIGHT

❦

WHEN GAGE RETURNED, HIS ARMS were filled with boxes. He handed a majority of them to her, but he had also gotten some treats for Kyla and Baba as a way of thanking them for caring for her.

Kyla opened her box and smiled. "I've been wanting to try these brownies but couldn't gather the energy to head to Peter's shop." She took a bite and sighed. "Wonderful."

Zoe, for the first time, could relate. Taking her own bite, she smiled blissfully. "Thank you, my mate."

Gage stood a little straighter. "I cannot tell you enough how sorry I am for upsetting you. I wish I could go back and censure my words better. When I started explaining things, one tragic story led to another. I could not seem to unravel the mess."

"Gage, I don't think there was a happy way of telling me such things, and leaving things vague may have created more anxiety. I have a feeling. Maybe, your way was the best."

He looked doubtful

She couldn't stand the look of pain in his eyes, so she stood on tiptoe to kiss his cheek. "Honest."

"You are too good for me," he kissed her forehead before turning to the older shop owner. "Baba, one of the robes is to be billed to the palace as a present from Her Majesty, but everything else goes to my account." He sat down and picked up a magazine from the basket by his chair. "Ladies, have fun." He nodded his head toward his mate.

Kyla sat forward. "Seriously?"

"Zoe, darling, tell them what clothes you have," Gage suggested.

Zoe gave a half shrug. "Just a couple temple robes. I don't need much."

Baba and Kyla exchanged looks and started moving in opposite directions.

"Baba, if you could show her your dress robes, I'll assemble a selection for everyday wear," Kyla suggested, looking through a rack by the window.

"Zoe, dear, this way," Baba steered Zoe toward the section of the store that had its own dressing room.

Zoe turned to look at her mate. "Gage?" She didn't want him spending too much.

Gage nodded as if understanding her concern. "Baba, she also only came with a single suitcase, so she must need other things as well." He looked back down at his magazine.

Zoe felt her mouth drop. That wasn't what she was worried about.

Baba patted her arm. "Gage, in addition to being a unit warrior, comes from a Noble House in Noctem Falls. We won't even be able to put a dent in his accounts, so never you mind about the costs."

Gage simply nodded absently, then turned the page and continued reading.

The next couple of hours was a whirlwind of fabric and accessories. Every time she went to decline something, she'd catch Gage looking excited about whatever she was wearing and couldn't say no. By the time they left, they had spent a godsawful amount of money.

"Gage I…"

"Yes, my darling?" He beamed down at her.

She had a feeling if she fussed or confessed to feeling guilty, she would dim his happiness. Smiling, she took his hand. "Thank you."

"You're very welcome. I can't remember spending a more pleasant afternoon shopping. We'll have to do this often."

She stopped in the middle of the sidewalk. "No way. I have enough clothes to last for the next hundred years!"

Gage just smiled.

"I mean it, Gage."

"Maybe next year we can do an entire wardrobe in greens. I told Baba I felt like there weren't enough emerald tones to go with your eyes."

Shaking her head, knowing this was a fight she'd probably never win, she followed him to the closest spell center. Surprisingly enough, it wasn't that far from Baba's. Gage stepped to one side to give her room to work.

Kneeling down, she took a deep breath and sent her magic through the crystals just as she had last time, only now she was looking for the imprint of the spell that made up the primary workings of the light. As she worked, the outside world fell away.

In her mind's eye, the spell gleamed like a shining tattoo along the crystal. Each rune and symbol was clear and accurate. Slowly, she extracted herself, and when she went to sit back, she collapsed on her backside.

"Zoe! Are you okay?" Gage asked, looking pale.

"I'm fine. Coming out of the crystal, my spatial awareness was a bit skewed, so I toppled a bit." When she went to stand, she was surprised at how weak her legs were. She looked up to Gage. "I think I may need some help standing."

He ignored her and simply lifted her into his arms. "You were in that trance for close to two hours, Zoe."

"What? It didn't seem that long."

"You need to check in with the queen, but more than that, I want Kendrick to look you over," Gage said as he walked at a quickened pace toward the palace.

She knew better than to argue. Besides that, she was tired. "I hope they have coffee when we get there."

"Are you fatigued?"

She nodded. "It took more out of me than I care to admit."

"Would having another witch with you help in any way?"

She shook her head. "I use my own magic to locate Appleblossom fire magic. It acts like a homing beacon. Once I find the spell, I ensure all the sigils are intact. I'm afraid it's a one-person job."

"And one only an Appleblossom can do."

"Afraid so."

"Zoe, there are twenty-three other spell centers to check."

"I'm well aware. This may take a bit longer than I had originally anticipated. But it has to be done. Maybe I could do one in the morning and one in the evening."

"Absolutely not."

"Gage…"

"You can barely stand after doing one. There's no way you can do two. There just aren't enough hours in the day to do that safely."

She yawned and rested her head on his shoulder.

"You're right."

"I'm not trying to rule what you do, Zoe. I'm just worried," he admitted.

"I know, and that's why I'm agreeing with you. It was a foolish suggestion, but one made out of impatience."

"You'll see it done, Zoe, and I'll help you every step of the way."

"Thank you, my mate."

He grinned down at her. "No charge," he teased, echoing Meryn's quip from yesterday.

"Wake me when we get there."

"Rest, Zoe."

"I'm just going to close my eyes while you walk."

"Sure, darling, whatever you want."

Zoe closed her eyes, and his rhythmic strides had her dozing in no time.

❦

"Is she well?" she heard Kendrick demand.

"Exhausted. Half my fault for scaring the hell out of her by getting her caught up on what's been happening, and the other half was her checking one of the spell centers. Kendrick, she was concentrating for over two hours," Gage explained, as he gently set her down on a soft sofa.

She yawned and opened her eyes. Kendrick, Gage, and Neil were staring down at her with varying degrees of concern on their faces. "It's the trace signature my family used in creating the spell. It's practical to keep interference with the spell to a minimum, but it makes maintenance a chore."

"Why didn't you utilize one of the other fire witches to act as an anchor?" Kendrick asked.

"A what?"

Kendrick's mouth worked like a fish. "An anchor. A secondary witch in a magical working used to keep the primary witch safe and to lessen the load on whatever spell you're casting."

She struggled to sit up so she could participate

in the conversation properly. "I've never used a second before."

Kendrick looked to Thane and pointed at her. "She's never used a second!"

Thane looked unsurprised. "I keep telling you that you should have left your ivory tower sooner, librarian. Justice, Law, and I have been combating this kind of negligence for years."

"I've sent spells," Kendrick began.

Thane nodded, then cut him off. "And how useful were they truly considering," he indicated to her.

Kendrick began muttering to himself, with Thane chiming in, so she decided to ignore them both by turning to the queen. "Good day, Your Majesty," she said brightly.

The queen chuckled. "And good day to you, Lady Zoe. Besides major mental and emotional trauma, how has your day been?"

"Fairly productive. My mate spoiled me with an entirely new wardrobe and even ran to get me brownies when I was upset."

Brennus smiled at her. "Sounds like a good remedy to me."

Zoe offered her hand to Gage, who helped her stand and escorted her to the table, where they both sat. Behind them, Kendrick and Thane were still bickering as Neil watched on, looking fascinated.

Zoe looked around for a coffee bar similar to what she'd seen at the warrior villa. Instantly Cord was at her side. "What can I get you, Lady Zoe?"

"Do you have coffee? I tried some this morning, and I have to confess, it was amazing."

He smiled and turned to Izzy. "Not only do we have coffee, but thanks to our Izzy, we have a full-service espresso bar."

"I haven't tried espresso yet."

Izzy tapped her lips. "You said you liked chocolate, right?"

"Oh my, yes."

Izzy turned to Cord. "I'd suggest a double shot served with a top layer of cream, drizzled with chocolate."

Cord inclined his head. "I'll get that started."

"I'm not sure what that is, but it sounds heavenly," Zoe confessed.

"Trust in Izzy. She's our Coffee Goddess," Meryn said.

Gage looked to Izzy. "Could I ask a favor?"

Izzy looked confused. "Sure, I'll help if I can."

Gage sighed in relief. "The owner of the Brick Oven has been trying to get espresso machines in his bakery for quite some time. Do you think you could help?"

Izzy's eyes lit up, and she spun to face Meryn. "A new place of worship."

"All hail Izzy, Coffee Goddess of Merytopia."

Beside Meryn, Nigel and Pip folded their hands at their chests, closed their eyes, and intoned. "Amen."

Meryn eyed Zoe. "That's the place with the brownies, right?"

"Yes, and apple fritters. Oh! And I tried this

flakey layered honey creation he sent over. It literally melted in my mouth."

"Baklava? He freaking makes Baklava!" Meryn demanded, practically bouncing in her chair.

"I'm not sure what it's called, but it was a favorite."

"Izzy! Tomorrow we're going on a field trip," Meryn said excitedly.

Neil jogged over and sat down between his brother and Pip. "We're going to that bakery?"

Meryn nodded. "It is a journey that must be undertaken."

Zoe wished she could go too. Spending the afternoon with Meryn and the twins sounded fun.

Something must have shown on her face because the next thing she knew, Meryn was turned back to her. "You have to show us da way."

Zoe looked from Gage to the queen. Both were nodding before the queen spoke. "Zoe, you're not a prisoner here. I am not expecting you to work yourself to exhaustion. In fact, I insist on you taking it easy tomorrow with Meryn."

She turned to Gage. "Darling, don't worry about me. I need to participate in more drills using the goggles. Enjoy your day with friends."

"Friends?" she whispered.

"Duh," Meryn said, popping a chip in her mouth.

"Duuuuhhh," the twins and Pip repeated, making Zoe laugh.

"I'd like very much to participate in your religious excursion."

Meryn's face scrunched up. "Sometimes, you sound more formal than the vampires or the fae."

Zoe thought about it a moment. "It could be because I was raised by scholars."

Kendrick plopped down in his chair. "Outside the Magical Academy, the Fire Temple is one the best centers of learning in Storm Keep." Turning to her, he leveled his gaze. "Day after tomorrow, pick an anchor witch, and I'll walk you through the process."

Zoe felt flustered. "I couldn't ask anyone to trouble themselves…"

"I'll help," Kincaid and the twins offered together.

Gage turned to the witch. "I thought the palace made you nervous? But you've been spending a lot of time here."

Kincaid ducked his head. "It's not that bad. I'm learning a lot with the twins."

"He is," Aiden agreed. "So much, in fact, I've excused him from drills for the time being."

Gage smiled. "Good for you!"

Zoe thought about it a moment. "If Kincaid is willing, I think it might be easier for him to help since he has some fire magic."

Kendrick nodded. "Good choice."

Kincaid looked nervous and pleased. "I'll do whatever I can to help. You're my unit brother's mate. I'll keep you safe."

Zoe sat back and turned to the queen. "I was able to, as you probably heard, check on the first spell center today. Everything was clearly etched and working perfectly. It may take a bit longer than expected, but I will try to get through them as quickly as possible."

"It's already making a difference," Ari said from across the table.

Zoe frowned. "The lights aren't any brighter."

He shook his head. "No, but seeing you working for hours on the lights made a huge difference to the people. Priest and I heard them talking when we made our rounds today. You, my dear, are being likened to a living flame."

"It's this robe Gage picked out. I normally don't wear red," she rambled.

"I think you look amazing in red," Amelia said soothingly.

Meryn looked from Amelia to Zoe and back before she pointed. "Is she an empath too? Is that why she's always so chipper?"

Amelia's eyes softened. "First of all, Meryn, someone being pleasant doesn't necessarily make them an empath."

"You're like that."

Amelia pinched the skin between her eyebrows. "You can't equate all happy people to me."

Meryn rolled her eyes.

"Secondly," she hesitated. "I think her wanting everyone to be happy isn't borne out of empathy. Her people-pleasing seems to be a survival mechanism."

Gage and Kendrick leaned in. "What?" they asked in unison.

Amelia shook her head. "I won't go into too much detail, Zoe deserves some privacy, but if she's willing, I'd like to have a session or two with her."

Zoe looked around. "Session? Are you a therapist?"

Amelia shook her head. "I'm a psychologist."

Under the table, Gage took her hand.

"Amelia, you can divulge what you suspect. I don't have any dark stories of abuse or trauma that would demand privacy."

Amelia exhaled and took a moment before she continued. "I think you may be wrong about the trauma. You are exhibiting every key indicator of a long-term domestic abuse survivor."

Zoe looked around the room. "But I was never beaten or anything like that."

"No, but you were trapped," Meryn said softly. "You were entirely dependent on someone else for your day-to-day needs."

"You even used the term locked up before you corrected yourself," Neil added.

"But that, that's normal…" Zoe looked around, and it was the looks of pity that had her heart racing. "I'm fine!"

Through her body, heat raced. "I'm fine!" she repeated, clutching at her chest.

Amelia shook her head, tears in her eyes. "No, you're not, but you will be."

Under the table, Gage jerked his hand back as sparks flew between them.

"I'm sorry! I'm sorry!" She had hurt her mate!

Before she knew what was happening, Meryn

was on one side, and Amelia was on the other. They joined hands and held her. Unlike when Kendrick used a spell to calm her, the ease started in her mind, then spread.

"Meryn!"

"Amelia!"

Around the table, people were scooting away as flames licked up her body.

In her mind, she wasn't alone. Meryn was there baring her teeth at the council in her memories. "Fucking douchebags."

Amelia held her hand and pointed to a smaller version of herself. Scenes from her past flew by. One of her being sent to another room, running away from her home, and her parents crying in frustration. This time with Amelia at her side, she could see these memories as an adult.

As they fast-forwarded through her life, they soon came to the most recent years and being moved to the Fire Temple. Her heart shied away from the image of the building.

"I don't want to go in there."

"We have to."

"Yeah, so we can bust you out," Meryn said, pulling her toward the door.

Once inside, memories of all the verbal abuse began. Having to ask for food, for permission to go outside. Every demeaning instance meant to break her.

Seeing herself smile brightly and give them what they wanted infuriated her. "I didn't want to do what they wanted. I was scared and alone!"

Amelia nodded. "We know."

Zoe watched as Meryn flipped her desk upside down. "Burn it."

Amelia sighed. "Really, Meryn?"

"What? That seems to be her forte. Burn this shit to the ground."

Zoe walked over to the desk that represented endless, mindless days and lifted her power hand. "*Inferno*."

The desk exploded in splinters of wood and flame.

Zoe turned back to the two women that had helped her face her own mind. "I'm free."

"Got that right! Hey, can you blow up the wall too?" Meryn asked.

The moment she began to laugh, the images began to fade, and all too soon, they were back in the queen's chamber.

Around them, chaos reigned. She turned to Meryn. "Oops?"

Meryn giggled. "That was kickass!"

Aiden and Darian were released by Kendrick and Thane and ran over, each scooping up their pregnant mate.

"What did you think you were doing!" Darian demanded.

Amelia flicked his ear. "I know you're not yelling at me, princess."

"I swear to the gods. I'm going to put you in one of those damn bubbles Gavriel wants," Aiden threatened, trying to catch his breath.

Meryn pointed to Ryuu. "Was he freaking out?"

Aiden grunted.

"Then you knew I was fine."

"Amelia, there was fire everywhere. You have to be burned," Darian set his mate down to inspect her closely.

Zoe looked around, wondering where her own mate was. He was being healed by Kincaid on the other side of the table. "Gage! I'm sorry, this is my fault!"

Kincaid glared at Gage. "No, it's his fool-ass fault. He kept reaching into the flames to try and get to you."

She watched as the blistered skin shrunk down, lightened, and healed.

"Wasn't the whole room burning?" she asked, looking around.

Everyone was shaking their heads. Thane answered. "The fire was centered on you. At first, we thought Amelia and Meryn were getting burned, but we didn't see them getting hurt. If you look at the table, the cloth burned, but not the wood."

Zoe dropped her head back. "Cord is going to ban me from the palace."

No sooner had she said his name than he appeared with a tray of drinks. "Don't be silly. Lady Zoe, your espresso." Smiling, he handed her her drink. "And for the gentlemen, shots of Forbidden Fruit and Blessed Chamomile." Cord kept smiling until he saw Darian spinning Amelia round. "For goodness sake, Darian, leave the poor girl alone. You'll make her sick, spinning her like that." He walked over and handed first Aiden, then Darian their drinks.

Darian sat down and simply pulled Amelia into his lap. "What happened?"

Amelia kissed his cheek. "Remember me telling you that I use my gifts to help people."

He nodded. "You said you could take on some of their pain," he paled. "Are you hurt."

She sighed. "No, I'm fine. I think I inadvertently used Meryn as an anchor."

Kendrick turned to his godsdaughter. "When did you learn about anchors?"

Amelia waved her hand. "Just a few minutes ago when you were ranting about them."

Kendrick sprung to his feet. "Did you not hear me tell Zoe I'd walk her through how to do it!"

Amelia shrugged. "It's not like I did it on purpose."

"That's not any better!" he shouted.

Cord looked from Kendrick to Gage. "I'll be back with more shots and tea."

Zoe looked at Meryn. "I think your bracelet kept you and Amelia from being burned. Dav's bar didn't burn earlier either, remember?"

Meryn's eyes widened. "I'm fire-proof?"

"No."

"But…"

"No," Aiden repeated.

"This is too cool not to play with," Meryn refuted. She turned to Zoe. "Can you try and burn me later?"

"Can my mate, perhaps not burn anything for a little bit?" Gage asked, reaching for Zoe. Before she knew what he was doing, she was ensconced in his lap in a similar fashion to the way Aiden and Darian were holding Meryn and Amelia.

Meryn shrugged. "That's okay. I still have that flamethrower Magnus got me."

Aiden dropped his forehead to rest on the back of Meryn's head in defeat.

"What happened?" Gage asked.

Suddenly all eyes were on her. "Amelia helped me face my past, but through the eyes of an adult. What I thought was normal, I think I always knew was wrong. I just lied to myself because it hurt too much to acknowledge how scared I was." She took a deep breath. "The Witches' Council abused me to keep me compliant. It was never physical, but maybe, the other ways that hinted of something worse was more terrible than if I had been hit."

Cord returned from the kitchen and refilled Darian's glass.

Gage tightened his arms. "Are you okay to discuss this?"

She nodded. "Amelia's gift is amazing. I know I'll probably need to actually talk through this, but she gave me a solid platform to begin. I'm insulated enough from the trauma of my past to begin the healing process."

"What did they do?" Gage asked through clenched teeth.

"They owned me. Every minute of every day. Growing up, it wasn't so bad, just council-mandated decisions my parents had to abide by. But when I got older, after my parents left, they had me on a strict schedule to keep my affliction under control. Once I moved to the Fire Temple, the verbal abuse began with Andrei."

Gage held her close. "You won in the end."

"I want to do magic like that!" Meryn exclaimed. "Zoe made her desk explode." Holding out her hand, she stared down at the table. "*Inferno*."

A tiny blue spark popped and fell harmlessly to her plate.

"Meryn!" Aiden and Kendrick roared.

"I did it!" she crowed.

Kendrick stood and cleared the table in two seconds flat. "What possessed you to try such a thing!"

Meryn was staring at her hand. "That was so cool!"

"Do you have any idea what you could have done?" Kendrick demanded.

"Blown up the table?" Meryn asked, tilting her head to look up at him.

"Meryn, please, my mate, I'm begging you, please never attempt magic again," Aiden begged.

"But what if it saves me someday?"

Aiden and Kendrick exchanged looks before Kendrick collapsed in a chair. "Cord." Kendrick pointed to himself and Aiden.

Without a word spoken, Cord simply poured the two of them a shot of Forbidden Fruit.

"This calls for a celebration! My niece can use magic!" Brennus announced proudly.

Kendrick scowled at him. "No, it does not call

for celebration. It calls for water sprinklers and asbestos."

"That shit will kill ya," Meryn warned.

The queen lifted her tea cup. "Never a dull moment."

Zoe rested her head against her mate's chest and let his heartbeat soothe her. "I feel like I can breathe freely for the first time since I was a child."

"You scared me to death, and seeing you face your fears without me had me feeling helpless, but I wouldn't exchange your expression of peace for anything," Gage admitted before kissing the top of her head.

"Even if I may have inadvertently taught Meryn fire magic?" she asked smirking.

"Even then."

Meryn looked up from where she had been staring at her plate and glanced around the table. "So, on a scale between one and ten, how angry do you think Sascha would get if I set him on fire?"

Cord sighed, then poured more shots.

CHAPTER NINE

AFTER MERYN'S QUESTION IGNITED LAUGHTER and multiple looks of concern, Gage simply stood and carried her toward the door.

"Get her home. We'll be right behind you," Ari said, indicating to Priest and Kincaid.

"We'll see you there," Gage replied.

"Zoe, keep your foods light tonight and drink Blessed Chamomile. Rest is the best thing for you," Kendrick advised.

"That sounds wonderful to me. Good night, everyone," Zoe said, waving. When she caught Amelia's eye, she mouthed the words, '*thank you*'.

Amelia just nodded.

"I'm going to forget how to walk," she observed as he turned the corner and started down the long hallway toward the exit.

"That's fine by me."

As they walked back, she thought over what she had learned. What amazed her was she had the knowledge the whole time. Amelia didn't reveal anything she didn't already know, just framed it in a new light.

"I think the worst part about how I was treated was that it made me doubt my own mind and strength. Their conditioning had me relying on them for everything."

"You don't have to concern yourself with them anymore," he said, his voice harsh.

"You can't go after the entire Witches' Council, my love."

He nodded. "You are right. But my uncle, and through him, our Prince can start inquiries."

"Is that necessary? You can't change the past, and they can't hurt me anymore."

He stopped in the middle of the sidewalk to look down at her. "Do you really think that I am the only one planning something? Both Kendrick and Aiden were barely containing their rage as you explained what your life had been like. I am merely opening the door for them to barrel through."

When they arrived at the warrior villa and walked in, Leon saw him carrying her and immediately frowned. "Is she okay?" he demanded in a loud voice.

Within moments the foyer was filled with warriors. Aeson lifted her from Gage's arms and carried her to the sitting room. Behind her, Gage leaned against Leon yawning as the fox shifter steered her mate into the wingback chair next to her.

Aeson placed his hands on his hips. "We already know how you scrambled her brain this morning with feral talk. What's happened now?"

Zoe snuggled under the chenille throw Ramsey tucked around her. "Amelia used her gift and helped me face my past. Let us just say that the Witches' Council has much to answer for."

Gage held up his pink hands. "She caught fire, and I stupidly reached for her."

Leon jogged toward the kitchen.

Aeson turned to Ramsey. "Find Ari and check in with our commander. I want to know what is planned."

"Yes, sir," Ramsey replied and headed for the door.

"Thank you, Aeson. It sets my mind at ease knowing my brothers are looking out for us," Gage admitted.

"We'll get you both fed so you can rest," Aeson pointed to the kitchen. "Jace, can you get some soup and sandwiches started?"

Jace nodded and passed Leon on his way out. Leon went to Gage and handed him a towel-wrapped ice pack. Exhaling in relief, Gage held onto the pack.

Ian shook his head. "I would have offered when you first came in, but I didn't know it was that bad, but seeing your reaction to the ice pack, changed my mind. Gage, come with me to the living room so I can look at your hands. Kincaid is good at healing, but I'm better."

Gage stood then looked to her. She waved him on. "I don't want you in pain."

He dropped a kiss on her forehead and walked away with Ian.

As soon as he was out of sight, Matthieu sat down next to her. "Listen, he won't say anything, but if he feeds, he'll heal faster."

She nodded. "I would never deny him."

"Yes, but he may hesitate as feeding can become very... um... sensual."

She blushed but kept her chin up. "We're mates. I don't see a problem with that."

"In case he hesitates, say, 'Gage, it is my right and duty to provide for you; I offer all of myself to you.' Those are the words spoken between vampire mates when they feed," he explained. He went to say more but stood quickly and sat back down next to the window where he started.

Seconds later, Gage walked back in, rubbing the palms of his hands. He looked at her and titled his head. "You're flushed. Are you well?"

She went to speak and had to clear her throat. Images of him claiming her kept distracting her. "I think I'm finally feeling better. This blanket has helped," she lied.

He looked relieved and sat down at her side again.

The other men kept the conversation light as soup and sandwiches were passed around. The men ate either standing or where they sat with her in the sitting room.

She managed half a sandwich and was sipping her chicken noodle soup when the door opened, and Ramsey and the rest of the Tau unit returned.

Gage looked up at his unit leader. "Well?"

Aeson stood to allow Ari to sit closer to Gage

as Priest, Kincaid, and Ramsey plucked sandwiches off the platter by the fireplace.

Ari sat, resting his elbows on his knees. "Aiden and the queen are opening an inquiry at the council level."

Zoe shook her head. "The Witches' Council operates outside the Elder Council, they will listen to what is said, but they rarely act on anything asked of them."

"How does Storm Keep have two councils anyway?" Leon asked.

Carson sighed. "It was first suggested as more of a public works type of committee. It then evolved as a way of governing the city proper. It's never been an issue before now as they don't really go against Elder Council dictates."

"Seems Prince Magnus was apprised of the situation already from a Caroline Edelweiss when she had to explain why she suddenly wanted to accept a standing job offer he extended over a hundred years ago," Ari said.

Zoe sat up. "Is she okay?"

He nodded. "Prince Magnus made sure to send the Eta unit to collect her. He had already reached out to Byron to discuss options when the queen contacted him." He looked to Zoe. "There is a major concern that a member of what is Storm Keep's equivalent to a Founding Family could be treated in such a manner."

"No one should be treated as I was, Founding Family or not," she protested.

Ari held up a hand. "We have to start somewhere. If your family's standing helps resolve this and puts in place measures for it never to happen again, it will be used."

"Right now, the larger problem is keeping Meryn and the twins from retaliating," Kincaid informed them, winking at her.

Zoe had to smile. Even though she had only known Meryn a few short days, it felt longer. They had truly bonded when the smaller woman helped to free her from her own mind.

"You're smiling now, but I heard a rumor that they sent a drone into the holding cells and cast a diarrhea spell on Ivan DeLaFontaine," Bastien said, grinning.

Ian and, surprisingly, Carson burst into laughter.

Kincaid smiled. "They see magic differently. I can't tell you how much I have learned from all three of them."

Ari stood and stretched. "Ryuu and Portia will be heading to Japan tomorrow to secure your attendant. That should help take the validity from the argument that you need the Witches' Council's help because of your magic."

She went to respond and yawned instead. Gage stood and scooped her up again. "If you gentleman will excuse us, I want to make sure my mate gets some rest."

Ari clapped him on the back. "We won't let this go, Gage. For tonight, let us worry about it for you."

Gage smiled and inclined his head to his unit leader. "Thank you."

Zoe waved goodnight to the room and stuck

her tongue out at Matthieu, who was wagging his eyebrows at her, causing him to laugh.

"What was that about?" Gage asked.

"Just the guys acting like brothers," she said vaguely.

"They're good at it," he responded.

It didn't take him long to get to their rooms. He opened the door and closed it behind them. When he went to set her down, she noticed the sheets were no longer black. They were now a scarlet red. "Did you change the sheets?"

He rubbed the back of his neck. "Aeson helped me with them. Baba knew where to get fire-proof fabric and whipped these up for us. Not that I'm expecting anything," he said, waving his hands in front of his body. "I know how innocent you are. I would never presume."

Zoe huffed. Maybe she was innocent, but she wasn't dead. She'd have to take brutally direct steps for him to see her as a woman.

Nonchalantly she began removing her clothes.

His eyes widened. "I'll go into the bathroom while you…"

"You don't have to."

She tried to hide her shaking hands as she slipped off her bra, then her underwear. Laying back on the silky red sheets, she felt reckless. She wanted her mate.

"Gage, my mate. Won't you come lay down?" she asked sweetly, reaching for him.

He stood stock still, just staring. She could see his throat working hard, and he kept swallowing.

Remembering Matthieu's advice, she came up

on her elbows. "Gage, it is my right and duty to provide for you; I offer all of myself to you."

She heard his quick inhale as his eyes seemed to bleed crimson in seconds. "You don't know what you're offering."

She smiled seductively. "I am offering you my everything, meaning the blood in my veins and the warmth of my body." She reached down and let her fingers trail between her breasts. "I have this funny ache down here, Gage. Do you think you can help me with it?" she said, twirling her fingers over her mound.

He moved quicker than she could track. One moment he was standing several feet from the bed, then she heard cloth tearing, and the next thing she knew, his naked body was looming over her.

He leaned down and licked up the column of her neck. When he captured her lips, she sighed, and he rocked his hips against her. He pulled back, breathing hard. "I am going to feast on you, my mate. I will plunge my fangs deep into your neck. Then I will extract every ounce of honey your cunt will give. Are you ready for that?"

"If that means I'll also be able to experience what it feels like to have that hard, hot length deep inside me, I'd say we'd both be getting what we wanted."

His smile turned wicked as his knuckles grazed her peaked nipple. When she closed her eyes to enjoy the sensation, he struck without warning. With his hands, he pulled her legs apart and around his waist. He leaned down and buried his fangs in the side of her neck.

At first, there was a blinding, burning pain, but then there was nothing but bliss. Each pull from his lips sent an electrical current to her clit, causing it to throb out of control. She bucked against him, needing more friction.

Cradling his head against her, she lifted her hips against him. He pulled back, his fangs peeking out over his lip. "Which would you like first, my love? Do you want my cock driving into you, or would you prefer my tongue to scrape each sensitive spot inside your channel until you're begging to be filled?"

She reached between them and grasped his hard flesh. "Claim me, my mate. Let tonight be the first night of my free life. Let this be the first and best decision I make for myself."

She felt his fingers brush hers as he grabbed his length to guide it between her slick folds. "I swear to love you forever. You will want for nothing, and I will always put you first," he whispered before he drove deep.

Like with his bite, there was a sharp pain, but it didn't last long. Feeding him had aroused her more than she knew it would. She was more than ready for him.

She felt her magic swirl, and she looked up at Gage, scared. He only winked and licked her breast. When he blew air across it, it felt cold. Slowly her errant magic calmed. "Yes," she breathed, closing her eyes to enjoy the pounding sensation his body was giving her.

When she felt close, her hand snaked down to her clit. He saw her movements and his thrusts increased in number and intensity. Her fingers had barely grazed her swollen flesh when she screamed.

Next to them, the glow-crystal exploded, and Gage roared his release. She felt a coolness swirl in her chest. It spun as it encountered the warmth of her own until a small cyclone whirled between them. When Gage shuddered and went to withdraw, the cyclone collapsed, sending two blended essences flying into their chests. He was with her now. Now and forever.

He collapsed to one side and immediately pulled her close. "Gods, I love you."

"I love you too, my mate."

She'd be walking funny tomorrow, but it'd be worth it.

After a few minutes, she pushed at him.

"What? Did I hurt you?" He propped himself up on his elbow to inspect her.

"Yes, but in a good way. That's not why I want to get up. I'm all sticky, and I hate it."

He laid back down, chuckling. "I must not have done a good enough job if such a thing worries you."

"It's sticky, Gage. It will always worry me."

He leaned over and kissed her. "I'll get a cloth. You stay in bed."

"The sheets will be a mess."

He stood, and she once again got to admire the view. Just enough muscle, so she wanted to trace the sleek lines with her tongue. He winked at her. "Whatever you're thinking, I agree, and no, the sheets are fine. They're self-cleaning like the robes. It's the same fabric, after all."

She checked around with her hand. "How remarkable."

He gently cleaned her, taking his time to kiss along her inner thigh. When he was done, he simply sent the washcloth sailing across the room. She heard it hit a wall and slide to the floor. "Oh, Gage."

He yawned. "I'll take care of it in the morning. Sleep, my mate."

She snuggled into his chest, tucking her head under his chin until she could rest next to where his heartbeat. As usual, its steady beat calmed her, and before she knew it, she followed him into slumber.

C

At breakfast, she couldn't help but notice that the men's cheeks tinged pink when they met her eyes. All at once, she realized they had heard her being claimed. Heat flooded her own cheeks.

A hand tapped hers under the table. She looked over, and Carson leaned in. "I'll handle the soundproofing today while the two of you are out," he promised in the barest of whispers. "The men won't breathe a word, so don't feel ashamed for what comes naturally between mated couples."

She gave a slight nod, then took the cup of coffee Ramsey passed her. Unlike the other men, he simply grinned at her. Shaking her head ruefully, she let the men ignore the awkward elephant in the room like the gentlemen they were.

Balder walked in from the kitchen, holding a frying pan. "Zoe, scrambled eggs?"

"Yes, please."

He easily slid a portion onto her plate. "Meryn sent a runner down earlier this morning. Despite her mate's worry, she has invited you to go shopping with her."

Gage put his cup of coffee down. "Why is Aiden concerned?"

"Because her squire Ryuu left for Japan at dawn through a portal with Portia," Balder explained.

Ari yawned. "Gage and Pierce have guard duty. It made sense as Zoe would also be going. Kincaid will continue his lessons with the twins and Kendrick."

Zoe bit her lower lip. "I was supposed to attend lessons too."

Kincaid smiled. "You won't be missing anything today. It will mostly be earth magic criteria."

Gage stood and kissed her forehead. "I'll be right back down."

She nodded, and he walked away.

"Did Meryn's message say what she wanted to shop for?"

"Something about religious supplies," Balder explained, looking perplexed.

"Ah. Brownies."

Broden leaned forward to look at her. "How is that religious supplies?"

She shrugged. "I don't know how Meryn meant it, but I feel like I experience something spiritual when I eat brownies. It may be something like that."

Broden didn't look convinced. "Our commander did say that chocolate helped cure women."

Zoe could only smile and sip her coffee. If the men truly believed that, she wouldn't tell them any different, especially as she had gotten brownies recently for reasons very similar to what they were describing.

She looked down at Gage's empty seat and wondered what her mate was up to.

☾

Gage stared down at his phone. Sighing, he tapped a name he knew better than his own. Moments later, he heard a soft feminine voice.

"Gage?"

"Good morning, mother."

"It is wonderful to hear from you, my son. Is it true you have found your mate?"

"It is, and the reason I am calling," he replied, slipping quickly into his more formal mode of speaking.

"What is she like? I want to hear all about my new daughter."

Gage pulled the phone away and looked at it. He wasn't expecting this reaction. He thought for certain she'd lament losing her baby boy.

He put the phone back up to his ear. "She is wonderful. Bright and warm, sweet and kind. I could not have asked the gods for more."

"She loves you, right?"

The question broke his heart. He knew that his parent's mating had been a loveless one. "She shows me every day, in thousands of ways, how much she loves me."

A ragged exhale had him wishing he was in Noctem Falls. He couldn't help the storm of tears about to happen whilst in Éire Danu.

A quick sigh later, his mother shocked him again. "Good. Now, when can I visit and meet her?"

"Mother?"

"Yes, darling?"

"Are you... well, are you on drugs?" he asked, completely at a loss for words for the change in his beloved mother.

Her tinkling laughter further confused him. "I am so very sorry to confuse you." She sighed. "Recently, here in Noctem Falls, Prince Magnus opened up the city to refugees."

He gritted his teeth. He had been one of the ones that had tried desperately to return home when the city suffered from the virus. "I know. The queen kept us apprised of the situation in Noctem Falls when we realized we could not open the portals."

"Good, there will be less for me to explain. Now, when that happened, a few vampires met their true mates and revealed to Prince Magnus a long-standing custom for Founding and Noble family members to arrange matings to keep bloodlines strong."

He did not like where this was leading.

"Gage, I have left your father. With Prince Magnus' support, I have realized that although I was blessed to have you, I do not have to stay within House Fabre. I moved in with your aunt and uncle weeks ago. I asked them not to say anything since I was still coming to terms with my new life."

Gage gripped the phone so hard he heard it crack. "Did he ever hurt you?"

She chuckled in a self-deprecating manner. "Not in the way you mean. It was his lack of affection that caused the most hurt. Everything else was treated like a business transaction."

Gage sagged in relief. He got along well with his father, though they were never close. He would hate to see his father as an abuser. "I would like you to meet my mate, mother. Can you please visit me in Éire Danu?"

He heard a sniffle, then laughter. "Of course, baby boy. I can leave this evening after taking care of a few things."

Smiling at the fact that his mother visiting wasn't anxiety-inducing, he shook his head. "You can stay here at the warrior villa or the Lionhart estate. Ari's parents have extended an invitation for you."

"Oh, my. Really? Gage, son, please do not take this the wrong way, but as much as I would like to stay with you, it would be a tad awkward you being so freshly mated and all. Besides, I would love the opportunity to get to know Catherine Lionhart, I have heard she is an amazingly strong woman, and I think this would help me."

Gage truly wondered if he was living in a strange parallel dimension. "I do not mind at all, mother, but well, I fully expected you to want to stay by my side."

"You are grown, Gage, and correct me if I am wrong, but I feel I did a fairly decent job raising you."

"You did."

"Well, now it is time for me to learn about myself and what I can do. I will not be able to get my years back, but I can move forward."

"Mother, words cannot express how proud I am of you. If I could ask a favor?"

"You have only to ask."

"Could you share some of your newfound strength and insight with my mate?" he asked, before unburdening his heart with the story of his mate's past.

"You tell that young lady to keep her head up. I will be there for the evening meal," his mother said in a firm voice. "I will get with Simon and see what can be done about this Witches' Council."

"It is already being handled, mother."

"Humph! Not to a concerned mother's standards. Now, go spoil that mate of yours. I will see you soon."

For the first time in his life, he was able to draw strength from his mother's words. "We will be waiting."

She hung up first, and he stared at the phone. Shaking his head, he stood, then walked down stairs. When he sat down next to his mate, he heard the room quiet.

Her hand on his had him looking up.

"Gage, what is it? What's happened?"

"My mother is coming to visit."

Ari chuckled. "Do you need us to run interference?"

He shook his head and looked at his unit leader. "She left my father. Evidently, they weren't true mates. She sounded like a completely different person."

He heard multiple sharp inhales from around the room.

"What do you mean they weren't 'true' mates? A mate is a mate," Aeson asked.

"She said that when Prince Magnus invited the wolves, certain already 'mated' vampires found true mates amongst them. This brought to light the fact that many of the Founding and Noble families had been arranging matings for years to maintain bloodlines." He exhaled and sat back. Grinning, he looked around. "She sounded happy."

Zoe squeezed his hand. "Of course she did. She's free now."

He brought her hand up and kissed it. "She said she can't wait to meet you. In fact, I am under orders to spoil you shamelessly."

"Wow, she does sound different," Kincaid said.

He turned to Ari. "She said she'd prefer to stay and your parent's estate and get to know your mother."

Ari's mouth dropped open. "I thought we'd have to pry her from your side. Damn, this is great news!" his eyes widened. "I don't mean about your parents, just that she's doing so well."

Gage nodded, laughing himself. "She said she wanted to get to know herself and what she's capable of. She's even going to my uncle to cause a fuss on Zoe's behalf."

"Me?" she squeaked adorably.

"Yes," he mused over the entire phone conversation. "She sounded very fierce when defending you. I can't wait to meet this new version of my mother."

Zoe leaned and rested her head on his shoulder. "Me too."

He was actually looking forward to his mother's visit. Shaking his head, he started to eat his breakfast. Gods knew he'd probably need all his energy and strength today with two feisty women in his life.

CHAPTER TEN

𝒞

ZOE STOOD NEXT TO GAGE in front of
the palace. Aiden was giving Meryn a laundry list of things she couldn't do. Meryn, on the
other hand, was ignoring him and fussing over
Pip's parasol. Izzy was saying goodbye to her
mate, who looked like he was close to pouting.
Evidently Nigel and Neil were staying behind
to help Kendrick with his portal energy project
after their earth magic lessons.

Pierce watched the entire scene with a smile.
He saw her looking his way and walked over. "I
know Aiden and Ryuu mean well, but they forget she's a grown woman half the time."

Gage winced. "I've heard stories of what that
grown woman is capable of doing. Maybe she
does need some rules set for her."

Zoe poked her mate's arm. "Just because they
are mates, that doesn't mean he gets to set rules
for her."

Gage sighed. "Zoe, I'm speaking of setting
boundaries on her not electrocuting people and
avoiding grenades, not that she can't spend a
certain amount of money."

Zoe looked to Pierce for confirmation. He nodded, grinning. "Maybe just a few pointers," she conceded.

Meryn walked over with Pip and a resigned-looking Aiden behind her. Heaving a huge sigh, he picked up his mate, kissed her, then set her back down. "Try not to level the city, baby."

"I will make every effort to acquiesce to your request," Meryn replied, smiling sweetly up at her mate.

"Pierce!" Aiden grumbled loudly.

"I'll watch over her, sir. I wouldn't want to disappoint Ryuu," Pierce promised.

Aiden shook his head, and he and Oron walked back toward the palace together, looking worried.

Meryn grinned and rubbed her hands together. "The overlords have retreated to their combat arena, now is the time to strike!"

"Zoe, show us da way," Meryn said, pointing to the sidewalk.

Zoe nodded and led them down the walkway she was now familiar with. When they were in sight of the Brick Oven, she heard Meryn whisper, 'whoa,' under her breath.

Gage opened and held the door for them, and they all walked inside.

"Zoe! I hope your mate didn't mess up again," Peter said, before releasing his booming laughter.

"No, he's been good," she teased.

Gage swatted her bottom, causing her to gasp

and cover her butt with both hands. Again, Peter laughed.

"Oven," Meryn said, swaying slightly.

Izzy came up on one side and Pip on the other.

"What else?" Pip said, guiding Meryn.

"Hot, embers, coal, oven, no… furnace." Meryn shook her head. "It's a place to cook and create, but it can be for food or weapons." She stared up at the large baker. "You're a furnace."

He eyed her from over the glass case. "What was that, Your Highness?"

Meryn just nodded. "I have stupid empathy, but I can't control it yet. However, your image came through loud and clear. You're strong, but not like muscle strong, though, obviously you're pretty badass; it was more like you're versatile and dependable."

The large man's cheeks tinted pink. "Your Highness, I don't think I've ever received such a compliment. Pick anything you want on the house."

Meryn scowled. "I wanna pay."

He looked over to Izzy. "Then you can help your friend figure out my espresso machine scenario."

Meryn beamed up at him. "Izzy is the Coffee Goddess, I am the Empress of Merytopia. We were hoping to turn your store into a new place of worship."

He frowned, then blinked, then blinked again before shrugging. "Whatever, as long as I can add espressos to the menu, I'll be happy."

"Excellent. Izzy, what do you think?" Meryn asked, pointing to the store.

Behind them, a few fae walked in and went to the counter.

Peter looked at Meryn. "Be right back with you," he said, then turned to help his customers.

Izzy and Meryn walked around the case and into the kitchen area. Zoe looked at Gage, who just shook his head. Moments later, when they returned, Izzy was pointing to the counter behind Peter.

"The problem is space. I have a feeling he needs all he has back there for dough and stuff. But, if he sacrificed this back wall bar seating area and extended his kitchen, he'd have the space for everything."

"Space for what?" One of the fae asked while their friend was getting rung up.

"We're looking at adding espresso machines here," Meryn replied, stepping from around Izzy.

The fae's eyes widened, and he bowed from the waist. "Good morning, Your Highness."

His two friends turned, saw who he was speaking to, and immediately bowed. "Good morning, Your Highness."

"Umm, good morning."

"My name is Ilan Vi'Exleden. These are my friends, Janlor Airston and Dean Li'Morlin. Did you say you were adding espresso machines here? Are you now the owner of this fine establishment?"

Meryn shook her head quickly. "No, I'm here with Izzy, my brother Oron Vi'Eirlea's mate. In the human world, she was a master-level barista. Peter asked for her advice on adding espressos to his menu."

The men bowed again in unison. "Lady Izzy."

"Gentlemen," Izzy responded.

Ilan extended a card to Peter. "If you need assistance with financing, don't hesitate to reach out to me. I frequent here enough that I'm surprised I'm not turning into the apple fritters I devour so much. I would love to see espressos and coffees added to the menu."

Peter took the card, looking gobsmacked. "Are you sure?"

Ilan nodded. "If Lady Izzy and Princess Meryn are this interested, I know it will do well." He inclined his head. "I wish you success in your planning discussions." He then gave a little wave, and he and his friends walked out.

Peter reached up and pinched his own cheek. Flinching, he looked to Meryn and Izzy. "The rumors are true. The two of you cause waves of change around you."

Meryn's expression turned thoughtful. "Most people say chaos instead of change."

Peter gave her a sly smile. "For creatures that eschew any deviation from the norm, change is viewed as chaos."

Izzy dug into her ever-present backpack and pulled out a notebook. She began scribbling down things.

Peter stared. "Did she say something about moving a wall?"

Meryn nodded. "Where did you think the

machines would go? Your kitchen area is kinda tight as it is."

Peter winced. "Space is at a premium here in the city."

Gage looked at Meryn. "What was it you told us? Go up."

Meryn brightened. "Yeah, you could do that." She pointed to the ceiling. "Do you think you could add an entire cafe on a second floor?"

Peter looked up, and his mouth moved silently. "If I could hire a few witches to add some basement storage, I could add on upstairs."

Meryn smiled. "I happen to know two very good earth witches who can help."

Peter shook his head. "I won't be able to afford them for a while."

Meryn took out her phone and tapped a message. Moments later, there was a ding. "You don't have to pay them. They said they needed a large project like this to test some new things they learned. So, just toss them some sweets, and they'll get it done in record time."

Peter's hand slammed the counter. "You can't be serious!"

Meryn frowned. "I am. Why?"

"These things don't happen."

"What things?"

"You coming in, willing to help, then Ilan Vi'Exleden of all people offering financing, then you arranging for few earth witches!" he exclaimed.

Meryn glanced around the room, looking confused. "Weren't we supposed to help?"

Pierce cleared his throat. "Most people would be considered kind just for stopping by. They would be considered amazing for providing the numbers for trustworthy vendors. What you and Lady Izzy are doing borders on miraculous. He is well within his rights to be flabbergasted," Pierce explained.

"Oh." Meryn scrunched up her nose. "I just wanted a place to eat donuts and drink coffee when I visited Uncle Bren."

Peter slapped his forehead with his palm.

Izzy ignored his high emotion and walked over to where he stood behind the case. Casually she ripped out several sheets of paper. "I have my recommendations. Two options, really, depending on what you can secure for financing. One is you extend the counter all the way around that wall. You'd lose seating, but from what I've observed, not many stick around to eat. That would give you room for some machines and supplies. Your second option would be pricer. Covert your upstairs space into a cafe. You'd gain more seating, but remodeling may be too expensive." She pointed to the lower half of the page. "Here's a human website to apply to that will distinguish you as a distributor. Once you get that, it's easier to order from wholesalers. I can help with that later." She handed him the papers.

"Worth the occasional brownie?" Gage asked, raising an eyebrow.

"More than worth it," Peter whispered, wiping his eyes.

"Can I have a cinnamon roll?" Meryn asked.

Peter sniffed and nodded. "Aye, you can. You young ladies can get whatever you want whenever you want it."

"You'll go out of business giving away treats," Zoe chided softly.

"I'm pretty sure a brownie or cinnamon bun here and there won't put me under." He turned to Izzy. "What can I get you?"

"Got anything with raspberries?" she asked.

"I have a raspberry cheese danish," he replied.

"Sold!" Izzy said enthusiastically.

Peter handed Meryn and Izzy their snack, then looked over to where Pip had kept quiet in the corner. "And for you, lad?"

Pip's eyes grew wide. "But I didn't do any planning."

"But, I bet you help these two ladies all day, don't you? That more than deserves a treat," Peter explained in a gentle tone.

"He is in charge of cuddles, and he's terrific at taking care of us," Meryn said, pulling Pip closer to the case.

Pip blushed. "I…I like chocolate. Meryn introduced me to chocolate. It is my favorite."

"How about a dark chocolate truffle brownie?"

"A what?" Zoe asked, along with Meryn and Izzy.

Peter chuckled. "One of my most addicting creations." He wagged both eyebrows.

Meryn crammed the entire cinnamon roll in her mouth and chewed quickly. "Wanna try that too!" she said, with a mouth full of the half-eaten roll.

Laughing, Peter looked at Zoe, Gage, and Pierce. "Interested?"

Next to Meryn, Izzy downed her danish.

Zoe nodded, but the men shook their heads. Peter pulled out four brownies and handed them out.

Zoe holding her wax paper-wrapped treat, looked at Pip, then Meryn and Izzy. "On three?"

Meryn nodded. "One... two..."

They all took a bite at the same time. Moans filled the small bakery.

"Gods above," Zoe said, this time actual tears fell from her eyes.

Meryn and Izzy moved to sit at one of the tables on shaky legs.

Zoe joined them as Pierce helped a shaking Pip to sit next to Meryn.

"This, this is life," Zoe said reverently.

Izzy began to tremble. "Imagine this with a mocha."

Meryn pulled out her phone and held it to her ear. "Hey babe, you know that thing you wanna try? The Brick Oven has dark chocolate truffle brownies. For every night I get a half dozen you get to try, you know what," Meryn promised.

"What!" was the loud, startled explanation.

Meryn sniffled. "Aiden, it's so good I wanna cry," she said before moaning.

"Pierce!"

Sighing and shaking his head, Pierce took the phone.

"No, sir, they're just eating brownies. No, sir, just brownies." There was silence. Then he began to laugh. "Yes, sir." He tapped the phone ending the call.

He cleared his throat and looked to Peter. "Unit Commander Aiden McKenzie would like to place an order for ten dozen dark chocolate truffle brownies."

Seconds later, Izzy's phone went off. "H… hello?" Izzy answered. Her eyes were still closed. "Oh Oron, it's so good. I want more in me," she whimpered.

"Godsdammit! Pierce!"

Unable to hold back his laughter, Pierce plucked Izzy's phone from her hand. "Yes, Your Highness? Yes, sir, I understand." He once again ended the call and lay the phone next to Izzy's hand.

"And Prince Oron would like to order six dozen dark chocolate truffle brownies," he announced.

Peter dropped the tongs he had been holding. "What?"

Pierce smirked. "If you don't have that much, maybe just send two dozen up to the palace every day for a while."

Peter looked from him to where the women sat in the thralls of ecstasy. Turning to Gage. "Any for you?"

Wiping away tears of laughter, Gage turned to Zoe. "Well, Zo?"

She licked her fingers, satisfied. "I like the treat I got last night better."

Gage's heated gaze had her blushing.

Laughing, Peter started pulling out boxes for the insane orders he had just received.

Leaning in, Gage nipped her neck. "Last night was just as addicting."

She turned and kissed his nose. "Agreed."

"I kinda want coffee now," Meryn complained.

Izzy pointed back toward the palace. "We can always head back early, and I can make you whatever you want."

Meryn shook her head and eyed both Gage and Pierce. "You guys have credit cards, right?"

Gage nodded, and Pierce pulled out his wallet. "I have yours. Ryuu gave them to me when he knew I'd be watching over you today."

"Let's go," Meryn said, heading down Main Street.

Gage's eyes widened. "Go where?"

"To Madison."

"Oh, hell no! Aiden will gut me if I take you there," Gage objected.

"We're just going for coffee. Besides, we have you and Pierce with us. No one would be stupid enough to try anything," Meryn countered.

Zoe followed, sticking close to Meryn. She had never been to a human city and was dying to see what it was like.

"What part of 'Aiden will gut me' is unclear," Gage asked, crossing his arms over his chest.

Meryn just kept walking. "It's not like I need permission. I can go wherever I want as long as I'm not stupid and try to go alone."

Pierce just followed along behind her. He

pulled out his phone. "Code Menace, I repeat, Code Menace." He tapped his phone and put it away.

Zoe had a feeling the warrior knew the score. Meryn was going to Madison, one way or another.

Gage walked beside Pierce. "What's Code Menace?"

"Code Menace is the phrase the vanguard came up with when we heard she was visiting with Aiden. It means she has flown the coop, managed to escape Aiden, and needs an escort," Pierce explained.

Meryn turned, so she was walking backward. "I love how the vanguard gets me."

Pierce winked. "Remember, Meryn. Most vanguard are in an inactive status because we've completed a long term serving as unit warriors. We've seen a thing or two."

"Noice!"

Pip, walking backward, looked worried. "Meryn, will humans like me?"

Meryn stopped and turned to Pip. "What's there not to like? You're freaking adorable."

Zoe edged closer. "I heard humans can be cruel."

Pip nodded quickly. "And that they're judgemental, even amongst their own kind."

Meryn's expression morphed into sadness. "It's true most humans are assholes, but, for the most part, they're decent. When push comes to shove, they tend to do the right thing." She eyed Zoe. "If you have to accidentally start a fire, try to make it near something that can be explained as the source, like a grill or cigarette or something."

Zoe swallowed hard. "I can't really control it that much."

Meryn shrugged. "Do your best." She then resumed walking toward the city's main portal. When they got there, the fae snapped to attention and, with their hands over their hearts, bowed low.

"Your Highness."

"I'd like to go to Madison, please," Meryn announced.

One of the guards looked apprehensive. "Are you sure, Your Highness? The ones killing the fae are still out there."

Meryn pointed to Pierce and Gage. "I'm going with unit warriors and will be meeting up with vanguard on the other side of the portal. We won't be gone long."

The guard gave a half bow. "As you wish."

Together, they activated the portal, and the second guard held out his elbow. "I will escort you and wait on the other side to open it for you when you return."

Meryn placed her hand on his elbow in a dainty manner. "Thank you."

Zoe felt her insides shaking in excitement. She reached for Gage's hand. Just the simple gesture helped to calm her.

Together they walked through, and Zoe found herself inside a building. Looking around, it seemed like they were in someone's family room.

Meryn looked around, confused. "Where are we? I thought this gate led to the woods."

The guard smiled. "It can, but it can also open here at the vanguard estate. We thought this might be easier for you."

"Kickass."

"Welcome again, Menace," a deep voice said from the foyer.

"Pay up, Cam," the man next to him demanded, holding out his hand.

Cam sighed, reached for his wallet, and passed over a bill. "Dammit, Liam, how'd you know she'd come back here?"

Liam blew on his nails and buffed them on his shirt. "Because I am one of Meryn's biggest fans."

Cam looked over to the guard. "Make yourself comfortable." Turning to them. "Okay, Meryn, what did you have in mind?"

"Will it be just you and Liam?"

He nodded.

"That's not too bad. First order of business is tech gear for Zoe and some jeans. Then we indulge in coffee."

Zoe looked down and realized that compared to Meryn, Pip, and Pierce, she and Gage stuck out a bit.

Liam pointed to a side hallway. "Extra clothes are down there, Gage," he frowned. "We don't have anything for Lady Zoe, though."

Meryn grinned and reached into her bag. "She

can wear this until she gets her own clothes," she said, holding up a satin bag.

Zoe looked at the smaller woman. "Meryn, I appreciate the thought, but I don't think I would fit in your clothes."

Meryn swung the bag back and forth. "This is my super gown. The Gown of Éire Danu, it will adjust to fit you."

Gage eyed Meryn. "So, those are your clothes?"

"Yup."

"And you packed away the gown instead of wearing it?"

"Uh, yeah."

"Then you were planning on coming here all along," Gage stated, sounding a bit exasperated.

"Look at you, thinking and stuff," Meryn teased. "Zoe, reward him later."

Zoe covered her mouth to hide her smile. "Thank you, Meryn." She walked over and kissed the tiny woman's cheek, causing her to sputter. Taking the bag, she smiled at Cam. "A dressing area?"

He pointed to the same hallway. "Laundry area on the left for Gage, bathroom to change on the right for you, Lady Zoe."

Holding the bag close to her chest, she walked with Gage to change for their afternoon outing.

❦

First order of business had been clothes shopping. After discovering jeans and sweaters, she returned Meryn's super gown to her. Once she had tried jeans on, she vowed to wear them more often. They were more comfortable than they looked, and fashionable. The girl at the store showed her how they could be 'dressed up' and she ended up buying half a dozen pairs.

Despite the fun, Zoe was torn. She loved that the entire city was comprised of things she had only ever read about. Cars, tall buildings, and technology everywhere! But as excited as she was, she also hated it. There was too much of everything. It was too loud and too bright, and the noxious smells made her nauseous.

Meryn's concerned face looked up at her. "I'm sorry. I forgot how loud it was. Can you hang in there long enough to grab some coffee? We got most of your stuff already."

Zoe looked over at Gage and gave him a wan smile. Her poor mate was loaded down with shopping bags. She had no idea what tech gear she now owned, but Meryn assured her it was all very necessary.

"Maybe someplace quieter?"

Izzy took her hand. "I know just the place. I applied there once because it was cute, but took the other job because it was closer to my apartment. It's about a five-minute walk from here."

Zoe squeezed her hand. "That sounds lovely."

They started walking and Meryn, for the fourth time, pulled Pip out of the street and away from the cars whizzing by.

His eyes were wide, and he looked around with a childlike wonder. The entire time they explored the city, he stayed under his silken parasol. "Meryn, that man over there, he had metal in his face!" Pip exclaimed.

"It's like earrings, but you can put them any-where," Meryn explained.

"It's a decoration?"

She nodded.

When the man with multiple piercings and tattoos walked by, he noticed how Pip's eyes followed him. He turned, scowling. "Whatcha lookin at?"

Zoe went to step between him and the strange man, but to her surprise, Pip moved forward. "I was admiring your metal decorations. My sister says that they are like earrings, but they can go anywhere." Pip pointed to the man's tattoos. "Is that like a warrior tattoo?"

The man went from hostile to friendly when faced with Pip's sincerity. "Not that one, lil man. That one I got when my dog died." He lifted his sleeve and pointed to an elaborate piece. "This is the one I got when I joined the service."

Pip swallowed hard. "To have so many metal decorations and tattoos, you must be very brave and very strong."

The man laughed. "It's not so bad after the first couple." He looked around and saw Gage, Pierce, Cam, and Liam. He gave a masculine-type nod acknowledging them. "I wouldn't stick around here. Not many are as understanding as me," he advised them. "Cops been dealing with more missing folk lately."

Pierce looked to Izzy. "How much further?"

Izzy turned to the stranger. "We're heading to Mugs."

He pointed to the right. "Cut up Seventh and go from there. If you keep going down Market, it gets dicey."

"We appreciate the heads up," Gage said.

"Always willing to help a fellow serviceman." Gage chuckled. "How'd ya know?"

Zoe watched as her mate fell into a lazy mode of speech.

Pierce clapped Gage on the back. "I swear, even when you get out, there's a permanent stamp on ya. I can always spot a brother in a crowd."

The man laughed. "Ain't that the truth." He ruffled Pip's hair. "Y'all stay safe." He waved and resumed walking down the sidewalk.

"Well done, Gage. You fell into that role perfectly. Maybe when you're done in Éire Danu, you can join us in Madison," Cam complimented.

Gage just shook his head. "I won't be done in Éire Danu for quite some time."

Pip turned to Meryn. "You were right. Not all humans are nice, but some are."

Pierce steered them down Seventh, and Izzy walked them to a nicer section of Madison. When she stopped and pointed, they were standing outside a large brick building. "This is Mugs."

Gage held the door, and they walked in.

Zoe, along with Meryn and Izzy, inhaled deeply.

Without wasting a second, Meryn walked up to the counter.

"What can I get started for you?" the young man asked.

"I'd like to start a tab," Meryn said, staring up at the menu.

The man stared. "Ma'am, we... we don't do that here. Wait, how much were you going to order?"

Izzy stepped up. "She'll have a quad shot decaf bittersweet mocha latte, thick. I'll have a white chocolate raspberry mocha, and this young man will have the vanilla bean latte." She turned to Zoe. "Did you know what you want?"

Zoe stared. "What language are you speaking?"

Izzy laughed. "More coffee or more chocolate?"

Zoe thought on it for a moment. They had brownies at the Brick Oven. "More coffee, please."

Izzy turned back. "And she'll have flat-white ristretto."

The young man exhaled. "Thank you!"

Izzy laughed. "Trust me, I know. Nothing's worse than a customer that doesn't know how to order."

"I'll get those started." He looked behind them. "Gentlemen?"

Pierce turned to Gage, Cam, and Liam. "Black coffee?"

They nodded.

Pierce held up four fingers. "Four black coffees."

The barista nodded and got started.

Meryn turned around. "How can you come here and get something boring?"

Pierce shrugged. "I'm a simple guy Meryn."

One by one, the drinks were placed on the counter, and Izzy paid for them. They found a table by the window and sat down to enjoy their drinks.

Meryn took a sip and sighed. "Perfection."

"Just think, if Peter gets his machines, we could get this every day without taking over Cord's kitchen," Izzy pointed out.

Gage sipped his coffee. "I thought Dav had machines as well."

Izzy shook her head. "He has one machine that can draw espressos and make basic drinks. I gave Peter plans for a cafe, which means more complicated drinks, like the flat-white."

Zoe sipped and sighed happily. "I think this is my new favorite."

Meryn was about to speak when her phone dinged, then dinged, then dinged again. "Shit," she muttered. She pulled out her phone and winced.

"Gig's up. We should start back, like soon."

Pierce chuckled. "Time to pay the piper."

Meryn took another drink. "It was worth it. I wanted Zoe and Pip to experience a bit of freedom."

Pip laid his head on Meryn's shoulder. "I loved it!"

Zoe sat back. It had been overwhelming and loud, but she had been able to go anywhere she chose. "Thank you, Meryn, for everything. Even the technology I don't quite know what to do with."

Meryn laughed. "No charge."

Her phone dinged, and she sighed, rolling her eyes. "We really need to head back."

"Aiden?" Pierce asked, standing.

She shook her head. "No. That one was Ryuu."

Pierce winced. "Ouch."

CHAPTER ELEVEN

☾

THE FAE WHO OPENED THE portal must have received orders from the queen, because when they walked through, they were now standing in front of the palace and a very irate-looking Unit Commander.

"Madison? Madison!" he roared.

"Yeah, so?"

"Where people have gone missing?"

"Yeah, they already hit Madison, so, statistically speaking, we were safer there than here with shadow portals popping up," Meryn pointed out.

Aiden ran his hands through his hair.

Pierce rubbed his chin. "You know, Commander, when she puts it that way, it really does make a lot of sense."

"Quiet Pierce! You're just as bad as Ryuu, going along with her crazy schemes," Aiden grumbled.

"Even I would have balked at going to Madison," Ryuu said dryly, his arms crossed. He looked down at his charge with a flat expression.

Meryn went to him and hugged him around

the waist. "I had to stay really busy because I missed you," she said quietly.

Ryuu exhaled as his face softened. "Oh, *denka*."

Zoe watched Meryn with her squire and realized that the smaller woman had been facing her own anxiety all day without her squire at her side. "You did really well, Meryn," Zoe said.

Aiden pulled Meryn into a hug of his own. "I thought you said you were okay?"

Meryn rubbed at her eyes. "I was, well, I knew I had to be because what Ryuu was doing was important, but I never want to have him leave again, like ever."

Ryuu gave a half bow. "I swear to you, *denka*, I will remain by your side from here on out."

Zoe couldn't help but look around. Where was the individual that had Ryuu gone for most of the day?

Ryuu caught her eye and nodded. "They are waiting for you in the queen's chambers." He smiled. "The queen is quite taken with them."

Zoe took Gage's hand and practically drug him into the palace. Together everyone made their way to the queen's personal chambers.

"Auntie, I'm home!" Meryn announced.

"Good, I feel better knowing you are in Éire Danu," the queen replied.

Zoe eyed the two new individuals at the table.

Ryuu walked around the table to stand behind them.

"*Denka*, Lady Zoe. This is Ame and Yuki. They are the ones who will be assisting Lady

Zoe in her day-to-day life," Ryuu placed a hand on each of the boy's shoulders.

Zoe stared. They were just children, and why were there two of them?

"How comes there's two? Was it buy one get one free or something?" Meryn asked.

Ryuu shook his head, then nodded. "Something like that. My old house had already expressed an interest in Ame. His gift is with rain, so he, of course, was highly sought after. We, however, asked after Yuki, whose gift is with snow."

"And? I feel like there's more to the story," Meryn prompted.

Ryuu inclined his head. "As you know, my old house does not treat their people well. House Fujiwara was hesitant to let Ame go to them. By offering for Yuki, we were able to protect both of them."

"How?" Zoe asked.

"Because you cannot have snow without rain," Ryuu replied.

Like Ryuu, the boys had gorgeous Japanese features, but unlike the squire, their eyes were bright blue, and their hair was white. They watched them with wide, unblinking eyes. To Zoe, they didn't look older than five or six.

"Ryuu, are they old enough to serve?" she asked.

He nodded. "Though they look young, they are, in fact, several hundred years old."

Zoe watched them, watching her. They presented as children, so she would treat them that way. "Will they both be coming home with me?"

Ryuu looked down. "Well?"

The boy on her right spoke first. "I can assist around the home. Yuki is better amongst people," he replied in perfect English.

Zoe had an overwhelming urge to scoop them up and keep them safe. They were so cute and so tiny. "You must be Ame. We will be living with the unit warriors of the city. Will you be comfortable with that?" she asked, keeping her voice soft and gentle.

Ame stood, causing Yuki to pop to his feet. They held hands and walked over to stand in front of her. "We are contracted to serve you. You tell us where to go."

She didn't care that Ryuu told her that they were several hundred years old. She saw how desperately they clung to each other and how their small bodies trembled. Looking up, she met Ryuu's eyes, and he smiled. He had done everything he could to keep them safe, and it was up to her now. Who better to expose them to the world than someone just learning it herself?

She bent down, and though it was somewhat a struggle at first, she propped up each boy on either hip. "We're going to be family from now on. You take care of me, and I'll take care of you. So, if you don't like something, tell me right away, okay?"

Gage placed a hand on her lower back, supporting her. "My name is Gage Fabre, I am Zoe's mate, so I guess we're family now too. It will be my job to protect you from anyone and anything. We'll be working together to keep Zoe happy and healthy. Do you think you can do that?"

Both boys nodded enthusiastically.

"*Hai*!" they responded in piping voices.

"Gods, I'm half in love with them already." She mock scowled at them. "You're going to have me wrapped around those tiny fingers of yours, won't you?" she asked playfully.

Both boys beamed up at her before Ame buried his face in her hair.

Zoe turned to Ryuu. "Have they eaten?"

He shook his head. "We were just about to when we got the message that you all were on your way."

Zoe walked over to the table and sat the boys to her right. "Let's get you two fed. Then we can head home." She looked over to Gage. "The guys are going to lose their minds."

Gage blinked, then laughed. "Technically, I think Ari is still the youngest, but I don't think that will matter," he said, pointing to the small boys.

"Fuck you," Ari growled.

Brie smacked his shoulder. "Not in front of the babies."

Ari pointed. "They're older than me."

Brie crossed her arms. "Doesn't matter."

Ame tugged on Zoe's sleeve. "What do we call you?"

"What do you want to call me?"

"*Aneue*."

"I'm sorry, I don't know what that means."

"It means honorable older sister," Ryuu interpreted.

Zoe inhaled. "I would love to be your sister!" she pulled both boys close. She understood Meryn and Pip a bit better now. Cuddling a younger sibling was nice.

Ame pointed to her. "*Aneue*," he then pointed to Gage. "*Aniue*."

Gage looked to Ryuu. "Honorable older brother?" he guessed.

Ryuu nodded. "Exactly."

Zoe leaned her head against Gage's shoulder as he choked up a bit. "I think I'm going to like being the older brother for a change."

"Are they twins like us?" Neil asked.

Ame shook his head. "No, I am twenty years older."

"I am more outgoing. Ame likes to stay at home," Yuki added.

Zoe looked down. "Do you wish you had stayed in Japan? Everything is different here. Will you get homesick?"

Both boys shook their heads back and forth repeatedly. "No! Ryuu-sama said we could have a real home here. A real family. He is honorable. He did not lie." Ame held onto her sleeve with both hands. "We are not things to you."

"I won't ask again. Instead, I'll share with you everything about this place as I learn it. I have just arrived, and before that, I was kept alone, so everything is new to me too. We'll discover things together."

Ame and Yuki exchanged glances, then nodded to her. "We'd like that."

Yuki leaned back to look up at Gage. "What do we do to keep *Aneue* safe?"

"Her fire magic gets out of hand sometimes. Your main priority is to ensure she's safe. Your second priority will be to minimize damage to any structure we're in or around," Gage explained.

"Gage, that sounded too much like orders," Zoe said, fussing at him.

Yuki and Ame half bowed in their chairs. "We appreciate clear orders so that we can best serve you."

"I want you to have time to yourselves too. Is there anything you want or want to learn?" Zoe asked.

Ame looked to Yuki, who nodded his support before Ame's eyes fell to his hands in his lap. "I would like to learn more about cooking and serving a house in the same manner a squire would."

Yuki looked at Gage. "I would like to learn how to fight. That way, I can keep my *Aneue* and my brother safe."

"Ame is more than welcome to come to the palace on his days off. I can show him recipes and what I do to support the queen," Cord offered.

"I will also help for as long as I'm here," Ryuu added.

Gage turned to Aiden, looking a bit lost.

Aiden raised a brow. "Not so easy, is it? Look-

ing after a younger warrior." He sat back and
looked at Yuki. "We can come up with some
abbreviated drills for him. Sascha has studied
martial arts and can help," he eyed Yuki. "I don't
say that because you're from Japan, but martial
arts are one of the best equalizers I have seen in
battle. Your size would not be a hindrance."

Yuki bowed. "I will be guided by my *Aniue's*
lord."

Aiden's eyebrows shot up. "Lord?"

Yuki tilted his head. "Is that not the term?"

Aiden cleared his throat. "You can just call me
commander. It's what I am."

"Thank you for correcting my words."

Pip tugged on Meryn's sleeve in much the
same manner Ame had to her. "Can I do introductions?"

Meryn gave a nod. "Good idea. You're the
best at them."

Pip's chest puffed out, and he stood. In his
own way of speaking, he went around the table
and introduced everyone, including interesting
observations from his time with them. Zoe found
his simple words and phrasing to be enchanting.

Looking down, she noticed that Ame and Yuki
were nodding as they listened. Pip's easy way
of speaking meant the boys could follow along.
When he was done, Ame looked up at her and
pointed to Oron. "That one changed his name to
Vi'Eirlea, becoming Lady Meryn's brother, but
he was already tied to her because her cousin is
mated to Oron's adopted brother?"

Zoe frowned. "Yes, exactly. It is a bit of a tangle, isn't it?"

Meryn looked around for something, then smiling, grabbed the small pot of jam and set it next to her plate. "I don't really care about all the particulars. It just meant more family for me." She poured half the jam onto her plate and mixed it with the clotted cream Cord made, creating a purplish mixture. Picking up her scone, she dunked it and began eating.

Aiden stared. "Meryn, can I try a bite?" he asked, licking his lips.

"Only because you bought me brownies," she said, holding one up for her mate.

He took a bite and nodded approvingly. "Perfect."

Brennus sighed, looking down at his plate of scones. "She always figures out the quickest way to eat those." He then reached for the jam.

Cord brought out two bowls of soup and set them before the boys. "I felt maybe a vegetable soup would be a good way to ease them into western foods. This should also leave them enough room for dinner later."

Ame reached for his spoon and took a bite. His expression changed to one of pure joy. "I do not know most of the seasonings, but I can tell they were chosen because they blended together well."

Cord nodded. "When you visit, we'll start with the spice cabinet."

Ame was practically vibrating in his chair

with excitement. Yuki was smiling softly at his brother's happiness.

There was a knock at the door before a pale Portia hurried in. She immediately looked to Kendrick.

Without saying a word, he cast a soundproofing spell.

The queen looked up, concerned. "Portia?"

"Your Majesty, please excuse the interruption, but I have Karl Brugmansia and Andrei Jessamine demanding to see Lady Zoe. I would have taken them to your audience room, but they are making claims I thought best to be discussed in private."

Zoe couldn't help her reaction. Her body began shaking so bad the plate in front of her began to clank on the table.

The queen looked at Zoe. "Prepare yourself." Turning to Portia, she simply nodded.

With a pinched expression, Portia went to the door and escorted the two men inside.

Zoe's stomach flipped and clenched. She tried exhaling through her nose slowly, but it wasn't working to calm her nerves. Under the table, a small, cool hand took hers. When she looked down, Ame was watching her with a serene expression.

Closing her eyes, she took another deep breath and allowed the coolness from his touch to soothe her frayed nerves. When she opened her eyes, everything seemed a bit more solid. She smiled her thanks. Ame just gave a short nod.

Then both boys turned as one to stare at the new-comers.

Karl Brugmansia, one of the elders on the Witches' Council, strode forward with Andrei on his heels.

"Your Majesty, thank you for agreeing to see us on such short notice," Karl said pleasantly, bowing when he was close enough to stand before the queen.

The queen sat ramrod straight with one of the haughtiest expressions she had ever seen on the woman's face since arriving. "For your sake, I hope whatever it is you are about to say is worth intruding on my private time with my family."

Karl's eyes shot in her direction before he smiled ingratiatingly at the queen. "There seems to have been a mix-up in assignments. In looking at your request for the Fire Temple Head, it is clear that you were asking for an experienced fire witch. Zoe Appleblossom, though acting as the Temple Head, has only just come of age. She is maintaining that position with the full support of the Witches' Council. With your permission, I'd like to escort Lady Zoe home and provide two of our highest-scoring fire witches to Éire Danu to assist you in providing routine mainte-nance on the city's light system."

The queen simply raised a golden brow. "Were you unaware that only an Appleblossom can ser-vice the city's lights?"

Karl gave a little laugh. "I'm sure that the pro-prietary nature of the spells has been exaggerated by little Zoe. Any fire witch can strengthen the spells on the lights."

"Are you calling Lady Zoe a liar?" Brennus asked, in an almost amused tone of voice.

Karl backpedaled. "Of course not, but she is young and has much to learn. She may have simply wanted to extend her stay when making the claim that only Appleblossoms can provide service."

"And why would she be desperate enough to lie to me in order to stay longer?" the queen asked.

Karl hesitated as if sensing a trap. "Young people like to travel," he answered simply.

The queen sighed as if bored and waved her hand at him. "I'm afraid I cannot grant your request. It has come to my attention very recently that Lady Zoe is my son's godsdaughter. I wish for her to stay so that I can get to know her better."

Karl smiled. "Forgive me, Your Majesty. I had heard that our esteemed Unit Commander was claiming to be her *athair*."

"That is true. But Lady Zoe's brother named all of the Alpha Unit to be her *athairs*, including my son."

"Your Majesty, surely you jest. One cannot make an entire unit *athairs*. It isn't done," Karl refuted.

The queen's eyes narrowed. "Many things are being done of late that have never been done before."

He flinched, and she continued.

"In these troubled times, I do not see any reason to deny a young lady of multiple protectors."

Zoe looked around the table. In addition to the Ashleigh brothers and Kendrick, Aiden and Darian seemed to be hanging on to their anger by a thread.

"If you feel that strongly about the matter, we can, of course, arrange future visits with Lady Zoe, but for now, she is needed back in Storm Keep to perform her duties for the Fire Temple," he said firmly.

The queen frowned. "Are you demanding I relinquish one of my unit warriors as well? Only the Unit Commander can reassign warriors," she turned to Aiden. "Commander, are you willing to reassign Gage Fabre to Storm Keep?"

"No, he is needed here in Éire Danu. We couldn't possibly arrange for a replacement on such short notice," Aiden said, glaring at Karl.

If Zoe hadn't met Aiden previously and seen his softer side, his visage alone would have her wanting to turn tail and run. She hid a smile. It looked like Karl was equally affected.

Karl spread his hands. "I am confused, Your Majesty. Why would I be taking one of your unit warriors? I would never presume to tell the Unit Commander what to do." He met Aiden's eyes. "Overstepping and inserting authority where it doesn't belong can cause quite a bit of strife."

Aiden's nostrils flared at Karl's clever dig, and a small wave of power began to emanate from his side of the table. "Lady Zoe is mated to Gage Fabre. By forcing her to return to Storm Keep, you would either be separating her from her mate or pulling Gage from his duties to accompany her. As the queen previously stated, at this time, she cannot grant your request. Zoe stays here," Aiden growled.

Karl straightened. "Zoe cannot be mated to Gage Fabre as she is already mated to Andrei Jessamine."

❦

Gage felt his fangs punch through his gums as he stood and flew toward the ones trying to take his mate from him. Only his commander was quick enough to intercept him. He thrashed against the larger man. "How dare he!" Gage roared.

"Stand down, Gage! That is an order," Aiden yelled.

It took everything in him to calm himself, and only when his breathing returned to normal did Aiden release him from the bear hug that had held him captive. He looked up at his commander, and with Aiden's back to Karl and Andrei, Aiden mouthed the words, '*trust us*'.

He nodded, then looked past Aiden to Karl and bared his fangs. "You will take her from me over your dead body."

"Isn't that supposed to be over 'my dead body'" Pip asked quietly.

Amelia grinned and leaned down. "I think he said it right."

Pip thought it over a moment, then smiled. "Oh. I get it."

Karl reached into his robes and handed Portia

a scroll. "One month ago, after Zoe came of age, she mated Andrei Jessamine and moved into the Fire Temple to assume her duties. As her mate, he was reassigned to the Fire Temple to assist her in her day-to-day activities."

Portia took the scroll, unrolled it, and read. When she paled, Gage got a sinking feeling in his stomach. Without a word, Portia handed it to her queen.

The queen looked it over, then, with her hand bathed in blazing, golden light, she waved it over the scroll. Whatever she saw or didn't see had her frowning. "It is authentic. This is Zoe's signature."

Zoe jumped to her feet. "I would have never mated him! Never!"

The queen's expression softened. "It is your signature."

Zoe's hand went to her midsection. "He must have slipped it in my paperwork when I wasn't looking to get it signed." She shook her head. "I read everything I sign. I would have never signed that."

"Be that as it may, that document is legal and binding," Karl said, pointing to the scroll.

"Come along, Zoe, it's time to return home," Andrei said, smiling and holding out his hand.

Without conscious thought, Gage raked his claws over the man's arm.

Andrei howled in pain and clutched his forearm to his chest. "That man attacked me!"

Aiden snarled at Andrei. "You're lucky you're still breathing. Stay away from Zoe if you want to live. If you make any move toward her, I can't guarantee that I can hold him back."

Gage almost snorted. That was a blatant lie. His commander could easily restrain him if needed. In addition to that, there were four powerful witches in the room that could cast Tangled Web the moment the order was given.

Gage stilled and looked across the room. Kendrick's hand was over his mouth, and the Ashleigh brothers stood forming a semi-circle behind where he sat. So far, none of the witches had spoken up. Try as he might, Gage couldn't hear Kendrick breathing. It dawned on him that they had cast a secondary soundproof spell.

"Your Majesty, I must insist that Lady Zoe be returned to us," Karl repeated.

"No."

He blinked. "Excuse me?"

"Why should I explain myself to you, in my private chambers, in my palace? I wish for Zoe to remain, so she shall. Portia, have Malcom escort these two back to the portal to Storm Keep," she ordered.

Behind Gage, Portia stepped into the hallway, and moments later, Malcom and half a dozen gold-armored warriors stood at the ready. The queen's captain stepped forward. "Karl Brugmansia, Andrei Jessamine, if you would please follow me."

Karl went to retrieve the scroll from the queen but made the mistake of taking a single step in her direction. Faster than even Gage could track,

Malcom had his sword at Karl's neck. "I really must insist you follow me now."

Karl swallowed hard, causing his neck to flex against the blade and a trickle of blood to appear. His eyes darted to the queen. "May I have the scroll?"

The queen shook her head. "No. I will be presenting it to the Elder Council for consideration. Magnus Rioux has recently abolished arranged matings in Noctem Falls. I feel this sort of situation merits further discussion. You are dismissed." The queen looked at Malcom, who nodded.

Removing his sword from the witch's throat, he grabbed the back of the man's robes and physically removed him from the queen's chambers. Andrei was escorted by a warrior on either side, right behind him.

Once the door closed, Zoe bent at the waist, hands on the table. She looked like she would collapse at any moment. Gage flew to her side. Rubbing her back, he sat down and pulled her onto his lap. "Shush, my love. They are gone, and you are safe."

"I didn't sign it, I swear, Gage," she repeated over and over.

"I think you were right in that they more than likely had you sign this unaware." The queen tapped her lips with the scroll. "My concern, is the fact that they thought this would sway the argument in their favor. Why would an arranged mating take precedence over a true one?"

"I hate that we have the phrase 'true mating' now," Brennus said, spitting the words.

Slowly Zoe's trembles eased. "You aren't going anywhere," he promised.

Zoe looked up at him. "I want to go home with you and the boys. I want to feel safe again in the warrior villa."

The queen chuckled.

Zoe's head swung that way. "I meant no offense, Your Majesty, nor do I discount the protection you provided. It's just that..."

The queen winked. "I'd feel safer too, surrounded by dozens of unit warriors."

Brennus growled but didn't say anything.

Gage turned to Kendrick. "What were you four up to?"

Kendrick's eyes darted from Aiden to where Ryuu stood, both hands on Meryn's shoulders. Aiden saw Kendrick look to Meryn and his eyes followed. "Meryn?" he rushed to her side. "What is it, baby?" Like Gage, he scooped up his mate and set her in his lap.

Meryn just buried her face in his chest.

Aiden turned to Kendrick and Ryuu. "What happened?"

Kendrick sat back. "Meryn had an immediate and violent reaction to Karl and Andrei. It took myself, the Ashleighs, and Ryuu to keep it quiet."

Aiden, with his finger under Meryn's chin, tilted her head back. "Baby, what happened?"

Meryn swayed slightly, then heaved twice before turning her body to vomit on the floor.

Gage stared. What had they all missed?

CHAPTER TWELVE

C

ORD AND RYUU WERE THERE immediately taking charge of the situation as
Kendrick and Thane cast spells to deal with the
mess. Zoe watched as Aiden unraveled when
faced with his mate's distress. She shook her
head. The man could face down rampaging
ferals, but the second something was wrong with
his mate, he went to pieces. Once again, she felt
a cool hand as Ame rested his palm on her arm.
She looked over, and both Ame and Yuki were
silently giving her their support.

"Ryuu!" Aiden yelled.

"She is doing better," Ryuu assured him. "It
was much worse a few minutes ago."

Aiden held Meryn close. "Why didn't you say
something?"

Meryn closed her eyes. "Because Auntie was
doing politics."

"I do not care if I am holding a grand ball with
every elder present. You tell me when you are
ill, young lady," the queen admonished.

"Aleksandra, she did the right thing," Kend

rick countered. "It was very wise for her to hide her reaction. It gives us time."

The queen seemed taken aback at Kendrick's use of her name. It made Zoe second-guess exactly how powerful the archivist was. Not many were on the first name basis with the queen of the fae.

The queen looked from Kendrick to Thane. "Time for what?"

"Time to remove Karl from his position." Kendrick clenched his jaw. "Tell her what you saw, Meryn."

Meryn shuddered. "Blood. Rivers of blood, and this time I heard stuff. Screams. Constant screams. I could smell it," she said, gagging.

"Gods, Meryn," Aiden wrapped his entire upper body around his mate as if to shield her from the world.

"Screw removing him from his position. He hurt Meryn. He needs to die," Neil snarled.

"Can you kill someone for inadvertently causing a reaction?" Priest wondered out loud.

When Pip, Nigel, Neil, Aiden, Thane, and Brennus turned in his direction, the shifter held up his hands. "Just asking."

Kendrick sighed. "Priest is right. We have no proof that what Meryn saw meant anything. She does tend to deal in metaphors." He looked back to Thane, who nodded.

The witch turned to his brothers. "Law, Justice, get us what we need."

Both men nodded and dropped a kiss on Meryn's forehead as they walked out the door.

Pip scooted closer to where Meryn was ensconced. "Aiden, I am in charge of cuddles," he said, reaching his arms up.

Aiden blinked down at Pip, then, sighing, sat Meryn in the chair next to him. Pip wrapped his arms around Meryn and snuggled her close.

Meryn smiled. "He really is the best at cuddles. I don't mind them at all from him."

Nigel exchanged glances with Neil, who nodded.

"No," Kendrick said.

Both boys looked at him, distressed. "But…" Neil started.

"No, boys. Let me handle this."

"But…" Nigel said.

"But what exactly?" Kendrick asked.

"You don't love her like we do!" Neil exploded.

A flash of annoyance was replaced by understanding. Kendrick met the boys' eyes. "I don't love her in the same way that the two of you do, but that doesn't mean I don't love her equally. She's the mouthy, little genius that challenges me at every turn, and I cherish that more than you could ever know. I ask that you trust me to handle this for Meryn and Zoe."

"Make them suffer," Gage ordered.

Kendrick's eyes flashed with an eagerness that shocked her. "Oh, I plan on it," he promised.

Zoe leaned up and kissed the underside of Gage's jaw. Looking surprised, he returned the gesture by kissing her forehead.

Zoe feeling better, glanced over to where Meryn sat, still looking pale. "Meryn, don't forget, Aiden bought you brownies," she reminded the small woman.

Meryn blinked, then her eyes quickly focused on the table. She turned this way and that looking for Ryuu. "Where are my sex brownies?" she asked.

Ryuu stared. "If you are referring to the stack of pastry boxes that Cord was rearranging, they are in the kitchen. Would you like one?"

Meryn scowled. "One?"

Ryuu sighed. "Would you like a dozen or so?"

Meryn cackled evilly, seeming more like herself. "Yes, please." She turned to Nigel and Neil. "Brace yourselves."

Neil looked skeptical. "Really?"

Pip's entire body shuddered. "So-o-o good."

Both boys licked their lips.

Gage stood. "I'm taking my mate and new brothers home unless you need us." Across the table, Ari, Brie, Priest, and Kincaid also stood.

Aiden, the queen, and Kendrick all shook their heads before the queen responded. "You are safe here in my city Zoe. Put this horrible episode from your mind and enjoy your time with Gage, Ame, and Yuki."

"Thank you again, Your Majesty."

Zoe wiggled until Gage put her down. She curtsied, and the boys bowed in unison.

The queen smiled. "Aren't the children adorable?" she asked her mate.

Brennus wrapped his arm around the queen's shoulders. "The gods have been kind to surround us with so many young ones."

Taking her hand, Gage led them out of the room and toward the path that would take them home.

☾

As it was dinner time, Zoe knew they'd catch the guys in the dining hall. Sure enough, when they got home, they headed straight to where the men were getting ready to eat. Ari winked at her as he and the rest of the Tau unit filed in and sat down in their normal seats.

"Ho, ho Gage. What have you there?" Balder asked.

The men turned to where she and Gage stood in the doorway. Behind her, Ame, then Yuki poked the heads around her to look at the men.

"Did you have babies?" Broden asked.

Tiergan cuffed his fellow unit warrior. "That's not how you get babies."

Broden rubbed the back of his head. "Explain them then."

Zoe blushed. "They are here to help me. Ame controls rain and Yuki snow. They're the ones who will keep the villa from being burned to the ground," she said, introducing the boys proudly.

Aeson stood. "They're ours?"

Gage growled. "They're mine and Zoe's," he corrected.

Aeson whooped. "We have babies!"

He cupped his hands around his mouth. "Upsilon, Phi, Chi, Psi, and Omega unit fall in!" he bellowed.

Above them, the trample of feet that sounded like a herd of elephants heading their way was the men as they responded to Aeson's order. Gage quickly pulled them to one side as the men entered the room at a dead run.

"Aeson, did we get orders?" Corrin, Psi's unit leader asked, zipping his tactical vest.

"No, even better." Aeson waited until the men were either sitting or standing in their respective spots in the dining hall. "Men, we have babies," he announced as if he were a proud new father.

The men's mouths dropped open around the table.

Corrin looked at Zoe. "Doesn't that usually take longer?"

Rolling her eyes, she lifted both arms. "Boys?"

Yuki, then Ame, stepped forward to stand next to her. She wrapped her arms around their thin shoulders. "Gentlemen, this is Ame, and this is Yuki. They will be living with us from now on."

She heard more than one warrior suck in his breath as they turned to look at the boys.

Govannon, Omega's unit leader, turned to his men. "Brogan, Kane, Colin, Jacque, you're on furniture detail." The men stood and hurried out the door.

Corrin looked at his unit. "Head out to the shops. You all are in charge of clothes."

Aeson, not to be outdone, turned to the Chi unit. "Gentleman, scour the Border City for toys and books."

Balder stood and stretched. "Come on, men. We'll clear the storage rooms closest to Gage for the boys." Upsilon happily marched behind their unit leader up the stairs.

Nerius shook his head. "Guys, let's get the food on warmers for the idiots that flew out of here without thinking." Laughing, Kael and Bastien headed toward the kitchen while Jace and Ian started pulling out warmers from the cabinets along the wall.

Zoe stood and had to wipe her eyes. These men were the sweetest and most considerate people she had ever met. Ame and Yuki looked up at her, almost appearing to be scared.

She knelt down and pulled them close. "The men that live here are the warriors that protect the city of Éire Danu, but more than that, they are kind and thoughtful. They want to ensure that you feel welcome here because they cherish those younger than themselves."

Ame looked down at the ground. "We are older than we look," he confessed.

Nerius chuckled. "Are you over a thousand years old?"

Both boys shook their heads.

"Then you're still babies to us," he replied.

Zoe laughed. "They did the same for me. This is a city of immortals. Everyone here is way older than us."

Both Ame and Yuki relaxed. She realized they had been worried it would be seen as deception if their ages came out after so much effort was expended to spoil them.

Ari pointed to Yuki. "Our unit commander will be creating a training regiment for Yuki. He wants to learn how to fight so he can defend Zoe and Ame."

Nerius nodded. "Then we will see it done."

Zoe stood and led the boys over to where she had sat next to Gage that morning. "Let's get you two something to eat. Soup is good, but it doesn't stay with you long."

Jace held up a dish. "We have pulled pork and fixings for dinner. Is that kid friendly?"

Zoe pointed down. "Ask them."

Jace swallowed, then walked over to kneel down to talk to Ame and Yuki. "Do you guys like pork?"

Ame nodded, then tilted his head. "Why did you kneel down?"

Jace stood and indicated the height difference. "We realized when we met the commander's mate that it might hurt little ones to look up at us constantly." He quickly turned to Nerius. "Can they reach the toilet?"

Nerius palmed his face. "I guess we'll find out eventually."

Jace walked over and handed Ian the pan of pork. "I'm going to run out for step stools."

Ian nodded. "Good thinking."

Yuki looked up at her. "They are quite tall," he observed, in a deadpan voice that sent her into a fit of giggles.

Gage turned to the fae unit leaders that remained in the dining hall. "Can I speak with you all for a moment?"

The leaders all looked at each other, then noticed that Ari, Priest, and Kincaid had stood at Gage's request. With serious expressions, they nodded.

Gage ruffled the boy's hair. "I'll be right back. I'm going to update the unit leaders on what happened earlier. Can the two of you watch over Zoe?"

Ame and Yuki both sat a bit straighter. "*Hai.*"

"Good lads." Gage kissed her forehead and left with the others.

"That bad?" Ian asked, sitting down on her other side.

"Storm Keep's Witches' Council forged documents that I mated another and is trying to force me back," she explained in a detached manner.

Ian's eyes bugged out of his head. "And Gage didn't kill them?"

Brie laughed. "It was a close thing. Aiden damn near had to tackle him." She shrugged. "If someone was trying to take Ari from me, I'd have shot first and listened later."

Ian strummed his fingers on the table. "Who came?"

"Karl Brugmansia," she answered.

Ian sat back. "They're playing hardball. Karl is known for his smooth talking and political prowess."

Zoe had come to the same conclusion. Karl was known as the one who got things done in Storm Keep. "There wasn't much he could do when the queen said no."

Ian shook his head. "Think about it, Zoe, in any other scenario, wouldn't what he attempted have worked? If he had that forged document and presented it to the Elder Council of any of the other cities, their hands would have been tied. The only reason I bet you're still sitting here is because he wasn't about to take on the queen in her chambers in Éire Danu."

Zoe felt a sliver of ice slide down her spine. He was right. In any other scenario, politics would have gotten in the way. Only the queen's sovereignty had saved her.

"What can we do," she whispered.

"Kill him," Yuki recommended.

Brie and Ian nodded.

Zoe stared. "You can't just kill people!"

Brie held up her gun. "No, *you* can't kill people. After Meryn's reaction, I could double tap his ass then snuggle up with Ari to watch TV, no problem."

"Is the commander's mate well?" Ian asked.

"Her empathy sucker punched her when Karl and Andrei walked in. She really doesn't like those two. They caused her to throw up," Brie explained.

Ian shrugged. "Well, that's good enough for me. They need to die."

At her side, both boys nodded.

Zoe didn't know whether to be concerned or touched by the levels of bloodthirstiness in her loved ones. In the end, she went with touched because she wasn't one-hundred percent certain she wouldn't do the same for them.

☾

They made it as far as the foyer when the doorbell rang. Gage looked at Aeson and Nerius. "Did the guys forget their keys?"

Aeson opened the door and stepped back, looking surprised. He turned to Gage and pointed. "It's for you."

Gage stepped around Aeson to stand in the doorway and came to a stuttering halt. "Mother?"

Tierla Fabre looked around. "Well? Did you happen to leave your manners in Noctem Falls, young man?"

Gage moved back, accidentally stepping on Aeson's foot. "My apologies, mother, it has been a most trying evening. Will you not please come in?"

She nodded once and stepped inside.

Ari took his mother's hand and kissed it. "Welcome to the warrior's villa Lady Fabre…"

She held up her hand. "I am going by my maiden name now. It is Tierla LeBeau."

Ari placed his hand over his heart. "A thousand apologies, sweet lady. If you'll allow Kincaid to escort you to the dining hall, we'll be with you shortly. Unfortunately, you caught us just as we were about to go into a meeting."

Tierla looked up at Ari. "A meeting concerning my Gage." It wasn't a question.

"In a manner of speaking."

"Then I will join you," she advised, smoothing out her skirts.

"Mother, I…"

His mother stepped forward and placed a hand on his cheek. "You are pinched and pale. I have never seen you looking so stressed and wan. I will be sitting in on this meeting, and whatever is not covered, you will be apprising me of later."

"Not to sound inappropriate, but I am finding

this feisty side of you a welcome change," Nerius said, grinning.

His mother blushed slightly. "I find it refreshing as well. Speaking my mind when I wish has become somewhat addicting."

Gage turned to Ari, who shrugged. "Mother will fill her in later anyway."

Gage sighed. He had forgotten that his sweet mother would be staying with the lionesses. "Very well, but please keep in mind, mother, that both Zoe and I are fine."

His mother's expression turned stoic. "I see." She took Gage's elbow. "Then I suggest we start this meeting so I can figure out the best way to help."

Gage and Ari took turns, slowly going over what had been going on in the city for the past few weeks. Whenever they got to a point that needed clarifying, his mother had them stop so she could ask questions. In hindsight, he realized he should have done this for his sweet Zoe.

His mother turned to him, her anger visibly simmering just below the surface. "Let me get this straight. Karl Brugmansia and Andrei Jessamine are trying to claim that Zoe has mated to Andrei due to a piece of paper?"

Kincaid nodded. "It has an affixed official seal, and the queen has tested its validity. It was Zoe's signature."

"And?"

The men looked around as if unsure how to answer.

"Lady LeBeau, it does lend a bit of credence to their story," Ari explained.

"Young man, I care not if it is valid or forged. I was 'mated' for centuries to Gage's father and bore him a son, yet, I left as soon as I realized I had a choice, as he was not my 'true' mate. Do you not think that carries more weight and significance than a piece of dubious paper?"

Ari sat back, looking astounded. "How is it our women pick up on things we don't?"

Gage turned to his unit leader. "That is what the queen was referring to when she said she would be reaching out to Magnus."

Smiling, Tierla rose, causing each man to stand. She smoothed out her skirts again. "I will take my leave. As much as I wish to meet my new daughter and defacto grandsons, I must confer with Queen Aleksandra immediately. I can offer a unique perspective to this entire debacle. With the queen's backing, I feel like we can support Prince Magnus' desire to declare all arranged matings to be illegal. That would render their entire argument moot."

"You only just arrived," Gage pointed out.

She smiled brightly at him. "Am I will not be leaving any time soon. I would rather resolve this quickly so both you and your mate can rest easy." She stood on tiptoe and kissed his cheek. "Tell Zoe and the boys I only leave so that I can shop and spoil them later." She looked up into his eyes. "I am very proud of you Gage, for defending your mate. Never hesitate to show her how much she means to you." She dipped into a small curtsey. "Gentlemen."

They heard the staccato of the boots' heels as she walked out, then the closing of the door.

"Damn, what a woman," Nerius exploded.

Gage snarled in his direction. "That's my mother."

Aeson placed a hand on his shoulder. "I, in no way, shape, or form, desire your mother, but I will echo Nerius. Damn, what a woman."

Gage scowled at his unit brothers.

Ari laughed so hard he had to wipe at his eyes. "She hasn't even been influenced by my mother or aunts yet."

Gage buried his face in his hands.

"You may be getting a new father while she stays in Éire Danu," Priest predicted.

He bared his fangs at his best friend, causing him to join Ari in gales of laughter.

"Let's concentrate on welcoming the boys because your mother was right. They may call you big brother, but, for all intents and purposes, you just became a father," Aeson pointed out.

Wheezing, Gage let his brother steer him back to his new, small family.

☾

A couple of hours later, the men had returned with their respective items, and the boy's room was set up across the hall from Gage. Even though they kept claiming to be hundreds of years old, she caught both Ame and Yuki picking up the toys bought for them, their eyes bright with happiness. Maybe they just aged slower than most paranormals?

Her new family, warriors included, were now all sitting in the dining hall. She assumed the unit leaders had filled in the warriors of her predicament as they kept stopping by to lay a hand on her shoulder in a show of support.

When she caught Ame yawning and leaning against her, she nudged Gage. Smiling, he pointed down to where Yuki had done the same with him. They stood and gently picked up each boy. The men went to stand, but when the first chair scraped and made a noise, they all froze. Sheepishly, they just waved goodnight as they walked away.

She appreciated them putting the boys' needs over propriety. They made their way upstairs and lay the boys down on their beds. When they went to stand, two sets of arms came up to hold onto them.

"Boys, did you want to stay with us tonight?" Gage asked softly.

Ame, and, surprisingly, Yuki both nodded.

Zoe lifted Ame as Gage once again carried Yuki, this time, they retired to their own chambers. They settled the boys in the center of the bed and stepped back. In their sleepy state, the boys reached for one another.

"I don't think they had it easy," she whispered.

"I think you may be right."

"How can I care for them this much?" She rubbed at her chest where thoughts of the boys' suffering were causing a dull ache.

"Because I think they were meant to be with us. It feels right to have them here." Gage took her hand. "Aeson said we're more like parents than big brother and big sister."

She nodded. "I'll be whatever they're comfortable with."

He led her to a large nook off to one side of the main bedroom and sat her on the loveseat before he went to a small sideboard. He lifted two wine glasses and knelt down to look over his selection. Nodding, he chose a bottle and opened it easily. He poured her a glass, then himself, and walked over to serve her.

She took the glass, and he sat down next to her, wrapping his free arm around her shoulders to pull her close. "It's staggering how quickly one's life can change."

"Did we come crashing into your warrior world, shaking things up?" she asked playfully.

Smiling, he nodded. "My mother arrived just as I was about to update the leaders."

Zoe held still. Did she not want to meet her because she hated her?

He rubbed her arm, having noticed that she froze. "She told me to tell you that she only left to help the queen combat this ridiculous situation with the Witches' Council, and she needed time to shop to spoil you and the boys."

"Nothing against your mother, Gage, but how can she help?"

"I think she will be testifying, explaining how detrimental it can be to live day in and day out with someone who is not your mate."

Zoe inhaled her wine and coughed. "Gods Gage, I had forgotten about that."

"She made an excellent point. Even if that paper had been valid, once you met me, it because useless. She said that Prince Magnus has been working on getting arranged matings declared illegal. I have a feeling Ari's father and elder brother will also be weighing in on this as well."

She sipped her wine. "Why?"

"They almost lost Declan Lionhart when he tried to mediate between a vampire and wolf-shifter. The vampire had claimed that the wolf stole his mate when in reality, Rachelle was true mates with Peter Hernandez, the wolf-shifter. If Jedrek and Rex can argue that these types of conflicts can be deadly and dangerous to our society, it would be nearly impossible to argue against."

Gage shook his head. "What I don't under-stand is why they thought that scroll would get them what they wanted."

She rested her head against him. "Ian had to explain it to me too. Imagine this scenario, but what if I had been called to Lycaonia instead? Karl shows up in an official capacity, as a repre-sentative of a ruling faction in Storm Keep and with a valid document."

"To avoid political fallout, I would have probably been handed over, even if it was only meant to be temporary. That's all they would have needed. I have a feeling once I would have stepped foot back in Storm Keep, no one would have ever seen me again." She drew in a ragged breath. "But here, what the queen says goes. I don't think Karl is used to dealing with those who have complete sovereignty over their people."

Gage rested his chin on the top of her head. "Why do you think they are willing to anger the queen to get you?"

She shrugged. "I'm not sure. My entire life, I was told I was useless as a witch. Once I became Fire Temple head, Andrei said I was finally earning my keep because I was doing all the paperwork."

"Did he ever…"

She shook her head. "He never lay a hand on me. His words were venomous enough to keep me in line."

She felt Gage exhale in relief. "I'm still going to kill him."

"I know, dear. Thank you."

"You're very welcome, my darling."

She took another sip of wine. It felt good to have a family again.

CHAPTER THIRTEEN

❧

THE NEXT MORNING ZOE WOKE up, and when she opened her eyes, she had two sets of brilliant blue peepers staring down at her. "You boys hungry?" she asked. They nodded. "You could have gone downstairs. I'm sure the guys would have tripped over themselves to feed you."

Ame shrugged.

She looked past Yuki and shook her head. Gage hadn't moved. "Come on, let's leave Sleeping Beauty here and grab some breakfast."

Both boys smiled.

She went to the bathroom, washed up, and changed into a new robe. She held up one of the only green ones she had, smiling. She clearly remembered Gage's reaction to it. It was one of the few robes that rendered him speechless. Slipping it on, she waited while it adjusted, then twirled in front of the mirror. She loved how formal it looked yet remained as comfortable as pajamas.

She opened the door, and both boys stepped forward to take her hands. When they got to the bedroom door, Yuki opened it for them, so they wouldn't have to let go of her.

They made their way downstairs and into the dining hall. When the men saw her, they all stood. Paris hurried over and pulled out their chairs for them. The boys waited until she was sitting before they sat. Ame to her immediate right and Yuki on his other side.

"What will it be?" Govannon asked, from the doorway to the kitchen.

"What's available?"

"Eggs, toast, and bacon are standard. Kael managed to find probably the only box of cereal in all of Éire Danu yesterday. I've had to chase Ramsey away from it twice, reminding him it was brought in for the boys."

Ame looked up at her, excitement on his face.

Zoe sighed. "It's full of sugar, isn't it?"

"Absolutely," Govannon confirmed.

"Is there any fruit?"

He grinned. "It's Éire Danu. There's always fruit and vegetables."

She looked down at the eager faces of the boys. "You can have that gods awful cereal, but you have to promise to try and eat a bit of eggs and fruit to balance out the sugar."

They both nodded.

"And for you?" Govannon asked.

"Scrambled eggs with cheese and toast would be lovely."

"Coming right up," he said, before disappearing into the kitchen.

She looked around until she spotted Aeson. "I thought you were the cook."

He laughed. "I tend to pull kitchen duty more than most because I despise laundry, bathrooms, and yard work."

"So, you all rotate chores?"

He nodded.

"What can we do to help?" she asked.

Aeson sat back with his coffee. "I'm pretty sure Nerius and Balder are arranging for an obstacle course slash playground to be built in the back for the boys. If the boys can help maintain that, it'd be appreciated, as we don't have that on the chore list yet."

"Count on us," Yuki said.

"I-I want to cook," Ame declared quietly.

Aeson set his coffee down. "I heard that the queen's own squire offered you cooking lessons. Whenever you're ready, we'll add you to kitchen duties. I think we'll all be excited to try your cooking."

Ame's pale cheeks tinted. "I will do my best."

"And me?" Zoe asked, pointing to her own chest.

"Help maintain the lights and keep Gage happy," Aeson answered.

"I was going to do that anyway."

Aeson winked at Yuki, causing him to giggle for the first time.

She reached over and rubbed his cheek. "You have a wonderful laugh. I wish I could hear it all the time."

Blushing, he looked down into his lap.

"Speaking of Gage, where is he?" Ari asked. "We have drills to do later."

She smirked. "He sleeps like the dead. The boys and I left him in bed."

Ari nodded. "It's probably because he's been able to sleep without nightmares. I'll cut him some slack."

Zoe turned to Gage's unit leader. "What nightmares?"

Ari looked to Brie, then answered. "The spell that was cast to bring the warriors mates causes the warriors to dream of them in much the same way witches do to find their mates. For us, though, the dreams tend to drift into nightmare territory quickly. Towards the end, right before I found Brie, I kept seeing her picking up a gun and walking away."

Brie rubbed his arm. "That makes more sense now that he knows I was a deputy."

Zoe frowned. "I wonder what Gage saw."

"Fire. You engulfed in flames and screaming; then you behind a closed door," Gage answered from the doorway.

"Oh Gage, I'm so sorry," she said, standing.

He hurried to her side. "I'm not. I would have endured years of nightmares for the chance to find you." He kissed her gently and settled her back in her chair before sitting down next to her. "I think the dreams are meant to prepare us." He turned to her. "Did you dream of me?"

She thought for a moment. "I think so, though it was all very vague. In my dreams, I saw you standing next to a door, and you kept waving frantically, trying to get me to go through."

Kincaid nodded. "It could represent the portal here, telling you to come through to be free."

She nodded, then shook her head. "It was more than that, more than just images; there were also feelings. I knew that if I could just get to him, everything would be okay. He was safety and happiness." She looked over to her mate. "Hands would come up from the ground to hold me in place, to keep me from moving forward, then I would wake."

He held her close. "But, you found your way here. That's all that matters."

"But what if Caroline hadn't intercepted the request from the queen? I would still be trapped there, never knowing you were right here waiting for me!" Breathing hard, she closed her eyes as she tried to shake the feelings of fear and frustration. It was thinking of her mate alone that had her shaking uncontrollably. She could face her own pain, but not his.

"Zo! Calm down," Gage exclaimed.

Opening her eyes, she watched as sparks flew from her, hitting the table, then the wall.

"Carson!" Aeson yelled.

"Whoa!" Leon said, looking up.

"Beautiful," Brie added in a breathy voice.

Zoe watched in amazement as a lazy sifting of snowflakes appeared from the ceiling. They gently quenched the sparks and disappeared when they touched the furniture or floor.

Carson skidded to a halt as he entered the

room from the hall. "Looks like you don't need me after all."

Seeing the snow calmed her in ways nothing else had. She took a deep breath. She could even smell winter.

When she was breathing evenly, she looked at Yuki. "Okay. You boys can have as much cereal as you want."

"I'll say," Ari observed, eyes still wide.

"We will keep you and our home safe," Ame promised.

"No screaming in flames," Yuki added.

Gage stood and ruffled both boys' hair. "That earned you a present. What would you two like? You can pick anything. In fact, give me several ideas for presents in case my mother asks."

"Your mother?" Ame asked.

Gage nodded, then looked to his unit before blushing. "She has sort of claimed you two as grandsons, so she wants to spoil you terribly."

Both boys immediately turned to look at her, and it was her turn to blush. "We will be whatever you want us to be."

"*Hahaue*?" Ame asked, his blue eyes filling with tears.

She felt her own eyes fill as she guessed what that meant. "Do you want to call me mother?"

Yuki scooted in next to his brother, and both of them took her hands. Their desperate faces caused her tears to fall. "I would be honored if you were to call me mother," she said softly.

Ame's face twisted as he sobbed silently. Yuki held her hand so tightly that it bordered on pain-

ful, but she wouldn't let go. Without saying a
word, she opened her arms, and both boys flung
themselves at her, burying their faces in her neck
and chest. It seemed as if they were purging
themselves of the tears they had been too afraid
to shed before.

"*Hahaue!*" Yuki wailed.

She sat and cuddled each boy on either side of
her body. In that moment, she knew she would
die for them. More than that, she would kill for
them. "Shush, you're home now."

Gage sat down in Ame's empty seat. "Do I get
a special name, too?" he asked.

Yuki turned, tears trailing down his face. "*Chichiue!*" He threw himself at Gage, who caught
him easily.

Zoe heard sniffling and thought it might
be Brie, but was shocked to see half the guys
rubbing at their eyes. "Ame, Yuki, you have
a mother and father now, but you also have
many older brothers," she said, sitting back, so
she looked Ame in the eyes. Gently she wiped
his tears. "You will never be alone again," she
promised. "I swear to all the gods that from this
moment forth, I will be a mother to you, Ame,
and to you, Yuki. You will want for nothing, and
I will defend you til my dying breath."

Ame and Yuki stared at her in shock.

"I swear to all the gods that from this moment
forth, I will be a father to you, Ame, and to
you, Yuki. You will want for nothing, and I will
defend you til my dying breath."

Ame gave a ragged exhale and collapsed

against her, snuggling up in her lap. Yuki did the same for Gage. It was as if hearing those words had finally allowed them to let go.

Aeson stood. "We will be a family, so do I swear."

"So, do we swear," the men echoed.

Zoe met Gage's eye. He looked as surprised as she felt. The men had taken on their oath. "Thank you," she whispered.

Aeson sniffed as if simply clearing his nose. "It's nothing," he refuted, absently straightening his place setting.

Govannon stepped forward from where he had been listening by the kitchen. "Let's get these lil guys fed." He walked over and set a tray down on the table to pass out bowls and plates of food.

Ame and Yuki refused to unbury their heads. Finally, she gently spun Ame in her lap, so he was facing the table. She sighed when she saw the warrior size bowl of cereal. "Is this half the box?"

Ame peeked down and began to giggle.

Hearing his brother, Yuki turned around on his own to grin down at his breakfast.

Govannon shrugged. "I forgot."

"Okay, boys, first rule, try not to take advantage of your older brothers... too much," she said, winking at them.

"*Hai, hahaue*," they responded brightly.

Gage sighed. "We're in trouble. I don't think we'll be able to deny them anything."

"Oh, Gage," she chided.

"Look how adorable they are!" he said, pointing to the boys who were shoveling in the cereal, so their small cheeks were puffed out like chipmunks.

"I see what you mean."

"You can leave them here if you have work to do," Aeson offered.

Gage scowled. "Quit trying to monopolize my sons."

Yuki and Ame sat up straighter, having been claimed by Gage.

"You have drills," Balder reminded him.

"And Aiden said he was willing to help train Yuki. Maybe he should just come with me," Gage countered.

"If Ame is comfortable with it, he can come with me while I check the spell centers. It will be boring, quiet work, but you're welcome to come along. Or you can stay here, maybe learn the kitchen," she suggested.

Ame swallowed his cereal. "Today, I would like to stay with you. Maybe later I can stay home."

Zoe understood. Claiming one another as family was still new. She felt it too. She didn't want to leave him here but wanted to always give him a choice. "Then it looks like we have a plan for the day. Yuki gets to watch your *chichiue* doing drills, and Ame stays with me while I check the spell centers."

"I'll be acting as her anchor, so I get to hang out with Ame all day," Kincaid crowed.

Paris and Brogan threw their napkins at him.

Gage laughed. "Everyone eat up so we can start our day."

The boys dug into their cereal, and she started on her eggs. For the first time since being a child, she was looking forward to what the day held for her.

🚦

Ame held her hand as they walked toward the palace. She wanted to check the other spell centers, but they needed Kendrick to show them how to make Kincaid her anchor.

"Thank you for choosing me," Kincaid said, as they approached the palace.

"Of course, you were an obvious choice."

"Carson would have been better," he admitted. "My magic never goes right."

She just stared at him until he laughed. "Fair enough. But seriously, Carson has more control."

She looped her free arm through his. "And you have earth magic that may provide the security we both need. No one sets roots deeper than an earth witch."

He stopped, and she pulled him a bit to get him walking again. "I never thought of it like that."

"Just remember, Kendrick thought you were a good choice, too," she reminded him.

Smiling, he nodded, and they walked through the doors to the palace. Kincaid came to a halt, and she was about to nudge him again when she turned to see what he was staring at.

In front of them in mad dashes, palace servants

were carrying small houses and potted plants. "What's going on?"

Kincaid frowned. "I'm not sure, but it doesn't look good. Let's look for Portia."

She looked down and made sure Ame was holding her hand tight. Seconds later, Kincaid did the same to her. Grinning, they wove their way through the palace staff's frantic efforts.

In the center, directing everything, they found Portia. "Portia, what's going on?" Kincaid asked.

Portia, looking as harried as Zoe had seen her yet, indicated to the large courtyard. "We're having to evacuate the sprites to the courtyard."

She frowned. "Why?"

Portia dashed at the corner of one eye, wiping a stray tear before straightening. "It's becoming too cold," she explained, her voice cracking.

Zoe let go of Kincaid's hand to place hers on Portia's shoulder. "What can we do?"

Portia seemed to realize who she was speaking to. "Maybe, just maybe, your magic is different enough to help. Come with me," she ordered.

Zoe noticed no matter how distracted, the palace staff parted subconsciously to let Portia pass.

Zoe thought she was out of shape as she struggled to keep up with the queen's assistant, but she caught a glimpse of Kincaid huffing and puffing and didn't feel so bad. She looked down at Ame, who was keeping pace just fine.

Portia knocked on the door of the queen's chambers, then swung the door open. "Your Majesty, Zoe, and Kincaid are here."

The queen looking pale and distraught, looked

up. "I'm afraid I don't have an update for you, Zoe," she admitted, looking defeated.

"We're not here for that. How can we help?" she asked, pointing to herself and Kincaid.

The queen blinked.

"Your Majesty, I keep hearing how their magic is different. Mayhap they can accomplish what Lord Kendrick cannot," Portia suggested.

The queen gasped, then stood. "Come with me," she ordered.

This time, she and Kincaid had to jog to keep up. For someone so elegant, the queen moved like the wind. She led them to a large chamber with a stone table in the middle. Around the table, Aiden, Kendrick, Thane, and Brennus stood discussing something. Meryn, the twins, and Pip lounged around a smaller table, watching something on Meryn's laptop.

Meryn looked up from her laptop and smiled. "About time y'all got here." She pointed to the table. "Zoe, make that crystal hot."

Kendrick exhaled. "It's not that simple, Meryn. I'm a fire witch myself. To know the exact calculations to maintain a certain temperature for extended periods of time take meticulous…"

Zoe began to tune him out when he started going over formulas. She scrunched up her nose. Her magic never listened to such things. She assumed the crystal would be used to keep the sprites warm, so it shouldn't be too hot. She raised her right hand, her power hand, and focused on the crystal.

"Zoe, stop…" Kendrick moved toward her.

"Sauna," she said, focusing her mind on the warmth she remembered of the sauna at home.

The crystal in the center of the table flared a brilliant gold, then settled into a warm amber color.

Kendrick's mouth dropped. "How!" he screeched.

Kincaid nodded. "I get it." He looked at the other crystal and held up his hand. "Kitchen."

Like the crystal she had enchanted, Kincaid's flared, but instead of going from gold to amber, his started at amber and faded to an umber. Steady heat radiated from both.

"How!" Kendrick demanded again, walking back and forth between the crystals.

Meryn chuckled. "Aiden, you owe me two dozen more brownies."

Aiden, looking relieved, nodded. "I'm happy to be wrong and more than willing to pay up."

Thane stared. He walked over to the crystal and reached out a hand. He tapped the crystal. "It's warm, but not enough to burn." He looked to them. "How did you two manage to do something we could not?" he asked, pointing to his own chest and then to Kendrick.

Zoe shrugged. "I'm not sure. I think I just let the crystal know about how hot I wanted it, and it happened."

Kincaid nodded. "Same." He frowned. "It was surprisingly easy."

Kendrick made inarticulate sounds behind them. Thane ignored him. "We use formulas for a reason. Without strict guidelines, disasters can and do happen. What if your magic turned the crystal into a small sun? We would have been incinerated."

Zoe winced. "Thane, formulas, and math make my brain hurt. I had guidelines in mind when I sent my magic forward. I didn't want it any hotter than the sauna I used back home."

Kincaid pointed to her. "What she said. Except for me, I wanted it as warm as the kitchen gets when Aeson is baking."

"We just think differently," Meryn said, pulling something from her shirt.

"Hey Felix, how's this?" she asked.

Zoe blinked, then blinked again. A small light buzzed away from Meryn to circle the crystals.

Meryn turned to Portia. "He said it feels perfect."

Portia practically sagged forward in relief. "Thank the gods!" she stuck her head into the hallway. "Malcom, David!" Two warriors stepped into the room. "Have your warriors place these in the courtyard on opposite sides."

Malcom looked eager. "Thank the gods," he whispered. Heedless of his own body, he lifted the large crystal and began to jog out of the room, David with the other crystal right behind him.

Kendrick, still fuming, hands on his hips, faced them. "How long will that spell last?"

Again Zoe shrugged. "Again, I have no idea. I wasn't really thinking of a time limit."

Kincaid shook his head. "Me either."

"Kendrick, leave the children be. Whether by

design or some miracle, we have what we need to save the sprite population," the queen admonished.

She turned to them. "Unstructured spell casting is dangerous, but it can yield results. Try not to fall back on lazy thinking too often."

"Yes, Your Majesty," Zoe said.

"That's what I said," Kendrick pointed out.

"Actually, my love, you just screeched a lot," Anne corrected.

"We came here so Kendrick could show us how to use anchors so I can check the spell centers. If it's a bad time…" Zoe pointed to the room.

Kendrick's mouth became a straight line. "I will show you because gods only knows what you two would cook up without supervision." He ran his hands through his hair. "Gods! I sound like my father. I will beg his forgiveness in the hereafter for putting him through hell," he said, then scowled at them again.

Zoe blinked. "Your magic is like ours! Like Nigel's and Neil's! It's why you helped us when we were growing up. You understood what it was like trying to force a round peg in a square hole."

"Technically, a round peg can go into a square hole. It should be a square peg in a triangle-shaped hole or something," Meryn corrected.

"I just thought he knew everything, but that makes more sense," Neil observed.

"I swear I have aged millennia since meeting you, Meryn," Kendrick admitted sounding tired.

"Not my fault. I'm just trying to make it in this crazy paranormal world. You should be blaming the reapers," Meryn pointed out.

"You're right, forgive me," Kendrick said, then exhaled. "Alright, you two, let's check on your crystals on the way out, then start lessons at the closest spell center."

"The closest one is in the merchant district right outside the palace gates," Zoe informed him.

"Good." Kendrick turned and kissed his mate. "I'll be back soon."

"Be nice to the kids," Anne said, rubbing noses with him.

He sighed, then smiled. "Yes, dear."

Zoe was nervous as they headed toward the courtyard. What if her magic konked out and was no longer warm? She looked over to Kincaid and noticed he looked as ill as she felt. She gave him a half smile, which he attempted to return.

Portia opened the door for them. Along the walls, long workbenches were filled with multi-story dollhouses, and plants were everywhere she turned.

On one far side, an amber crystal glowed. The one closer to them was Kincaid's umber one. She felt a wave of relief that both crystals were still pumping out a good amount of heat.

At her side, Ame tugged on her hand. "I can help."

She knelt down. "What would you like to do?"

Ame pointed around the room. "It will be too dry." He swallowed hard. "Too dry." He looked up at the center of the room, and before her eyes, a sapphire flower bloomed that released a gentle mist. His expression eased. "Better."

Kendrick stared, then shook his head. "You know what, we'll save that for another day."

Portia looked down at Ame. "We never even took into consideration the effects of constant heat." She smiled at Ame. "Thank you, little one."

He smiled shyly and ducked behind her. Zoe remembering that morning, looked to Portia. "I know Gage has to make special requests to Noctem Falls but is there anything, in particular, we have to do to formally adopt Ame and Yuki?"

Portia's only reaction was a slight lifting of one brow. "You and Gage will need to come to the palace and make a declaration stating you wish to become their parents. Normally a clerk would handle such a thing, but I feel this is something that would brighten the queen's day. Would you mind it being slightly more formal if she were to accept your vow instead?"

"We made our own private vows this morning, so if it would help the queen, I don't think Gage would mind having her accept the official ones."

Portia smiled. "Ryuu made sure that their contract had a caveat that should you choose to adopt them, the contract is null and void." She shook her head. "I think he knew how much you all needed one another."

She looked down at Ame. "Well, you were

under contract for all of about a day. Does that bother you?"

He shook his head. "No. I'd rather have you as my *hahaue*. Yuki and I do not need the prestige of serving. We have only ever wanted a family."

She picked him up. "You have us now. Even a grumpy Uncle Kendrick," she said, pointing to where Kendrick still scowled at the crystals.

Kendrick coughed and cleared his expression. "What's two more children to add to the mix?" he said.

"Kendrick, you're not being honest with yourself. You would have looked after Ame and Yuki if only because it meant something to Ryuu," Kincaid pointed out.

Kendrick shook a finger at him. "Quit being cheeky." He took in the three of them staring up at him. "Well, let's get started."

Zoe winked at Ame, who surprised her by winking back. Laughing, they walked through the palace hand in hand to learn from the grouchy witch.

CHAPTER FOURTEEN

G AGE'S ATTENTION WAS SPLIT. HE was trying to run his own drills, but his eyes kept drifting to where Sascha worked with Yuki. The second time he was clipped by Ari's baton, his unit leader shook his head. "Go on, before I accidentally brain you to death, and your mate sets me on fire," he ordered, pointing to where his new son practiced.

"Thanks, Ari," he said, then jogged over to the small practice field Sacha was using. Yuki's movements flowed easily. His footing was sure, and he was limber. Smiling, he watched his son with pride.

The white tiger-shifter saw him approach and called a halt to their sparring. "Ramsey owes me twenty. I said you wouldn't last an hour."

Gage ignored him. "How's it going, son?"

Yuki stood straighter. "I am familiar with most of the movements, but I lack strength and stamina."

Sascha nodded. "I couldn't have put it better myself. Technique can wait. He's a natural at hand-to-hand. For now, we'll focus on strength training and building up that stamina." He looked around and winced. "We don't really have kid stuff here."

Leon jogged over. "Whatcha need?" he asked, having obviously been eavesdropping.

Sascha thought it over for a moment. "Smaller weights, maybe five to eight pounds. I wish we had an obstacle course designed for tiny legs."

Leon held up a hand. "It should be done by the end of next week." He thought for a moment. "Would one-gallon water jugs work for now? I can run get some."

Gage laughed. "They are both very beloved if you couldn't tell."

Sascha nodded to Leon, then ruffled Yuki's hair. "We have a girl about his age who helps us train back home. I swear, some days, I feel like she runs circles around us. She's just as beloved."

Gage was about to ask about Penny when an alarm began to sound. Ari must have hit it from his phone. As the alarm blared, Yuki looked up at him, fear clear to see on his little face. Gage picked him up and followed the men when they congregated at the center of the training field.

"Ari?"

Ari held up a finger, listening to whoever was talking on the phone. "Yes, sir." He listened. "All units are available, sir. The old guard has taken to doing patrols after that shadow popped up a few days ago." He nodded. "Yes, sir." He ended the call and looked to the men, then to Gage. "Aiden said that right after your mate enchanted some crystal that was needed for the sprites, Meryn got a hit on that laptop of hers. We need to gear up for another warehouse run."

Gage's heart leaped in his chest. If the units were doing a warehouse run, who'd watch his son? Ari turned to see why he hesitated and blinked when he realized Gage was holding Yuki.

"Call your mom," Ari ordered.

Gage felt a wave of relief. He had forgotten his mother was visiting. Reaching for his phone, he made the call.

"Gage?"

"Mother, I need you."

"Where?"

"The warrior villa. I have a mission, but there's no one to watch Yuki. I don't know what else to do," he explained, not even realizing he had kept his informal way of speaking.

"I will be there momentarily. Calm down, Gage. Yuki will be well taken care of," she assured him, then hung up.

"She's on her way," he told Ari.

"Good. Let's head that way, pick up Brie and gear up," Ari pointed toward the villa.

Gage jogged with the men, but when the others dispersed to their rooms to get their things, he waited downstairs with Yuki. They sat in silence on the bench in the foyer.

"If I were not here, you would not be worried," Yuki said in a quiet voice.

Gage sat him on his lap, facing him. "I would be worried regardless. These missions are dangerous." He heard the front door open but focused on his son.

"You don't distract me, Yuki. You, your brother, and your *hahaue* give me a reason to fight and come home. Now, I'll need you to watch over your grandmother for me. Can you do that?"

Yuki clutched at his arms. "What if you don't come home?"

Gage felt like he had been punched in the gut. In all the missions he had partaken in before, he had never felt pain and fear like this, not for himself but for this small child who relied on him.

"Welcome to parenthood," a female voice observed.

He looked up. "Mother."

There were thousands of things he wanted to say; he wanted to share how he understood her fears now, but they didn't have time.

She placed a hand on his shoulder. "I know. Trust me, Gage, I know." She lifted Yuki off his lap. "Is this my grandson?"

Yuki blinked, then nodded.

"I feel so much better knowing you will be looking after me," she said in soothing tones. "Now. You do not have to worry about your father. He has dozens of muscle heads around him that will help keep him safe," she said dryly.

Yuki smiled faintly.

She pointed to Gage. "Young man, your father is the third-ranked warrior in all of Éire Danu. Ferals would be hard-pressed to make him break a sweat, much less hurt him," she said, though

Gage could see the worry in her eyes even as she reassured his son.

"Well said, Tierla," Ari said approvingly. "We'll come home soon Yuki. While we're gone, you're the man of the house. Take care of your grandmother, and your mother and brother when they return. Okay?"

Yuki straightened with purpose and nodded. "I will."

Ari turned to him. "Gear up," he ordered.

Gage fought the urge to hesitate, but he knew if he did, it would only get harder each time he would go out on missions. He had to trust his unit leader, his mother, and his son. It was the only way he'd make it back alive. Otherwise, the worry would get him killed faster than any feral.

☙

After Kendrick explained the basic mechanics, she and Kincaid stood on either side of the spell center. She looked around and found that Kendrick had somehow pulled sidewalk chalk from his little bag, and her son was happily defacing public property.

"Concentrate," Kendrick barked.

She looked over at Kincaid, and they rolled their eyes in unison.

"I saw that," Kendrick observed.

Taking a deep breath, she sent her magic forward. Moments later, Kincaid's magic met hers, and when she started the mental image of a braid, his efforts morphed them into cables.

Feeling secure, she pushed forward to look for the Appleblossom signature.

At one point, she felt Kincaid's magic jerk, but she kept going. Finally, she found the spell. With meticulous effort, she examined each rune and symbol to ensure it was intact. Like the previous one, this spell center was fine.

Slowly she pulled her magic back and followed the cable back to Kincaid. When she opened her eyes, she was surprised at how good she felt. Spreading the load between two witches had helped enormously.

When she looked up at Kincaid, her smile dropped. "What?"

Anxiety was pouring off him in waves. "The guys got called out less than an hour ago. They're hitting another warehouse," he said tersely.

She looked around. "Who is watching Yuki?"

Kendrick held up a walkie-talkie. "Gage's mother is at the warrior villa with Yuki. I'll escort you there, then return to the palace. Kincaid, can you guard them?"

Kincaid nodded.

She went to Ame, who held up his arms and scooped him up. Laying a hand on Kincaid's shoulder, she gave it a squeeze. "I know you'd rather be with them."

"We're only a four-man squad normally, five counting Brie, but they went out one man short." He shook his head. "I'm glad I was able to help you, Zoe. I just wish..."

"That you could be in two places at once?"

Kendrick asked, then gave a short laugh. "Join the club."

Kincaid nodded at Kendrick's understanding. "Let's get them home." He smiled at Ame. "I bet we can figure out some snacks for the guys for when they return."

Ame nodded enthusiastically. "I want to help!"

Zoe was fighting to stay calm. Her mate was out there fighting, and she was here, where she had no idea what was happening.

Kendrick gripped her shoulder. "Your only responsibility right now is to watch over the boys and don't make them worry over you."

In other words, keep my shit together. She thought.

The walk back to the warrior villa was quicker than she remembered, but that could be attributed to her being distracted. When she opened the door, the first thing she noticed was how quiet it was.

"Yuki!" she called out.

"*Hahaue!*" Yuki came running from the family room. Behind him, a beautiful, dark-haired, woman appeared in the doorway, smiling at her.

Yuki wrapped himself around her legs, and Ame hugged his brother tightly. "It's okay, boys. Everything will be just fine." She knelt down and kissed each boy on the forehead. "Your big brother Kincaid has had a marvelous idea. He suggested we make some food for the warriors so that when they return, they have plenty to eat. Yuki, would you like to help us in the kitchen?"

"Rice," he answered.

She frowned.

"He means he wants to be in charge of cooking the rice," Ame interpreted.

Because Ame was the more timid of the two, she tended to forget he was older. Right now, his younger brother was upset, so he was stepping up. She was very proud of him.

Looking up, she gave a wan smile to the older woman. "Gage's mother, I presume?"

The woman laughed. "What a way to meet one another. Yes, I am Gage's mother, Tierla LeBeau. You have beautiful boys. I cannot tell you how excited I am to have two grandsons!"

"Thank you, for coming so quickly to watch Yuki."

Tierla waved off her thanks. "That is what grandmothers are for."

Yuki smiled at the woman shyly, then turned to his brother. "She is very nice."

Ame nodded and eyed Tierla carefully.

Tierla clapped her hands. "Let us get started. Young man, you will be our runner," she said imperiously to Kincaid.

Kincaid pointed to his chest. "Me?"

"Who else? If we need ingredients as we cook, you will be the one to fetch them for us," Tierla said.

Zoe pushed her sleeves up. "Come on, boys."

When they headed toward the kitchen, Tierla looped her arm through hers. "I am just excited to get a daughter too. I am looking forward to getting to know you better."

Blushing, she felt as shy as Ame. "Me too."

Kincaid followed. "What kind of ingredients? Will it be a lot? Will I have to go far?" he asked.

Tierla looked at her and winked. "Who knows?"

Zoe felt some of her nervousness dissipate at Tierla's teasing. She wasn't planning on getting to know her mother-in-law today. Still, given the circumstances, it might be just the thing to keep her mind occupied, so she didn't worry herself over her mate.

☾

Gage waited for the signal. Ari and Aiden had stationed two units at each of the three doors. Brie and Ari were responsible for securing a room in the warehouse as a fallback point to evacuate any wounded. Aiden was impressed with how Brie's mission went and decided to add that to their methodology for warehouse missions.

Priest tapped his shoulder, then pointed to his forehead. Gage grinned. It was also their first time using thermal goggles. In their drills, everyone agreed that two warriors would stand back-to-back, and everyone else would drop to initially clear the room, much in the same way Brie and Cam did. After that, the goggles could be used if attacked by an invisible assailant. Was it perfect? No. Could they still accidentally shoot each other? Yes. But it was the best plan they had for now.

Brie looked at them. She tapped her comms unit. "Menace, Gemini, night, night," she said, initiating the start of the raid. After a ten count, they began moving.

Gage and Priest's task, along with Upsilon, was to secure the hostages if they were still alive. Meryn had pinpointed a warehouse about one-hundred miles west of Madison. Both she and Brie agreed that if they kept the raids random, the ferals wouldn't know which ones to shut down to taunt them.

Clearing the door, he scanned the room. Being a vampire, his sight was better than Priest's but not by much. Priest was one of the rare harpy eagle-shifters that could shift their eyes for better sight much in the same way hands could be shifted for claws.

"Gage!" Priest yelled.

But Gage was already moving. They had live hostages in a cage in the corner. About twenty-feet from them, a fae lay strapped to a steel gurney screaming as a crystal above him glowed. On the other side of him, a line of fae cowered against the wall.

Raising his gun, he took out the feral manipulating the machines. Priest went to the gurney and began unstrapping the survivor. Behind him, Aiden gave the order, "Down!"

Immediately he and Priest dropped to the floor. A few moments later, Brie called out the all-clear to stand.

Gage was looking through drawers for the keys to the cage when he heard Priest scream his name. Looking up, he had just enough time to see Priest snarl before an arm snaked up behind him. "A goodbye present. Tell my little brother Oron thanks for the way in," a voice rasped in his ear, releasing a putrid smell. He was knocked to one side, and the tall fae hit a few buttons before giving him a mock salute. Touching his necklace, he disappeared.

"Son of a bitch!" he yelled.

He went to reach for his goggles to track him when Priest pointed to the ceiling. "Gage, he did something to the machine. We need to get these people out now!"

Gage looked up to see that the crystal now pulsated with a steadily increasing beat. He was taking no chances. He reached up to his comms unit. "Bomb! Clear the building!"

He heard exclamations as his unit brothers started grabbing fae survivors from the wall and began carrying them to the portal.

"Where are we at?" Aiden asked, running up to them.

"You are getting your ass through that portal, sir," Gage said. "You're too important to lose."

"That's not how I operate," Aiden refuted.

"Thane! We need help with the locks!" Priest called out.

Thane ran over, his hands already glowing. After a few seconds, he stepped back, shaking his head. "They've been magicked."

Ari and Brie were herding the remaining survivors through the portal near the front of the building. Ari met his eyes, and Gage jerked his head toward the portal. Ari snarled his frustration but did as Gage wanted. He got Brie to safety.

"Unit Commander Aiden McKenzie, as this is an Éire Danu sanctioned mission for fae citizens, I am taking command as the highest ranked Éire Danu warrior present. You are relieved of command and ordered back to the palace."

Aiden scoffed. "Yeah, right."

Gage placed his hand over his heart. "There was never an option where you would stay." Looking up, he swallowed hard. "Take care of Zoe and the boys."

Aiden's expression became panicked as he realized Gage was serious. "No. Now you listen to me…"

Behind him, Thane raised a hand and placed it on Aiden's shoulder, a pulse flared, dropping the bear shifter.

Darian sighed. "He is going to be so pissed."

Oron pointed to their Unit Commander. "Get him out of here, Dari. You too, Thane."

Darian shook his head. "Not without you."

"Right now, I am not your brother. I am your guard. Prince Darian, leave. For the sake of our people and our mother, you must survive," Oron said in a firm voice.

"I hate you for this," Darian said, from between clenched teeth.

Oron gave him a crooked smile. "No, you don't."

Darian gave him a fierce hug, and both he and Thane lifted Aiden up and carried him toward the portal. "You come back to us, Oron! You hear me? You come back!" Darian yelled back, before he disappeared through the portal closing it.

Gage looked up. The light was now blinking quickly. "We don't have much time."

Priest looked at him. "Go, Gage. Oron can get you out of here. You have Zoe and the boys. Let me be the one to stay."

"You have a mate on the way, and I outrank you, now hush. I'm trying to think," he said, looking over the panel.

"There have to be at least a hundred combinations of buttons. The chances that we get the right sequence to turn this off is slim to none," Oron said, shoving his hand through his hair.

"Prince Oron, one of the guards used a bracelet to unlock the cage," one of the prisoners called out.

"Quiet! He's an Eirson," another reprimanded fearfully.

"Technically, he's a Vi'Eirlea now," Priest corrected.

"That's not important," Oron said, pointing to the ceiling. "We have maybe thirty seconds."

"Fuck!" Priest yelled.

Gage looked at the cage. "We never found any cages."

Priest looked confused. "What does that have to do with anything?"

Oron clapped him on the back. "It means they're not welded to the floor."

Gage nodded. "Can you open a portal there?" he asked, pointing to the wall.

Using a silver signet ring, he opened a portal

on the other side of the cage. "It's not as fancy as my brother's, but it will get us the hell outta here."

Gage, Priest, and Oron dropped their shoulders and pushed. Just as the crystal became a steady stream of light, they shoved one last time as an explosion behind them flung them and the cage through the portal into darkness.

☾

Zoe watched from the kitchen doorway.

Ari had returned looking pale and furious. He spoke to Kincaid first, who dropped to his knees.

"No," she whispered.

Ari turned and hurried to her side. "We don't know for sure. I came to explain things and bring you to the palace."

Zoe spun to face Tierla. The older woman cuddled the boys close. "Go. Do everything you can, and go. We will be waiting for you here."

She kissed both boys and began running with Ari. Seconds later, Kincaid was right behind them.

"What the fuck happened!" he demanded.

Ari's expression twisted. "There was a bomb. Gage took command as third-ranked. Brie and I took charge of the survivors. He immediately relieved Aiden of duty and basically shoved him and Darian through the portal. He, Priest, and Oron stayed behind. We waited for them to come through, but they never did. Thane said based on what he saw of the bomb, it should have gone off minutes after we evacuated." He stopped speaking.

Zoe froze in the street. "What aren't you saying?"

Ari turned to her, his face a mask of grief. "We went back through, and there was nothing left."

Zoe swayed, and Ari was instantly at her side. He scooped her up and resumed running, Kincaid sobbing, ran beside them.

"No. He's alive. I would have felt it if he died, wouldn't I?"

"I don't know, but I wanted you with us for any updates. You have that right," Ari said, his face a mask of grief.

Once they got to the palace, Ari slowed his pace but didn't put her down. They went immediately to the queen's chambers. When they neared, they could hear bone-numbing roars from inside.

Ari winced. "Aiden's awake."

He opened the door, and they walked inside to face devastation. Aiden had flipped the table and stalked back and forth as he wrestled with his bear. To one side, the queen was seated between Darian and Brennus. All three of them were wrapped in palatable despair.

"Aiden, if you don't fucking calm down, I'm going to get upset. And that will probably make me puke, then I could hurt our jellerbean!" Meryn threatened.

Aiden snarled at her.

Her eyes narrowed. "Did you seriously just snarl at me?"

Aiden huffed, but his erratic pacing slowed.

Meryn turned to her. "We know nothing for certain."

"There was a crater, Meryn!" Darian exclaimed, tears streaming down his cheeks. He jumped to his feet. "I had to walk away for a second time! First with Keelan and now with my own brother. It should have been me!"

Brennus stood and pulled Darian into an unbreakable hug. Darian thrashed about until he lost strength, then sagged against the older fae.

Zoe looked around the room. "Kendrick?" she asked, her voice breaking. If anyone could make this all go away, it was him.

Kendrick shook his head. "It's been over twenty minutes. They would have contacted us by now."

Her knees gave out, and Ari easily lifted her and sat her down next to the queen. "He's alive. I can feel it," she said.

The queen nodded. "I will not give up hope. Though I am not his mother by birth, he is still my son. I would know if he departed from this world."

Around the room, the warriors lingering for news looked at them with a mixture of pity and grief.

Zoe thought things over. Gage was smart. He was resourceful and thought quickly. If anyone had a chance at surviving this, it was him. "It is rather concerning they haven't contacted us. What could cause that?"

Darian's head rose from Brennus' shoulder. He

gave her an incredulous look as if he couldn't believe what he was hearing.

Meryn scrunched up her face. "Well, if they aren't dead...because you know death could keep them from reaching out." She looked over at her laptop. "The only way they have to contact us is via cell phone, but if that crystal bomb thingie acted as an electromagnetic pulse, it could have fried their hardware."

Aiden swung his head in her direction. "There's a chance?"

Meryn nodded. "It's slim as fuck, though."

Aiden took a deep breath and centered himself. "How can we find them?"

"Aiden?" Darian asked.

Aiden looked at Zoe. "I won't give up on them. Not yet. In my heart and soul, I know that I would feel it if Meryn left this world before me. Until Zoe feels otherwise, we have a rescue mission to plan."

Darian straightened. "I'm scared to hope."

"Then let me do it for both of us," Aiden said. "You have carried the weight and grief for Keelan alone, I won't let you do that this time." He looked around the room. "Men! Gather round!"

With a sense of purpose, the men walked over, faces grim.

"Okay, baby, where do we start?" Aiden asked, turning to Meryn.

Meryn took a ragged breath and exhaled. Zoe realized that despite her flippant manner, Meryn was scared for her brother. "Did we check around the warehouse? Like in the woods and stuff?"

Aeson stepped forward, his eyes red-rimmed. "Yes, we scoured the surrounding area."

Meryn glanced around the room, looking a bit desperate. "Here!" Neil said, running in with a small, wheeled office chair.

Sighing in relief, Meryn sat on her knees in the chair and began spinning. "So, if they are on foot, they are well enough to get outside the zone the warriors checked. That's good. No one saw any blood, also good. I mean, there were people in the cage. There would have been some sort of splatter." She stopped spinning. "Did you see the cage?"

Nerius shook his head. "It was just a hole in the floor, and one wall was gone."

Meryn spun, then stopped again. "One wall? I thought you said it was in a corner."

Kael stepped up next to his unit leader. "The back wall was blown out, but the external wall took little damage. We think that the blast hit down and back."

Meryn spun, slowed, and kick spun again. "Or, something protected the wall."

Aiden frowned. "You lost me, babe."

Meryn stopped then looked up, turning to the queen, then Brennus. "What if Oron opened a portal? Would the blast have traveled through the portal before it closed?"

The queen gasped and covered her mouth with her hands. Sobbing, she nodded. Brennus went to her side and wrapped his arm around her. He turned to Meryn. "Keep going, little love."

"What if they opened a portal and tried to get

the cage through? I'm not sure how successful they could have been, but if they were on the other side of the portal when the blast went off, they could have been hurt and unable to contact us."

Zoe's heart stuttered. "How do we find them? They could be anywhere."

Darian slowly began to shake his head. "That's not true. My ring, which signifies I am heir, can open portals anywhere. But Oron's ring isn't like that. He can open portals, but only to established locations." He stood shaking. "Gods! Aiden, I think I know where they are!"

Aiden pulled out his cell. "Where?"

"The warehouse near Noctem Falls! Or Noctem Falls itself. Those two locations are the last portals he opened. In a blind panic, he might have linked up to one of them without thought," Darian walked off to one side and, using his own ring, tried to open a portal. He stepped back, shaking his head. "I can't open a second portal so close to an established one. We'll have to go to the building on Market Street to go through and check."

Aiden was already making calls. "Adriel, I need a sweep of Noctem Falls. We have men missing, and they might have used a portal to escape there."

Zoe reached over and clutched the queen's hands. Like Darian, she was afraid to hope.

"What!" Aiden looked up. "Adriel is reporting approximately twenty minutes ago, a loud boom was heard throughout the city. They are trying to pinpoint where." He returned to his call. "Adriel, expect incoming. I am bringing warriors to help search." He ended the call. "Darian, can you open a portal to Noctem Falls."

"You bet your ass I can!" Darian exclaimed. Seconds later, a golden portal shimmered.

"Ari, Brie, and Kincaid. Omega Psi, Phi, and Upsilon head through. Chi, take point here in the city."

Aeson looked like he was about to argue but ended up shaking his head. "We will."

"*Hahaue*?"

Zoe turned and sprung to her feet. Tierla stood with Portia and the boys. "They wanted to come, and to be honest, so did I. He is my son and their father," Tierla explained.

Zoe ran and knelt next to the boys, holding them close. "We have to look for him. He could be very hurt."

They both nodded. "We're going too."

"Absolutely not!" Aiden argued.

Zoe stood and kissed Tierla on the cheek. She now knew what she had to do. Find her mate.

"No," Aiden repeated.

When she and the boys walked past the queen, she reached out. "Please," she whispered.

Zoe nodded. "I will do everything in my power to bring them home."

"Is no one listening to me? I said no," Aiden waved his finger about.

Zoe, followed by the boys, walked up to Aiden, and she patted his cheek. "You're not cruel enough to say no to all three of us, are you?"

She looked down, and both boys were giving Aiden the biggest Puss in Boots' eyes she
had ever seen. Not wanting to be outdone, she
looked up at him with her saddest eyes.

"Argh! I am commander in name only. Either
that or your family has no respect for my authority! I can't wait to give Gage a piece of my mind
about shoving me through a portal. Fine!" he
threw his hands up in defeat.

"Respect my authoritai," Meryn mimicked.

Behind her, the boys took ahold of her robes.
Together they walked through the portal to look
for the missing piece of their family.

CHAPTER FIFTEEN

🌙

WHEN GAGE CAME TO, HE was in complete darkness and filled with indescribable pain. He listened carefully and heard ragged and raspy breathing around him. The cage! "Priest! Oron!" he called out. He stopped. He knew he had called out, but he couldn't hear his own words. He took stock of his situation. Moving slowly, he gasped as the pain got worse. He tried to make out his surroundings, but there was so little light. He felt a hand on his arm, and he went to swing. His fist was caught, and his hand was brought up to a face.

He blinked and saw that it was Oron leaning over him. As his eyes adjusted, he could see more.

"Are you okay!" he yelled.

Oron shook his head ruefully and held his wrist out to Gage. Gage could only stare before he shook his head. He wouldn't feed from his brother the way he felt. He'd drain him dry.

Scowling, Oron took out a knife and cut his wrist before thrusting it in Gage's mouth. He went to turn his head, but the aged fae blood began to race through his veins. Draw after draw, his strength began to return.

After a minute, Oron pulled his wrist away. "Can you hear now?" he asked, wrapping cloth around his wrist.

"You know I hate feeding from you guys."

Oron gave him a flat look. "You were close to dying. Get over it."

That sobered him. Gage nodded and started to move gingerly. "My back?"

"I'm not going to lie. It looks mangled. You were the last one through, so I think you took most of the blast."

"Priest?"

"I'm here, buddy," Priest said, from his other side. "Broken ribs, and something's wrong with my lower back, but other than that, I'm good."

Gage had to fight the urge to roll his eyes at Priest's flippant answer.

"The hostages?" he asked.

"Knocked out for the moment, which is probably a good thing. They got banged around in that cage. I bet we have several broken bones and concussions to treat," Oron said, looking over his shoulder.

"Oops, we forgot to pack a healer," Priest joked.

Gage went to laugh and inhaled sharply. "Gods, that hurts." He looked around. "Where the fuck are we?"

Oron winced. "Noctem Falls, I think."

Fighting back anger fueled by his pain, Gage breathed through his nose. "You think?"

ALANEA ALDER

Oron sat back against the stone wall. "I didn't have a clear destination in mind, so I'm hoping it took us to one of the last locations I opened a portal to." He looked around. "We're not in that other warehouse, we're surrounded by stone and caves, so I'm pretty sure we're in Noctem Falls."

Gage closed his eyes. He had grown up here and knew exactly how extensive the cave systems were. They could die down here, and they'd be lucky if their bodies were found in the next decade or so.

"How bad?" he asked.

Oron looked away. "If you don't get treated soon, I don't think you'll make it."

Priest went to whack Oron but couldn't reach him. "Did you have to say it like that?"

Gage shook his head. "We're past sugar coating." He tried to clear his mind. "Oron, you'll have to go get help."

Oron pointed down to his legs. "Both mine are broken. I'm not going anywhere."

Gage turned to Priest. "Can you shift?"

Priest shook his head, his face twisted in frustration. "I've been trying, but you know my bird…"

Gage nodded. "I know, brother, it's okay."

"It's not! You might die because I'm a failure as a shifter," he admitted bitterly.

"And Brennus spends more time at the palace than the warrior villa. Ari's time is split in a dozen different directions, and Kincaid's spells go sideways on him most of the time," Oron listed.

Both he and Priest stared at him.

Oron continued. "So what if you have shifting issues? Gage has confidence issues…"

"I do not have confidence issues!" he argued.

Oron shook his head. "Today was the first time I have ever seen you take charge. Ever." He gave a sad smile. "Like I was saying, despite all that, you five make up the highest-ranking unit in the city. I'm just a low-ranked fae from Lycaunia. I was counting on you two jokers to get me home," he teased.

Gage chuckled, then winced. "Please, please don't make me laugh."

Priest looked around their small cave. "Do you think anyone heard us?"

"It was an explosion. I hope to all the gods they did," Gage grunted.

Priest turned his way. "You said in some places in Noctem Falls, the stone between levels are like thirty feet thick."

Gage nodded.

Priest squinted as if trying to make something out. "I don't think we're that far from the city proper."

"Why would you think that?" Gage asked.

"I can see light, it's pretty far out, but I see it. That, and Oron hasn't been many places in Noctem Falls, right?"

Oron nodded.

"Then, even if the portal was off by a bit,

wouldn't that still put us close to the city center?" Priest explained.

"Priest, some days your brain belies that idiotic face you have," Gage teased.

Priest shook his head. "I'll get you back for that later. For now…" He grinned. "Do either of you know Morse Code?"

ℂ

All of Noctem Fall's units, plus the ones from Éire Danu, assembled in a large market area. Zoe watched as Aiden coordinated with a handsome vampire with a clipboard. There had been introductions, but she'd be lucky if she got half the names right later. She knew Serenity from Storm Keep and was relieved to know that she, along with Laelia and Radclyffe, were manning the hospital, ready to heal at a moment's notice. She looked around at so many people, unable to do much.

"Have faith, my dear. If anyone can find them, it's Aiden and Meryn McKenzie," a soft voice said from her right.

"Thank you. I trust them, of course. It's just…"

"It is your mate," the man said.

"Yes."

He looked down. "And who are these two little gentlemen?"

Zoe shook her head and dashed away her tears. "This is Ame and Yuki. Gage and I just recently adopted them."

"Recently?" he asked.

She sniffled. "This morning."

"Oh, dear. Sebastian!" he called out.

A tall squire walked over. "I was helping little Meryn."

"Perhaps Zoe and her sons could use some of your Magic Pudding," the kind man suggested.

Sebastian's expression dawned his understanding. "Of course, I have already brought some up for Meryn. If you would follow me, I will escort you to where she has her... what does she call it... her command-central setup," Sebastian said.

Feeling less lost, she smiled at the kind stranger that had seen her pain and reached out. "How can I thank you for your kindness?"

He wrapped an arm around her shoulders and steered her toward where Meryn sat. "You take good care of your mate. He is a beloved son here in Noctem Falls. I know you feel scared and alone, but you have family here." The man pointed to another set of individuals standing close to Aiden.

"Simon, Leana, Theo," the man called out.

The group turned and bowed to the stranger. "Your Highness, did you need us for something?" Leana asked as they walked up.

"Simon and Leana Géroux, Theo Fabre, this is Zoe Appleblossom, Gage's mate and his two sons, Ame and Yuki."

"Your Highness?" she asked.

He winked at her. "I am Magnus Rioux, Prince of Noctem Falls."

"Oh, dear," she whispered.

"Sons?" Theo asked, looking down at Ame and Yuki. "These two boys are my grandsons?"

She nodded, unsure of how he and Tierla parted.

He smiled wide and bent down. "Hello, boys. I am very happy to meet you. I am Gage's father."

Yuki stared. "Did you hurt grandmother?"

Theo stood quickly and looked at Zoe. "What have they heard?"

"They might have overheard that their grandmother Tierla was able to leave you when she had a choice. That she had been part of an arranged mating."

Theo's expression looked conflicted.

Simon and Leana each scooped up one of the boys. "We are your father's aunt and uncle." Leana cuddled Yuki. "Oh Simon, are they not darling?"

When they went to walk away. Theo quickly began to answer Yuki. "I never intended to hurt your grandmother. Times were different then. I always tried to treat her with the utmost respect. My only regret is that we were not true mates. She is a very fine woman."

Yuki smiled, then nodded before he reached for Theo.

The man's eyes bugged out. Laughing, Leana handed Yuki to the man, who immediately began to fumble. Yuki, being patient, waited for him to secure his hold. "Am I doing this right?" Theo asked no one in particular.

Zoe took pity on the man. It was obvious he had never held a child before in his life. Which made her wonder about Gage's upbringing.

She adjusted his hold, so Yuki sat easily on his forearm. "There."

"You have my thanks," he replied, staring at Yuki, who stared right back.

Simon shook his head and winked at Ame, who giggled. Watching the easy way Simon and Leana handled Ame, she realized that these two probably played a huge role in raising Gage. It made her feel better to know there had been some warmth in his life.

Yuki reached up and placed his tiny hand on Theo's cheek. "Will you find *chichiue*?"

"*Chichiue* means father," she said, translating the words.

Theo straightened. "Of course, I will. You do not have to worry about a thing."

Theo handed Yuki back over to Leana and strode over to Aiden. "What is being done to find my son?"

Leana shook her head. "Never, *ever*, have I seen him like this."

Simon shrugged. "Better late than never, I suppose."

Together they carried the boys over to Meryn's table. Sebastian was waiting on them with two smaller bowls of pudding for the boys. After the boys were seated, Sebastian handed each of them a spoon.

Zoe sat when Magnus, Simon, and Leana returned to the meeting with Aiden. She then turned to Meryn. "What are you working on?"

Meryn looked up. "How come you're not over there getting an update from Aiden?"

Zoe frowned. "Why would I go over there when obviously you will know something first?"

Sebastian chuckled, then covered his mouth with his fist and coughed.

Meryn grinned. "See, you get me."

"Anything?" Zoe asked, pointing to the laptop.

Meryn shook her head. "I don't see anything on the message boards from the city residents. I posted there when I knew we were heading this way. In addition to the warriors, the people of Noctem Falls are looking too. All I've seen so far are posts asking about the random rumbling they heard earlier."

Zoe sighed, sat back, and looked around. Up in the corner, near the high ceiling, she spotted a camera. "Meryn, could the cameras have caught anything?"

Meryn looked up sharply, her eyes wide. "I lurves you right now." Her fingers began moving fervently.

A small man with white-blond hair and a gigantic warrior walked over. "Avery, I need to be over there to get orders," the warrior protested, pointing to the crowd around Aiden.

"Warrick, you can go. I, on the other hand, will be getting *my* orders from Meryn," Avery countered.

Warrick sighed. "I'm not leaving you alone with this crazy quartet."

Nigel, Neil, and Pip wiggled their fingers at the warrior.

Zoe stared. Avery was an older, anglo version of her boys. All white hair and blue eyes.

"Meryn, please give me something to do to help," Avery begged.

"Shush a second," Meryn ordered, her eyes tracking something on the screen.

Avery nodded and waited.

She clicked, then clicked again. Zoe stood and walked around to see what she was doing.

Meryn was watching certain clips over and over again. She then brought up a second set of clips and watched those a few times.

"What are you looking for?" she asked.

"Movement."

Zoe watched. "I don't see Gage, Meryn."

"Not Gage, the cameras."

Zoe watched the clips over and over and over again. But she didn't see what Meryn was tracking.

Meryn sat back. "There!" she exclaimed, pointing.

Behind them, the large group of men quieted.

"There, there and there."

Meryn brought up three different camera angles.

Aiden walked over. "Babe?"

Kendrick moved beside Zoe, so he stood behind Meryn and had a clear view of her laptop.

She played the clips again and looked back at Aiden and Kendrick as if expecting praise, only to be greeted with confused expressions.

She scowled. "This is why I am smarter than you, by the way."

Aiden nodded. "I never doubted that, baby."

She pointed to the screen. "Zoe suggested I look at the camera footage."

Aiden nodded. "But in the clips you're playing, I don't see the men."

Meryn exhaled and kept going. "The first clip is transport tunnel Level Five, the second is the tunnel Level Three, and the last one is the tunnel Level Two." She replayed them. "The cameras shook a tiny bit on the first, more on the second, and the most on the third. Nothing was felt up here on Level Six."

What they were seeing was the stronger vibrations from the blast affecting the cameras differently based on proximity.

Aiden pointed to the screen. "Replay the last one."

She clicked her mouse.

Aiden turned to Magnus and Sebastian. "Did either of you feel anything on Level One?"

Magnus shook his head. "Sebastian and I were up here for a weekly meeting with the wolves."

Aiden looked around. "Was anyone on Level One?"

The ones closest to Magnus shook their heads.

Meryn turned to Avery. "You can be anything, right?"

Avery looked around nervously. "What do you mean?"

Meryn rolled her eyes. "You know I wouldn't out you like this unless it was an emergency." She bopped shoulders with him. "Come on, Avery, your last name is Therian. I looked it up.

If you wanted it to be a secret, you should have changed your name."

Warrick's brows disappeared into his hairline. "What is she talking about?"

Avery remained quiet.

Meryn placed her hand on his. "I wouldn't have said anything if it wasn't important. You know that."

Avery nodded but still didn't say anything.

Meryn looked around. "Therian, derived from therianthropy, defined as the mythological ability for a human to change into an animal. In the human world, one of the most famous examples is lycanthropy or werewolves."

Aiden nodded slowly. "And Avery is a shifter. That makes sense."

Meryn looked over to Avery.

"What she doesn't want to say is my shifting is different. I am not a lycanthrope or an ailuranthrope, not a wolf or a cat."

"Right, you're a red fox," Warrick said.

Avery shrugged. "But I don't have to be just a fox."

Meryn grinned. "He is probably the coolest shifter ever. He can become anything."

Zoe looked around. You could hear a pin drop.

Aiden shook his head. "You know what, lately, I refuse to question these new revelations." He looked down at Avery. "Can you help find Gage and the others?"

Avery frowned and looked to Meryn. "Can I?"

Meryn nodded and tapped on her laptop before

rotating it to show Avery. "Can you become a fennec fox?"

Avery nodded. "Easily. It's even close in size and shape to what I normally change into. Why?"

Meryn pointed. "Fennec foxes have like supersonic hearing and are best at hearing things underground. They can hear the vibrations of their prey scurrying around."

Avery nodded enthusiastically. "I can go searching for them!"

Meryn held up her hand, and he high-fived her.

Avery looked down at the floor. "I wasn't sure if I was going to tell anyone about my abilities. I think that's why my family was hiding. But, I never would have kept this to myself if it meant someone dying."

Meryn nodded. "I know. That's why you're amazing and super cool."

Nigel nodded. "Like super-super cool! I want to be able to turn into any animal. That sounds incredible."

Avery blushed but looked proud. Moments later, his form wavered, and he became the smallest fox she had ever seen. But, what was more impressive, was that his clothes shrunk down to fit him.

Magnus clapped Warrick on the back. "I do not think you will ever have to worry about your mate. He just stole the heart of everyone present."

Meryn rubbed Avery between his huge ears. "You're so fucking cute!"

Warrick gently picked up his mate. "I have my

walkie-talkie. I'll call out if he finds anything."

Nigel and Neil stood. Neil looked down at Meryn. "We'll go with them. If Avery finds them, it may be through a hole smaller than Gage and the others can get through." He paused. "The guys would probably have a time getting through a human Avery-shaped hole too." He grinned. "We can reshape the stone to create larger openings."

"Good call," Meryn said.

The boys jogged after Avery and Warrick.

Zoe watched as the impossibly huge warrior cuddled a fox that was smaller than his bicep. "How remarkable."

❦

Meryn chewed on her lower lip. "Shouldn't they have found something by now?"

The one introduced as Beth rolled her eyes. "I told you the city was bigger than you thought. We're talking about miles and miles and miles of caves."

"Stupid beehive," Meryn grumbled.

The area around them had thinned out after the men knew what level was best to start looking.

Meryn's cell rang, and she quickly picked it up. "'Ello? No, I never know why he doesn't answer his phone. What? Well, fuck. I'll see what I can do. Yeah, yeah, I'll stay safe."

Zoe waited expectantly. "Well?"

Meryn strummed her fingers on the table. "That was Dav. After Aiden realized the amount of ground they had to cover, he called in the units he had in Éire Danu from Lycaonia. That only left the Chi unit and the old guard and Auntie's imperial knights back in the city."

"Something has happened back home, hasn't it?" Zoe was scared to hear the answer. Were they ever going to catch a break?

"Yup. A new portal is trying to form. Right now, it's hazy, but it could solidify at any moment."

"And most of the warriors with thermal goggles are using them to find Gage and the others," Zoe guessed, feeling ill.

"Yup."

"What did Dav advise?"

"They need backup," Meryn said, then pointed to the now empty market area. "We're short on warriors right now."

Zoe debated it for all of about two seconds. Currently, everyone was doing everything they could to save her mate. She couldn't heal or search or shape stone, but she could use her magic to defend. She stood. "I'll go."

Meryn's brows lifted. "Bad. Ass."

Yuki stood. "Me too."

Meryn nodded. "Baby badass."

Zoe pointed to his chair. "No. Stay here and wait for your father."

Yuki just took her hand. "I promised I would look after you and the house and grandmother. I have to go."

"Oh baby, that doesn't mean you risk your life. You're too precious to us to chance you getting hurt."

"I can help," Yuki nodded once. "Yes. I can help." He turned to his brother, and a blue mist floated between them. Looking up, he smiled. "I'm ready."

"Fine, but you stay behind me the entire time. If for one second it becomes dangerous, you run. Do you understand me, Yuki Fabre?" she asked, using his full name for the first time.

He looked a bit surprised but smiled. "*Hai, hahaue.*"

She looked at Ame. "And you, Ame Fabre, you listen to Meryn. Don't get hurt, and help if you can."

Ame beamed. "*Hai, hahaue.*"

"Let's go," she said to Yuki, then turned to Meryn. "Call me…"

The smaller woman nodded. "The second anything happens."

Together she and Yuki walked toward the open portal that would take them home.

☾

Priest had been tapping out SOS for over an hour until he fell asleep. Oron was able to doze, but pain kept Gage awake. Burns were like that. They hurt too bad to let your mind shut down. In the cage, people would occasionally whimper, but for the most part, they stayed unconscious.

To take his mind off the pain, he thought of Zoe and the boys. He wished he could see them one more time. The little time they had together wasn't enough. He grit his teeth together as another wave of pain threatened to overwhelm him. He was scared that the pain would break him before they were found.

That's why he thought he was hallucinating the first time he heard the scurrying. But, as it seemed to get closer, he called out. "Help! We're down here!" He didn't know what the sound could be, but if by some miracle it was someone looking for him, he wasn't taking any chances.

He knew his instincts were right when the scurrying sped up and got closer to them. When it paused, he began yelling again. The running resumed. He did that a few more times before a tiny white fox in a sweater and corduroys wiggled through a crack.

"I've lost my damn mind."

"Keep it down. I'm trying to sleep," Priest complained, still half asleep.

When the fox wavered into the form of a small man. "Thank the gods we've found you!"

"Who are you?" Gage asked through dry lips.

The small man looked around. "Avery Fortier, my mate, is the Founding Family head of Level Five. Is there water nearby I can bring you?"

Gage shook his head. "We haven't been able to explore. All three of us are unable to move much." The man's words sunk in. "Why is the mate of a Founding Family head of a search and rescue team?"

Avery tilted his head. "Because Meryn asked me to."

"Gods all bless that woman," he said, closing his eyes.

"Don't close your eyes! I know that's bad. In the movies, people die after they do that," the small man fretted.

Gage opened his eyes. "Do you have a plan for getting us out of here?"

Avery nodded. "Give me a second. I left my bag in the cave on the other side of the crack. It has my phone in it. I'll call the twins. They were about a mile behind me."

"Gods, you really are here to rescue us," Gage said, suddenly feeling overwhelmed.

"Absolutely, so don't close your eyes. I'll be right back." He shifted back to the form of a tiny fox and disappeared into the crack.

Oron grunted as he opened his eyes. "I could have sworn I heard Avery."

Gage laughed. "You did, my friend. You did. They've found us."

Oron's eyes popped open. "Where are they?"

Gage pointed toward the crack. "He came from that." Relief flooded his mind knowing Priest and Oron would be okay. "Tell him I'm sorry," he whispered.

"Why?" Oron asked. "Sorry for what?"

"I don't think I can keep my eyes open after all," he admitted before they drifted shut.

He felt warm liquid against his mouth. He was simply too tired to drink.

𝕮

"Hurry!"

"Neil, open the crack wider!"

"Easy now."

"Gods above, look at his back!"

"We need to get him to Serenity. Now!"

Gage floated in and out of consciousness as his fellow warrior brothers worked to free them from their stone tomb. He must have lost track of time because one moment he could hear Oron yelling beside him, and the next, his eyes were blinking against the light as he was lifted up a transport tunnel.

"Bring him here," a female voice ordered.

He was lifted, then set down on a flat bed.

"I need his clothes off. I have to see what I'm working with. Laelia, Radclyffe you two concentrate on Priest and Oron. Vivi, Ellie and Marjoram are helping the survivors."

When they began to peel his gear off, he screamed and kept screaming.

"He needs blood!"

"I am here!"

"He's too weak to drink. I tried that in the cave," he heard Oron advise.

"Luckily, we have other ways. Lord Fabre, if you would lie down here."

Gage knew he was dreaming. There was no way his father was here. "Losing…"

"Losing what, Gage?" the female voice asked.

"Losing my mind, father not here."

"Where else would I be? You are my son. I may not know how to show it, but I will learn. I will do better, Gage, for Yuki and Ame," his father said.

Gage struggled to open his eyes. "Boys?"

In the bed next to him, his father lay with an IV and tube running from his arm. "That is right. I met your boys." His father actually smiled. "Your son Yuki did not hesitate to take me to task regarding your mother. He is a good lad."

"Zoe, boys, safe?"

Theo nodded. "Last I saw, they were on Level Six with Meryn."

He exhaled. Already he could feel the difference in receiving his father's blood.

"This may sting a bit, but I have to remove the debris and fabric from your wounds," the woman advised.

"Do it."

He felt the second her magic entered him. Each time her magic tried to clean his wounds, his body jerked. "Please! Please stop," he begged.

"I have to clean your back. You're healing too fast. The debris will stay in your body, fester, infect and rot," she advised. When he looked up, he could see the toll this was taking on her.

"Try again."

When her magic entered his body to force the debris out, the burning sensation started, then faded. "Whatever you're doing is working."

"It's not me," the woman said in wonder.

Gage opened his eyes and saw Ame standing at the foot of his bed. Above him, snow fell. Each flake driving away the heat and the pain. "Ame? What are you doing here?" He looked up. "I thought you did rain, and Yuki did snow."

Ame walked over to the opposite side of the bed from the healer. "I heard your screams, so I came down here by myself because *hahaue* said to help if I could. Yuki gave me some of his power in case I had to defend myself. We can shoot ice crystals."

Gage nearly groaned in relief as the snow, coupled with the healer's abilities, soon had his back feeling nearly whole. "Where are your brother and your mother? Why are you here alone?"

"Yuki and *hahaue* went home to fight ferals," he replied.

He went to sit up, and the healer shoved him back down. "She did what? They did what?"

Ame shrugged. "There was a hazy shadow portal, and everyone was here."

"What!" Aiden yelled and reached for his phone.

"Meryn? No.. No, you're fine. Ame is already down here. You want to tell me about a shadow portal in Éire Danu?" he asked, then put her on speaker.

"Oh, yeah. A shadow portal is trying to open in Éire Danu," she confirmed.

"And?" he demanded.

"And what? Dav requested backup, and Zoe and Yuki went to help. Though, I think Zoe is gonna be the one setting ferals on fire. Yuki probably went to make sure Zoe didn't get hurt and to prevent her from burning the city down," Meryn said.

"Sascha, Balder, get the men moving. We need to get back to Éire Danu," Aiden yelled.

"End the call before you start bellowing like a psycho. You about killed my eardrums," Meryn complained.

"Sorry, baby, we'll be right up," Aiden said in a much softer voice before ending the call. He then looked around. "Move it!" he roared.

Gage tried to sit up again.

"You have to lie still."

He looked over to the healer. "I'm sorry, but it's my mate and son. I have to go."

"Take from me, Serenity. Get him on his feet," a warrior said, coming to stand behind her.

"Micah. Are you sure?"

"Absolutely. It's either that or he'll undo everything you've done so far heading to his mate." Micah met his eyes and gave him a knowing look. "There is no force in this world that could keep me from you if I thought you were in danger."

Serenity threw her hands up. "Men! Fine!"

Gage felt the rush of power, and what should have taken hours took only moments. Swaying, Serenity pulled her power from him as Micah wrapped himself around her. "You'll still be tender, but you're out of the woods."

She removed his IV and he was left facing his father.

Theo Fabre looked anywhere but at him.

"Father, thank you."

Theo looked up. "Of course."

Gage swung his feet around and hopped off the gurney. Ame took his hand.

"Gage, I…"

Before Yuki and Ame, he would have walked away. But he recognized his father trying. "I will bring Zoe and the boys home for a visit soon," he promised.

He watched as Theo swallowed hard. "It is more than I deserve."

Ame tugged, and Gage was moving. He met up

with Oron and Priest in the hallway. "I thought you two needed more rest," he teased.

"Zoe is using fire to defend Éire Danu. Did you really think we'd miss that show?" Priest asked.

He shook his head. "Fuck you guys."

Oron laughed, and they joined the units returning to the city of the fae.

CHAPTER SIXTEEN

❦

ZOE STOOD NEXT TO DAV as the portal continued to waver in front of them. Every once in a while, Yuki would throw a rock at it. She turned to the older warrior. "Why is it doing that?"

Dav pointed to his chest. "You're asking me?"

Seemingly bored, Yuki spun around in circles, his hands raised. Moments later, snow began to fall.

"I'll be damned. Snow in Éire Danu," Dav whispered.

Yuki smiled at her. "It's cold enough now it won't melt." He pointed to where a fine layer of powdery snow began to cover the golden walkways of the fae.

Unlike the previous portal, this one opened up in the center of the Market district near the palace. Zoe took in the grim expressions of the older warriors around her.

After about an hour, Dav passed her a cup of hot coffee. "Fresh from the pub. Never thought we'd need to keep warm in Éire Danu," he mused aloud.

One of the warriors called Yuki over, holding a small cup. When he extended it to the boy, Yuki turned to her for permission.

"What is it?" she asked.

The warrior smiled. "Just a bit of hot chocolate."

She nodded, and Yuki took the cup happily.

By now, a good inch of snow covered the ground. Looking around, the white of the snow made the gold tones of the city look even more ethereal.

Suddenly bells began to sound all over the city. Zoe turned to Dav in a panic. "What does that mean?"

Dav exhaled and whooped. "Three bells sounded. That means Prince Oron is home! They found them!"

Zoe looked up at the palace. Did that mean they had found Gage too? Were they okay?

"Dav, Yuki, and I have to go to the palace…" she started before she heard cursing all around her.

Turning slowly, she saw the portal had solidified.

"I'd give my left nut for those fucking thermal goggles," Dav complained.

Yuki ran behind her. "I saved your nuts."

Dav looked down. "What?"

"Gods, look at the ground!" another warrior exclaimed.

Clear as day, a set of footprints were visible in the snow.

She raised her hand and let a fire bolt fly.

Around her, gunfire sounded off as the warriors fired where the footprints stood. Blood splattered the snow, and a large oblong imprint appeared off to one side.

"Contact the palace. We have incoming!" Dav roared, his gun aimed at the portal.

Zoe kept Yuki behind her with her left hand and kept her right raised to cast.

"No screaming, *hahaue*," Yuki reminded her. "We promised *chichiue*."

"You're right. How about battle cries instead?" she asked, keeping her tone light.

"I think that would be okay."

"Unit approaching in two minutes," Bryok called out.

"I don't think we have two minutes," Dav whispered.

Zoe watched as close to a dozen footprints appeared. She shoved Yuki at Dav. "Guard him with your life!"

She stepped in front of the men behind her who could not see their enemies.

'Okay, you've always flared up when I didn't need it. I need you now. Please!' she begged her magic.

Bringing up both hands, she simply let go. She didn't need to see her enemy if she engulfed the entire area in flame.

"*Inferno!*"

She heard the exclamations of the men behind her and the screams of the enemies in front of her. She kept the flames a solid wall of fire in front of the portal. It was surprisingly easy to use this much of her magic. Much easier, in fact, than using smaller amounts.

"Zoe!"

She turned to see her mate standing behind her as she heard the sound of shattering glass. The portal collapsed, and the only evidence that it had been there was the scorched ground.

"Gage!" she flew to him, and he caught her up in his arms. "I thought we lost you!"

Her mate winced but held her tight. "You nearly did, but thanks to Meryn and her band of misfits, we were found in time."

He pulled back and tilted her head back so he could look into her eyes. "Are you okay? That was a lot of fire."

She nodded. "I didn't scream, though."

"Let me check her," she heard Kendrick say before a large hand landed on her head. "I can't believe it."

"What?" she and Gage asked at the same time.

"I've never seen it looking better. It reminds me of a purring, contented kitten," he scrubbed his hands over his face. "It's like you were built to use larger amounts of magic."

"Cool beans?" she asked, using one of Meryn's phrases.

Kendrick scowled and walked over to where Aiden was getting reports.

Dav walked up, holding Yuki and Ame, and passed them to her and Gage. "Your boys are very special."

With Ame tucked close on one side, Zoe grabbed Gage's free hand and drug him over to Aiden. "Aiden! Yuki used snow so we could see the enemy. But it doesn't have to be snow, it could be flour, paint, memory foam, anything that would show footfall."

Aiden's brows rose, and he smiled. "Good job, Yuki! We'll make a warrior of you yet. You're already showing the men up."

"Hey!" playful protests echoed around them.

Gage leaned in. "Yuki was also able to pass some of his magic to Ame, which he used to help heal my burns."

"Burns!" she looked at him aghast.

He squeezed her hand. "I'm fine now. Tender and a bit sore, but fine."

As the afternoon wound down, Aiden gave orders for the old guard to continue patrols for the next twenty-four hours so that the units could recover.

When they reached the warrior villa, Aeson pulled both Gage and Priest into bear hugs, causing both men to protest as their abused bodies screamed at them.

Exhausted and hungry, the men sat down, and the Chi unit, along with Tierla, Yuki and Ame, brought the food out. Tierla and Aeson had been able to put up most of what the boys made.

When the men heard that the boys had made them dinner, Zoe thought it had become Longnight. Each bite was praised and treated like a present. Between her and Gage, the boys beamed.

Gage kissed the tops of each of their heads. "I am so proud of you two."

Zoe sat back and closed her eyes. The past few days were catching up with her.

"Aeson, brother, I think I may need help," she heard Gage say.

She felt herself being lifted and opened her eyes. Aeson was carrying her while Matthieu helped Gage and Leon led the boys up the stairs. "I can walk," she protested weakly, then yawned.

Aeson chuckled. "Now, you sound like your mate."

She looked over Aeson's shoulder and down the stairs behind them, where Matthieu was supporting a grumpy Gage on one side.

Out of respect for Gage, Aeson set her down in front of their bedroom door. Smiling, she nodded her thanks. Gage hobbled forward away from Matthieu, and she wrapped her arm carefully around his waist.

"Goodnight, you four," Leon said, waving.

"Goodnight," she responded, then looked down. "Yuki, can you grab the door? Ame, can you pull the covers down?" The boys nodded and quickly began to help.

"This is humiliating," Gage mumbled.

"You nearly died. I think it well within your perceived acceptable macho behavior to be assisted into bed by your mate and sons."

Gage grimaced at her admonishment. "You're right." After that, he dropped the strong facade he had been maintaining. She got him into bed and pulled up the covers. "Your father gets a pass on his bath since he was hurt. However, you two do not." She pointed to the bathroom. "Do you need help?"

The boys shook their heads and raced to get ready for bed.

She sat down next to where Gage lay and brushed the hair from his forehead. Leaning down, she kissed him gently.

"I wish I could make love to you," he whispered.

"We have the rest of our lives. Thank all the gods, we have the rest of our lives for that."

"I thought of you in that cave. You and the boys."

"I heard you made Aiden and Darian leave."

He opened his eyes. They were full of grief. "I had to stay."

She nodded. "I know. As much as I wanted to scream to the heavens how unfair it was, I knew you made the right decision."

"I didn't make it lightly. I wouldn't give up you or the boys for anything."

"I know," she repeated.

"Zoe, I almost couldn't do it," he admitted, closing his eyes.

"But you did. You're too strong to let fear rule you and I will be eternally grateful that fate gave me an honorable mate like you."

"I'm just going to rest my eyes for a bit. Remind me tomorrow. I have to talk to Oron," he said, before passing out moments later.

She changed into her nightgown while the boys washed up. When they emerged, she kept both of them on her right, so they wouldn't jostle Gage in the middle of the night.

"Good night, my little loves," she whispered.

"Good night, *hahaue*," they answered.

Snuggling close, it wasn't long before they all fell asleep.

☾

Zoe gripped Gage's hand as they walked through the hallways of the palace. She now had to use the gorgeous emerald wrap Gage had gotten her from Baba's. The city was dimmer, and there was a bite of cold in the air.

That morning she and Kincaid managed to recreate a warming stone for the warrior villa, which kept it comfortable, but once you stepped outside, the change in temperature was drastic.

Portia saw them coming and nodded before falling in step with them. "Ari and the rest of the Tau unit are here."

Gage nodded. "They left before us. We were getting the boys settled."

Portia knocked on the queen's door, then opened it for them. "Your Majesty, Gage, and Zoe are here."

To their shock, the queen stood and walked right toward them. First Gage, then Zoe, she reached out and embraced them tightly. "Thank you," she choked on the words. "Thank you, for saving my sons and defending my people."

She dropped into a curtsey as Gage bowed. "Of course, Your Majesty," they said in unison.

"Come, sit," Brennus ordered as he steered his own mate back to the table.

Once seated, Aiden glared in Gage and Priest's direction. "None of my warriors are replaceable," he began. "Neither one's rank or mated status changes the value of a life lived." He growled. "That being said, you two, along with Oron, will be receiving service medals in honor of your bravery and sacrifice."

"What he means to say is thank you for shoving my ass through the portal," Meryn added.

Priest laughed but quickly coughed when Aiden's ire swung his way.

Oron looked over to Gage. "Ari said you needed to talk to me? Something you forgot to say when we were in the cave?" he asked, smiling.

Gage stared. "Something I couldn't say because we were trapped in the cave."

The smile on Oron's face evaporated. "What could be that serious?"

Gage folded his hands on the table in front of him. "The feral that put the crystal into overload and turned it into a bomb, he said, 'Tell my little brother Oron, thanks for the way in'."

Oron looked like he was two seconds away from being physically ill. "I knew they were the ones responsible, but to know for sure that Callum turned," he hung his head low.

"What did he mean, a way in?" Meryn asked.

Oron shook his head. "I have no idea. I haven't had any contact with him since I was ten years old!" He shoved back from the table and began to pace.

"It's not like you invented the new portals or

ways into the city," Meryn said, reaching for a pretzel.

Beside Darian, Amelia gasped and clutched at her chest. Instantly, all eyes were on her. Both Darian and Oron knelt down next to her.

Darian took her hand. "Are you well? Is it the baby?"

Amelia looked up at Oron. "I'm so sorry."

Oron shook his head. "Whatever it is, it's fine."

"You don't understand. It's our fault."

Oron blinked his confusion.

Amelia looked to Darian. "We brought the first feral to Éire Danu, using my soul as an anchor. We discovered a way."

Oron stood, walked five feet, and screamed his anguish. His fist slammed into the wall before he strode from the room, crashing the door behind him.

Izzy jumped to her feet. "Thane, I'll need you. His hand! We have to fix his hand!"

Thane cleared the corner of the table, and they both ran after Oron.

The queen covered her face. "How much more must he suffer? Must we suffer?"

Zoe looked over at Meryn. "His hand?"

Meryn looked angry and sad. "He's an amazing artist."

"Gods," Zoe whispered to herself.

Darian cradled Amelia, who wept softly.

Zoe couldn't stand the oppressive despair in the room. "So what if they've figured out a way in? The second a portal forms, I'm roast every single one of them."

Meryn blinked. "Oh yeah. That was amazingly badass. I wish someone had recorded it."

"And we saved more of the captured fae," Anne added. "We're getting closer and closer every time we shut them down."

"You girls are right, but some days are harder than most," the queen said, looking at where her door now hung slightly off its hinges.

"Then we should have a party," Meryn suggested.

"A party?" the queen asked.

"Yeah, I mean y'all are focusing on the shitty stuff, but we've had a lot of good stuff happen too. We found more people alive. Ari, Oron, and now Gage have found mates. Brie and Zoe are badass, and Izzy has become our Coffee Goddess." She grinned. "Not to mention I found out about my mom and dad, and Oron got adopted, and the twins and Pip were able to get here," she continued rattling off things.

"And I caught two of our enemies in a box, and I may even have an idea on how to get them out," Kincaid said.

"And we just received the support of nearly everyone in Noctem Falls to find our missing warriors," Brennus said, rubbing the queen's back.

"My dad found his mate," Brie added.

"And we got Yuki and Ame," Zoe said proudly.

The queen sat a bit straighter. "You all are right. What could we do to celebrate?"

Zoe was struck by a moment of inspiration. "What about a Festival of Lights? People release lanterns into the sky with a message of what they're grateful for. I think in times like this, with the lights not working and people getting depressed, maybe that could help."

"Yeah, and since this is Éire Danu, we don't have to worry about the lanterns fucking up the environment," Meryn clarified.

Amelia looked up from Darian's chest, her expression brighter. "We can borrow Kari when she visits to help plan."

"Food. We need lots and lots of food," Meryn said, licking her lips.

"Dav's fish," Brie suggested.

"Peter's brownies," Neil said.

"Oh! And Leo's meat dishes. Maybe we could get a boar, like the goblins serve," Meryn said, reaching for her laptop. "I'll make a list."

Under the table, Zoe reached for Gage. He took her hand and kissed it. "You really are like a living flame, like a beacon of light and hope."

"If I'm a living flame, then you are the one that makes me burn hotter," she whispered.

He kept the neutral smile on his face, but she noticed a flush working up the back of his neck.

She sat back and watched as her idea for a festival began to take shape. Each suggestion was borne out of love and the desire for those around them to feel better. She knew that things were dangerous, that they had an enemy that shook the foundation of their world, but they also had each other, and that is what made them stronger and able to face each day with a smile.

EPILOGUE

❦

PRIEST WALKED STIFFLY BACK TO the warrior villa alone. Gage and Zoe stayed to help plan the festival. Ari and Brie had left to update the Lionharts on all that had taken place, and Kincaid was working with Kendrick to see if his idea about that clay box worked.

Ari's nightmare meant that Brie was a deputy. Gage's nightmare of seeing Zoe engulfed in flames meant she was an amazing fire witch. But what good could possibly come from seeing your mate ripped apart by dozens of grasping hands?

Shuddering at the memory, he kept walking. It was better to stay alone.

Dear reader –
   Thank you for reading!
I hoped you enjoyed *My Beacon*.

   For a full listing of all my books please check out my *www. alaneaalder.com*
   I love to hear from readers so please feel free to follow me on Facebook , Twitter, Goodreads, AmazonCentral or Pinterest.

SEND ALANEA A
HUG!

LEAVE A REVIEW

Hug me please!!

If you liked this book please let others know. Most people will trust a friend's opinion more than any ad. Also make sure to leave a review. I love to read what y'all have to say and find out what your favorite parts were. I always read your reviews.

IMPORTANT!!
   As you know Facebook strictly controls what shows up on your newsfeed. To ensure that you are receiving all my latest news and teasers you can to sign up for my newsletters so you

will receive regular updates concerning release information, promotions, random giveaways and future Live events.

I typically send only 1-2 updates per month and won't flood your inbox, promise! ;)

Alanea

OTHER BOOKS BY ALANEA ALDER

KINDRED OF ARKADIA SERIES

This series is about a shifter only town coming together as pack, pride, and sloth to defend the ones they love. Each book tells the story of a new couple or triad coming together and the hardships they face not only in their own Fated mating, but also in keeping their town safe against an unknown threat that looms just out of sight.

Book 1- Fate Knows Best
Book 2- Fated to Be Family
Book 3- Fated For Forever
Book 4- Fated Forgiveness
Book 5- Fated Healing
Book 6- Fated Surrender
Book 7- Gifts of Fate
Book 8- Fated Redemption

BEWITCHED AND BEWILDERED SERIES

She's been Bewitched and he's Bewildered...

When the topic of grandchildren comes up during a weekly sewing circle, the matriarchs of the founding families seek out the witch Elder to scry to see if their sons' have mates. They are shocked to discover that many of their sons' mates are out in the world and many are human!

Fearing that their future daughters-in-law will end up dead before being claimed and providing them with grandchildren to spoil, they convince their own mates that something must be done. After gathering all of the warriors together in a fake award ceremony, the witch Elder casts a spell to pull the warrior's mates to them, whether they want it or not.

Each book will revolve around a unit warrior member finding his destined mate, and the challenges and dangers they face in trying to uncover the reason why ferals are working together for the first time in their history to kill off members of the paranormal community.

Book 1- My Commander
Book 2- My Protector
Book 3- My Healer
Book 4- My Savior
Book 5- My Brother's Keeper
Book 6- My Guardian
Book 7- My Champion
Book 8- My Defender
Book 9- My Angel
Book 10- My One and Only
Book 11- My Solace
Book 12- My Warrior
Book 12.5- My Gifts at Christmas
Book 13- My Beacon
Book 14- My Salvation
Book 15- My Eternal Light

Coming Soon

THE VANGUARD

We Hold the Line.

Book 1- Inception

Made in the USA
Middletown, DE
06 July 2024

56965262R00184